THE FIFTH REFLECTION

Also by Ellen Kirschman

Fiction: Dot Meyerhoff Series

The Right Wrong Thing

Burying Ben

Nonfiction:

Counseling Cops: What Clinicians Need to Know (with Mark Kamena and Joel Fay)

I Love a Cop: What Police Families Need to Know

I Love a Fire Fighter: What The Family Needs to Know

THE FIFTH REFLECTION

A DOT MEYERHOFF MYSTERY

ELLEN KIRSCHMAN

ISBN 978-1-60809-250-5

Published in the United States of America by Oceanview Publishing
Longboat Key, Florida
www.oceanviewpub.com

10 9 8 7 6 5 4 3 2 1

PRINTED IN THE UNITED STATES OF AMERICA

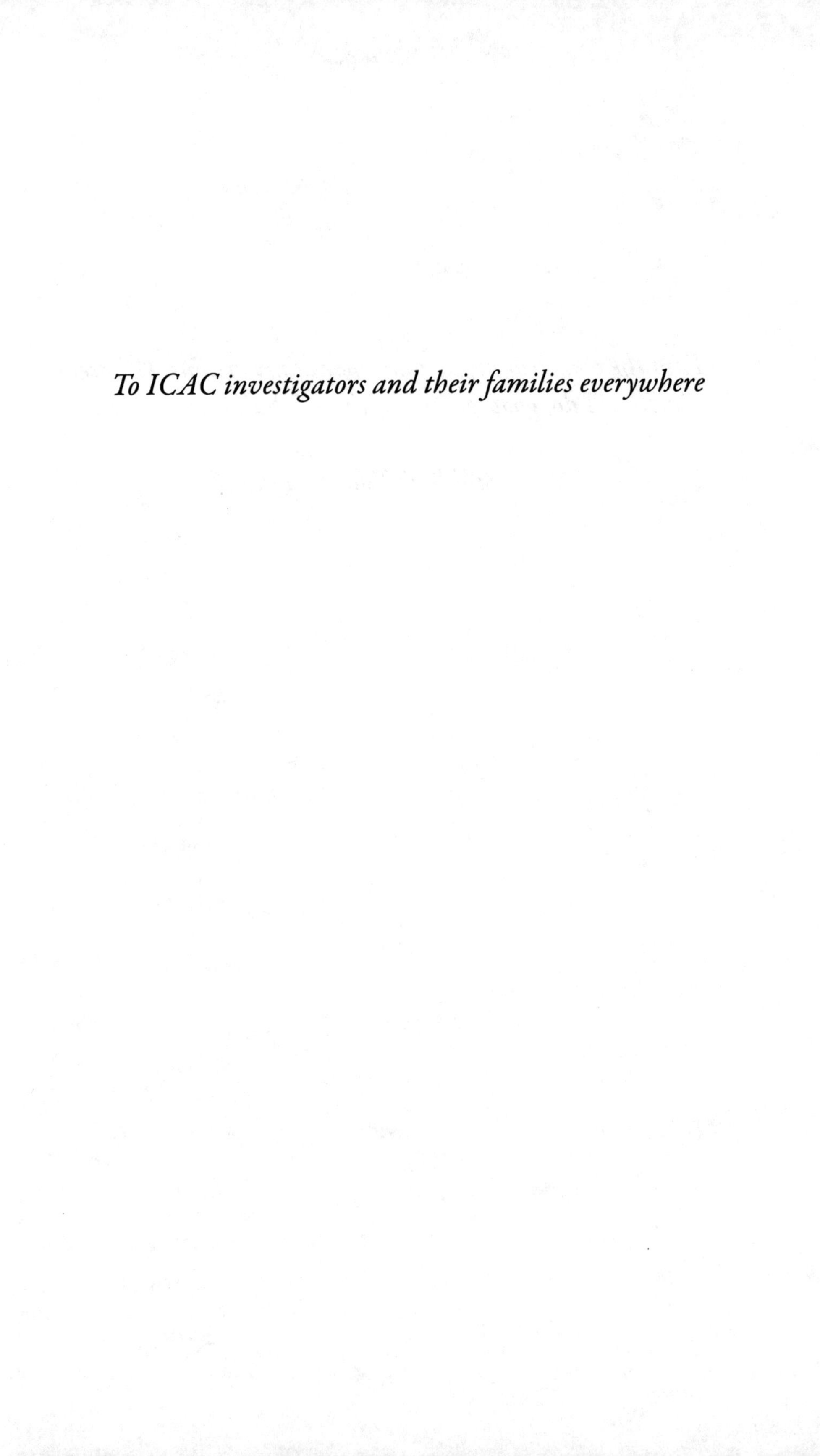

To ICAC investigators and their families everywhere

I am the owner of my actions, heir of my actions. Whatever actions I do, good or evil, of these I shall become heir.

—Buddha's Fifth Reflection

ACKNOWLEDGMENTS

AS A POLICE psychologist, I've always understood that investigating crimes involving children is one of the most emotionally difficult assignments law enforcement professionals can undertake. Fortunately, there are programs such as Shift Wellness (shiftwellnes.org) that support investigators with resources and training.

What I didn't know until I started researching this book was the magnitude of Internet crimes against children. Our cherished electronic gadgets, computers, webcams, smartphones, and tablets are playgrounds for pedophiles. Purveyors and collectors of child pornography, often one in the same, need not leave the privacy of their own homes to support a worldwide industry that trades in the suffering of children. I wrote this book to entertain. Still, I ask my readers not to forget the real human suffering that inspired me to write it.

I am the luckiest of mystery writers to have the support and help of so many law enforcement professionals, mental health colleagues, and subject matter experts. Thank you all for sharing your experiences and responding to my questions. If I've left anyone out, forgive me: John Averitt, PhD, Lisa Barrett, MD, Nancy Bohl-Penrod, PhD, Michael L. Bourke, PhD, Peter Collins, MD, Michael

Comer, PhD, Dan Dworkin, PhD, Joel Fay PsyD, Lt. Neal Griffin, Sherry Harden, PsyD, Chaplain Jan Heglund, Agent Anjanette Holler, Paula Kamena, Esq., Sgt. Daniel Ischige, D. P. Lyle, MD, Jon Moss, PhD, Lt. Zach Perron, Sgt. Adam Plantinga, Lt. James Reifschneider, Jane Stevenson, RN, Casey Stewart, PsyD, and coroner's investigator Andrea Whelan.

My apologies to Paul Ekman, PhD for taking liberties with his decades-long study of deception and micro facial expressions. For a serious look at his work, go to www.paulekman.com.

Special thanks to Gil Fronsdal, PhD, Buddhist scholar and co-teacher at the Insight Meditation Center in Redwood City; writer Ann Gelder who helped in the early days; my editor and beloved sister-in-law, Doris Ober; my calm yet stalwart agent, Cynthia Zigmund; and all the staff at Oceanview Publishing. Last, but never least, my husband, Steve Johnson, who is everything to me.

PROLOGUE

IOWA IN NOVEMBER is cold. The sky is as gray as the stubble in the fields, obliterating the horizon. Without a line to show where earth and sky meet, I feel as though I'm floating in space.

"You okay?"

My fiancé, Frank, and I are stumbling across a frost-tinged cornfield. Today is Thanksgiving. We've been out walking in the frigid air. Trying to move our food-besotted bodies after breakfast the size of a ceremonial banquet. It's below freezing and the air is so cold it hurts to breathe. There's a storm predicted, and we can see enormous black clouds boiling in the sky, illuminated by sudden snaps of lightning.

"If we don't move faster, we're gonna get wet." He grabs my hand and pulls me forward. I can see the back of his sister Daisy's house where we're staying, and behind it the houses belonging to his other sisters, Violet, Rose, and Lily. "Next time," he says, "we'll come in the summer in time for the corn and tomatoes. Did you know you can hear corn as it's growing?"

I know what he's doing. He's trying to take my mind off the cold and away from my sore feet. I should have brought hiking boots, but who wears hiking boots in Iowa? The place is as flat as a pancake. The highest point in Pick City is a 700-hundred-foot bump called The Knob. His sisters, all four of them, took me to see it the day after we arrived. Then we went to see the second most popular tourist attraction, The Bridge of Mystery, a railroad bridge built in the 1800s that spans a wide river. Its name derives from the death of a supposedly happy young girl who shocked everyone by jumping off the bridge to her death. Her story provoked a slew of questions about what psychologists, like me, know about people who commit suicide. Why do they do it and what could be done to stop them? My first thought was that the young girl probably jumped out of boredom, but their questions were so earnest I bit my tongue.

Frank's sisters, their husbands, their children, and his mother have all been bending over backwards to be nice to me. It's just that I'm not used to so much conversation or having someone jump up and ask me if I need anything every time I move. I'm an oddity to them. I can feel it. Forget being Jewish—what's strangest about me is that I have no children and I don't cook, bake, sew, or can vegetables. Therefore, I don't have much to talk about. They seem mildly interested in the books I've written and happy to talk about the books they're planning to read come winter when they can't work on the farm. Any time I compliment their cooking, I get a recipe to try at home, many with Jell-O as the main ingredient. I had no idea Jell-O could be prepared in so many ways and for so many different uses. Add cucumbers, it's a salad. Add marshmallows, you have dessert. My mother used to make Jell-O for me when I was a kid. Her idea of getting fancy was to add a dollop of whipped cream from an atomized can. I learned everything I know about cooking from her.

Daisy's expecting almost thirty for Thanksgiving Dinner. If I was feeding a crowd that size, I'd be curled up in a fetal position under my dining room table. Not Frank's sisters. Cooking for family is what they love. I can hear them laughing and talking before we even open the back door and step inside.

The house is in chaos. Tables and chairs squeezed into every available space. Linens, glasses, silverware, and handmade table decorations from four different households laid out on each table. Nothing matches and no one seems to care. Everyone remembers who made which napkins and used them on what occasions, the meals they served and the time Frank, the baby of the family, ate so much sweet corn he was covered in melted butter and had to take a bath.

Lily asks me to help with the salad; I'm glad to have something to do. She hands me two heads of iceberg lettuce, a tomato, a cucumber, and a bottle of salad dressing for each table. This would be heresy where I live. The only acceptable salad in Silicon Valley is locally sourced, organic kale tossed with hand-pressed olive oil from a boutique orchard in the Napa Valley and imported vinegar that costs forty dollars a bottle. Thanksgiving is the season my friends run themselves ragged cooking gourmet versions of traditional dishes that need no improvement.

Forty-five minutes before the guests arrive, Rose realizes she forgot to make the seven-layer bean dip. Violet goes to the store and returns home with four cans of beans, a bag of grated cheese, and a tub of sour cream that she layers into a casserole and puts in the oven before going home to get dressed for dinner. She's a stout woman with short, blunt-cut gray hair. When she returns, she's wearing clean jeans and a different sweatshirt hand decorated with dancing turkeys. I decide not to wear the silk top and crepe pants I bought for the occasion and go for something more casual.

The guests arrive. More friends. More family. More food. There are so many I give up trying to remember anyone's name or how they are related to Frank, who is seated across the table from me grinning so hard his lips might be permanently stretched out of shape. Dinner is noisy, disorganized. There are mounds of food plated in the kitchen, please-help-yourself-to-seconds. Frank hardly gets a chance to swallow before someone slaps him on the back and peppers him with questions about his life in California as though it were a foreign country.

We never had Thanksgiving when I was a kid. My mother, social as she is, still thinks holidays are corporate tricks designed to get people to eat too much and spend money they can't afford. My long-dead father—ever the student radical—considered Thanksgiving and Columbus Day to be monuments to the genocide perpetrated by white settlers against Native Americans.

Frank's sister Rose, sitting next to me, asks me for the third time if I need anything more before they serve dessert. As soon as she stands to go to the kitchen, Frank's mother takes her place. She's a tiny woman. Probably doesn't weigh more than a hundred pounds. Her apple doll face wrinkled with age and cigarette smoke.

"Having a good time?"

I nod "yes" because, despite my fears about fitting in and the elitist West Coast attitudes I hate to admit I have, I'm enjoying myself a lot.

"I'm glad to finally meet you. I've been worried about Frank, living alone. He's so much happier now that he found you. Wish my husband was still alive. You'd like him. He'd like you." She puts her hand on mine. Her skin is soft as chamois. "I'm getting on. I feel good, but who knows? It makes me happy to see him settled. I can tell, you're good for him." She blushes. "Listen to me yammering. This is a party. Let's go get us some dessert."

Sometime between the apple pie, the Jell-O ambrosia, and the pumpkin cheesecake, Daisy tells Frank she heard his cell phone go off in the bedroom. He excuses himself and wedges out from the table making jokes about how much more room he had to move around in before he ate dinner.

"Dot's the police psychologist. She's usually the one who gets called in the middle of a party. Not me." There's a chorus of jests from the table about screws coming loose and other construction-related calamities befalling one of Frank's clients. This leads to a long, funny story involving lug nuts and tires. So funny I don't realize Frank has been gone for nearly ten minutes until he comes back into the room, paler than I have ever seen him. Instead of sitting down again, he stands in the arch separating the living room from the dining room, picks up a water glass, and hits it with a spoon.

"Sorry, everyone. Hate to interrupt. That call was from my friend JJ in California. Something terrible has happened. She put her daughter to bed last night and when she went to wake her up this morning, she was gone. She's been missing now for hours. Nobody knows where she is."

There's a chorus of "for cat's sake" and "great snakes."

"Maybe she ran away," Lily says. "I did that once, didn't I, Mom? Scared the poop outta you."

"Chrissy's only a toddler."

There's a collective intake of breath. Including mine.

"I hate to cut our visit short, but we need to leave." He looks at me. "I called the airlines and got a flight out of Des Moines. Leaves in three hours. We'll make it if we get going. It's been great to see everybody."

I don't move.

"Come on, Dot, we have to pack."

Frank's eyes bore into me for a second too long before he walks back into the bedroom. Then all the eyes and all the questions are on me.

"Who's JJ?"

"Her real name is JoAnn Juliette. She's a well-known photographer and Frank's teacher. Actually, she's his mentor. He's been studying with her for nearly a year. He was planning to show you his photos tomorrow. He's very good."

"His teacher? Not his friend?" Rose's perpetually pink cheeks redden with the audacity of asking a personal question. "I never had a teacher call me in an emergency."

"They're close."

"How close exactly?" Now her cheeks are scarlet.

It's the question I've been asking myself from the day I first met JJ last April.

"She's taken a special interest in Frank; thinks he has a lot of talent. She's very charismatic. Enthusiastic." I stumble over my words. Irritated that I'm the one trying to explain Frank and JJ's relationship to his family when I don't fully understand it myself.

Frank leans into the room and taps the face of his watch with his finger.

I walk into our bedroom. Frank's throwing clothes on the bed. My bag lays open and empty next to his. He balls up a shirt and jams it in his suitcase. I've never seen him agitated like this.

"Can we talk about this for a minute?" I say. "I can see you're upset. JJ must be in a panic."

I know what it's like to have to listen to another person's pain. It's what I do for a living. Frank's an action person. When something breaks, he gets out his tools and fixes it.

"You can't fix this, Frank. A missing child is police business. I'm sorry. It must be terrible for you to stand by and do nothing."

"That's why I said I'd go back. She didn't ask. I volunteered. It's the only thing I could think to do." His eyes well with tears.

"Doesn't she have anyone else to call? Somebody closer maybe? What about the child's father?" I feel like a grinch just asking the question.

"So far as I know they aren't together. I don't think she has many friends. She spends most of her time working or with her daughter."

He closes the lid to his suitcase and zips it shut.

"I just wish you would have discussed this with me first—privately. You've been asking me to come to Iowa with you almost since the day we met. Now that I'm finally here, I hate to leave early."

"Why aren't you dying to get home to help your cops? You've always said the worst cases cops have to deal with involve children."

"They're not going to need me in the middle of an active investigation. Nobody's even called me to tell me what's going on."

He puts his hands on my shoulders. "I'm sorry we have to cut this short. It's just something I feel I have to do. JJ's more to me than a teacher."

I stop myself from asking what that might mean.

"She tried to talk me out of coming home early, but I could tell she was relieved when I insisted. I'm flattered that she called me and happy to be able to give something back. Stay longer if you like, but I'm going to go."

"Well then. There's no more to say. Let's pack, say our goodbyes, and get out of here." A whopping sadness fills my chest. It hardly compares to losing a child, although nothing in the comparing makes the feeling go away.

Frank sets his suitcase on the floor and straightens up, his eyes on me. His face fixed and somber.

"I know what you're thinking, Dot. I hope you don't say it."

"Say what?"

"'I told you so.' Because that's what you think, isn't it? That if anything ever happened to Chrissy, it would be JJ's fault."

CHAPTER ONE

I DIDN'T BECOME a psychologist like some of my colleagues who went from BA to PhD on Mommy and Daddy's credit cards. My parents didn't have credit cards. Didn't believe in them. My father thought bankers were Shylocks who cheated the poor with exorbitant interest rates and balloon payments buried in the small print. My mother was for simplicity and against needless consumerism.

I worked my way through college and grad school waiting tables, serving cocktails, and pleading for scholarships. Turns out I am better at reading people than serving them food. I acquired this skill trying to anticipate when the sins of the rich and powerful would send my father on a rant, barging around the house for twenty-four hours, spewing letters to the editor. While my mother, for whom all life's challenges contain lessons to be learned, regarded my father's tantrums as an opportunity to practice patience and understanding. With righteous indignation for the underdog combined with the ability to normalize bizarre behavior as my parental legacy, how could I have not become a psychologist?

Currently, I work as a paid consultant for the Kenilworth Police Department. It's a moderate-sized agency, seventy-five sworn, located in the heart of Silicon Valley. I didn't intend to be a police psychologist. I was aiming to be an academic, dazzling graduate students and writing acclaimed books. That was until I got a taste of graduate school, which was only slightly less treacherous than swimming in a shark tank. I fell in love with my advisor, Mark Edison, while I was helping him write a book. We married, wrote two more books together, and when I got my PhD, I joined his forensic practice. Kenilworth PD was his biggest client. Years later, I wrote a book on my own. Mark was happy for my independent success. Or so I thought until he left me for Melinda, his psych intern and twenty years his junior. We divorced. He got the forensic practice. I got Kenilworth PD.

Police officers are not eager consumers of therapy. They think it makes them weak to have problems. I think it makes them human. Almost every cop at Kenilworth PD regards me with skepticism, worried that I'm reading their minds and getting ready to report them to the chief as unfit for duty. They are not as standoffish as they were when I started three years ago, but it's still an uphill battle to win their trust, let alone put a dent in the male-dominated culture of rugged individualism. My biggest skeptic is Chief Pence. Maybe he doesn't like psychologists. Maybe he doesn't like me. All I know is that we've been in a push-pull battle since before he was promoted to chief. He can't live with me and he can't live without me. He wants my advice when I least expect it and when I have something to offer, he avoids me.

I'm not saying that Pence is to blame for what happened. He couldn't have predicted the future and he didn't mean to offer anyone a convenient narrative. But, in retrospect—pardon me for dredging up that tired saying about hindsight having 20/20 vision—his blundering ego may have started the ball rolling last spring, the day I met JJ for the first time.

* * *

It is springtime, seven months before Frank and I go to Iowa for Thanksgiving. Pence has called a special session of the city council.

He's invited the public and the press. All members of the Kenilworth Police Department, including me, are encouraged to attend. In Pence-speak, "encouraged" means show up because he'll be taking names. He cloaked the subject of his announcement in secrecy, responding with a Cheshire Cat smile to any questions that "all will be revealed." Pence likes drama and will do anything to get his name in the paper, provided the press is positive. If it isn't, then he is as tight lipped as a double agent. I sit in back of the council chambers looking at my watch. I'm supposed to meet Frank at an opening reception for his photography teacher's new exhibition.

I've been hearing about this woman for months. He's described her as an extraordinary photographer and a wonderful teacher. Innovative, daring, inspiring, and—I took note—exceptionally beautiful. Frank is passionate about his photography. I'm relieved that he has something absorbing in his life besides his remodeling business and me. We're quarreling less about the hours I spend at work and how often I change plans at the last minute because police departments are open 24/7. He's known this from the time we met. I think he hopes that when we get married, my priorities will change. They won't. Police psychologists don't have nine-to-five jobs. When cops work, we work.

This is a red-carpet affair. The mayor is here, as is the city council. Chief Pence greets them one by one, his silver hair gleaming in the overhead lights. He's a handsome man if you like your men looking like they stepped off the cover of *GQ*. I don't know much about men's clothes, but if I totaled up what Pence spent on his outfit, it would equal the down payment on a small car. I prefer shaggy men like Frank, who orders his jeans and work shirts online by the half dozen. He can look spiffy when he wants to, but mostly he just looks touchable. There's nothing touchable about Pence or his wife, Jean, who is sitting in the front row, coiffed, buffed, and color-coordinated from head to toe. Not a hair out of place. They are a matched pair, age-adjusted versions of Ken and Barbie.

Cops, dispatchers, and records clerks file into the chambers, some in uniform, some in jeans and t-shirts. No one looks happy with this mandated show of support for the chief when they could be at home with their families, catching up on their sleep, or out catching crooks. I see Manny and his wife, Lupe, sitting in the front row. He's wearing a suit and tie. Lupe is wearing a dress and high heels, her tiny figure snapped back into shape after having a baby. I'm very fond of Manny and take pleasure in watching him mature on the job. He's always been a quiet, serious young man, who kept his own counsel, even when it meant standing up to popular opinion or to the chief. He was never one of those rookies who tried too hard to fit in and be one of the boys. He's well liked and served a term as president of the Kenilworth Police Association. I haven't seen much of him recently and I wonder why he isn't sitting with his buddies.

The mayor taps the microphone, asks everyone to take their seats, thanks us for coming in at the last minute, and promises that we will be rewarded for our efforts by being the first to hear about an innovative new police program. He hands the microphone to Chief Pence who's been smiling and nodding at people in the audience. As soon as he takes the mike, Pence's smile disappears. He sucks in his cheeks, furrows his brow, and takes a deep breath.

"The announcement I have to make this evening concerns crimes that are perpetrated against our most vulnerable citizens. Our children. Day after day, the citizens of Kenilworth go about their daily activities feeling safe, thanks to the dedicated employees of my police department." There is a smattering of applause. "Silicon Valley is the birthplace of a technological innovation, so profound that it has changed the world. It was here, in our backyard, that the microcomputer revolution began." He looks at his notes. "Hardware, software, data storage, networking, data sharing and delivery—I have to ask my ten-year-old neighbor what these things mean." He waits for a laugh that doesn't come. "Our lives have been significantly and positively affected by technology. We've all come to depend upon our electronic gadgets." He waves his cell phone in the air so everyone can see it.

"But there is a dark side, too. One that is difficult to understand and impossible to tolerate. These same technological advances that enrich our lives have enabled pedophiles to distribute child pornography around the world with the click of a mouse. Pedophiles trade images the way you and I used to trade baseball cards. They use chat rooms to lure unsuspecting children away from the safety of their homes. Every month, sixty thousand new images are added to these websites. Sixty thousand. Think of it." He looks at the audience, gauging his effect.

"In 1998, the United States Department of Justice initiated a task force to provide state and local law enforcement with the tools to catch distributors of child pornography and stop sexual predators who solicit child victims through the Internet."

"Has something happened to a Kenilworth child?" someone in the audience shouts. Everyone looks around to see who is talking out of turn.

"No. And I am determined it will never happen here. Not on my watch." His wife starts to applaud and stops when she realizes no one else is joining her. "But, forewarned is forearmed. Therefore, ten months ago, in a trial run, I committed staff from KPD to join the county Internet Crimes Against Children task force, part-time. Something my predecessors were unable or unwilling to do. Officer Ochoa, would you stand please and face the audience." Manny stands up and turns toward us. A red blotch seeps up his neck. He waves once, turns around, and sits down. "That moving blur was Officer Manuel Ochoa. Known to most of us as Manny. He is a dedicated young officer, who in his three years on the department has shown himself to be a hardworking, effective professional. When I asked for a volunteer to join the task force, he was the first to respond."

No wonder I haven't seen much of him.

"Today I am making this trial effort public and official and I am increasing Officer Ochoa's hours to full-time." There is another smattering of applause. "This will be a major commitment for Officer Ochoa and for his wife, Lupe, as well." He smiles at Lupe and bows slightly in a mock show of gratitude. "Even being assigned part-time to the task force, his hours have been long and irregular. Pedophiles peddle their wares in all time zones. Assigning Manny to work full-time on the task force means other officers will have to work harder and longer to fill in. No doubt this will increase the overtime budget. But I believe, with all my heart, that it's a small price to pay for keeping our children safe." He pauses to let this sink in. "Now, are there any questions?"

Hands fly in the air. There is a lot of shouting. I don't have time to stay for the answers although I have plenty of questions of my own. The first one being, why all the secrecy around the task force? Money's tight. If no crime has been committed, how is Pence going to justify an increase in overtime? And most irritating of all, why didn't Pence consult me before appointing Manny? Investigating child pornography is one of the most stressful assignments in law enforcement. No one should be placed in a stressful specialty without first being screened. Manny has a small child of his own. That brings everything closer. Makes him vulnerable to over-identifying with the victims, losing whatever emotional Kevlar he needs to investigate these horrendous crimes. Had I known what was going on, had Pence told me, I could have helped innoculate Manny, prepared him to deal with the stress. Strategized with him and Lupe both about how best to minimize the emotional contagion that comes with such an assignment.

My cell phone vibrates with a reminder that the reception for Frank's teacher starts in twenty minutes. I want to stick around and talk to Manny and Lupe. Before I'm even out of my seat, it vibrates again courtesy of the damn calendar app Frank installed after telling me my Day Runner was so retro it made me look out of touch.

"We need to keep up," he had said. "We live in Silicon Valley."

* * *

Frank is waiting for me at the front door of the gallery. He's leaning against the wall like a cowboy. All he needs are boots and a ten-gallon hat. His eyes flicker back and forth, looking for me, anticipating that I'll be late. The minute he sees me, he breaks into a grin. He's a truly good guy. I'm lucky to have found him. Pickings are slim for women in their fifties. After Mark and I divorced, I figured I'd be single the rest of my life. A more appealing alternative than pairing up with the men my girlfriends were meeting online, most of whom were depressed widowers with bad teeth and a penchant for golf clothes with contrast stitching. I debated signing up for an online dating program but couldn't think of how to describe myself in five sentences. I got as far as "thick in the waist, not in the head" before I gave up. That was when my colleague Gary introduced me to Frank who was remodeling his house.

"Right on time. Thanks." Frank bends down to kiss me. He's at least a foot taller than I am. "JJ's photos will blow your mind. They are amazing. You've never seen anything like them before." I wonder if anyone says "blow your mind" anymore, but decide not to ask. "Controversial. Cutting edge." He takes me by the elbow and steers me into the gallery.

In an instant I move from the warm summer air and the dimly lit night into an air-conditioned cavern with refrigerator white walls and ceilings. It's so bright my eyes water. A woman with neon red hair and a Celtic chain tattooed on her arm offers me a glass of champagne. I take it. Then a skinny young man with a partially shaved head holds a tray of stuffed mushrooms and kale chips under my nose. I refuse.

"This way." Frank has to yell at me to be heard over the din. We move through the crowd to a wide doorway leading to a large room filled with a veritable rainbow of people. Once again California's lure of bottomless opportunity and fortune has sucked people from around the globe. Spilled them out in a place once covered in apricot, plum, cherry, and almond orchards, now covered with condominiums and sprawling corporate campuses. More than half of all Silicon Valley start-ups have a founder who was born outside the United States and more than half of the people who work for them in science and engineering were born in another country. A large percentage of whom are standing in front of me munching on kale chips.

I shoulder my way to the back of the big room where the lighting is softer. My eyes adjust again. People are walking around, talking in whispers, heads together, eyes gauging each other's reactions. I move to the nearest image. Three children with pouting, sultry faces cling together in a wilting triangle. They are naked.

I move to another. A single child, perhaps a prepubescent girl with an amorphous sexuality, lies facedown on a bed of wet leaves. Some are randomly stuck to her body. She could be dead; she could be sleeping. Next to her is a waist-up portrait of a stick-thin boy. He looks directly at the camera, his eyes blazing with the angry intensity of a powerful secret self. He appears furious with the photographer. She has interrupted a private moment. Exposed his puny little body to the world. The photos are gorgeous, evocative, drawing me in and repelling me at the same moment.

"What do you think?" Franks whispers.

"I don't know what to think."

"Do you like them?"

"I honestly don't know. They're erotic. Bordering on pornographic."

"Sensual," he says. "Not sexual. These are works of art, carefully composed. The lighting is fabulous. The images are crisp. Look at the photo of the boy. Look at how she blurs the background so your eye is drawn to his face. Masterful. Or this one." He takes my hand and walks me across the room to a photo of a young girl, perhaps three years old. She is sitting on a log in the middle of a stream, her knees pulled up to her chest, looking down at the water swirling in circles under her. "If this was a painting, it would be hanging in the Met."

"She's naked."

"So is Venus rising out of that clam shell. And all those naked cherubs in the Italian masterpieces. And the Odalisque. I've gotten interested in art since I've been studying photography with JJ. Now I see the naked form everywhere. Imogen Cunningham, Georgia O'Keefe, they all photographed naked women."

"Women, not children."

"How are these images any different from what you see every day on television? Victoria Secret's ads, *Sports Illustrated* swimwear edition . . ."

"Those are adults. They can give informed consent to being photographed."

"Do you think she forced these kids to pose?"

"I have no idea. Kids are pliable. Under the right circumstances they'll do anything. Whose children are they?"

"My brother's." JoAnn Juliette's voice is soft and smoky. Her presence so light I never sensed her standing behind us until she spoke. She is as described, breathtakingly beautiful, tall and willowy with high cheek bones and a wide mouth. Her long dark brown hair, parted off-center, hangs over her shoulder in a thick braid. She is wearing wide black pants, a kimono top hand-painted with birds and butterflies, and long earrings that swing when she moves.

"JJ. This is my friend, Dot." I notice he doesn't say 'fiancée.'

"Dot. This is JJ."

We shake hands. Hers is warm and firm.

She loops her arm over Frank's shoulder. "He's my favorite student. Came late to the game, but he works very hard and shows considerable talent." I wonder if she'd feel as positive about him if he weren't so positive about her.

"Your brother's children?" I say.

"I wouldn't presume to take pictures of children I didn't know. I lived with my brother, his wife, and their kids on the family farm where we both grew up. We ran around unsupervised and usually unclothed when we were children. His kids are lucky to do the same. Most children today can't walk to the bus without a parental escort." She shudders and shakes her head. It's a small movement. Nothing dramatic. "His kids were like my own. Until I had one of my own."

"Is your child in this exhibit?"

"Chrissy? Of course." She loops her left arm through mine and steers me across the room. Walking next to her, her perfect form emulating the unreal ideal foisted on us less-than-perfect women, I am suddenly self-conscious, wondering if Frank, walking behind us, is making comparisons.

Chrissy's photo is hanging by itself. She looks to be about two years old. Her arms are at her sides and she's dangling a toy dog by the leg—it's head drags on the ground. She is naked, wearing only a white headband with a large floppy bow. Her face is turned and she looks over one shoulder into the camera as though asking, *Who am I? What am I? Am I a child or a woman or the woman in a child?* Her eyes are huge and her skin flawless. I have no children of my own, but the image is so powerful I can literally feel the sensual appeal of Chrissy's smooth skin, imagine how it would be to cover her plump, pillowing body with kisses.

"I wanted her to wear something else, but she wouldn't have it." JJ's voice shakes me from my reverie.

"And the pose?" I ask.

"She posed herself. I took about fifty shots. This is the one she chose."

"Isn't she self-conscious?"

"About her nakedness? Not at all. It's a natural state. She's quite comfortable with her body."

Frank leans in. "Dot's a psychologist. She likes to analyze things."

Something shifts in JJ's eyes. "Really? Wish I had known. I spoke to several psychologists before I mounted this show. And I had the children meet with a child therapist. I wanted to be sure that I wasn't doing any harm. None of the psychologists I consulted were concerned. They felt the older children understood the project and were cooperating of their own free will with the full understanding that they had veto power over any images."

A small group of people press in on us, eager for JJ's attention. She seems not to notice.

"I even consulted a world-famous expert on pedophilia, Dr. Charles M. Randall."

"Did you? I studied with Dr. Randall when I was in graduate school. He was one of my favorite professors. I haven't seen him in years."

"He thought a few of my photos might be of interest to pedophiles. At the same time, he said some people, given their predilections, are aroused by anything. The only way to avoid them was to stop taking pictures altogether. I loved his attitude. He warned me not to be put off by law enforcement types or right-wing zealots, religious or otherwise, because my photos were gorgeous. Rather than charge me his usual consulting fee, he asked for a photo instead."

That's the Dr. Randall I remember. Warm, kind, and avuncular. The stereotypical absentminded professor, bumbling and rumpled. An iconoclast who valued common sense and decency over small-mindedness. He had a cynical view of his fellow psychologists as fussy, self-inflated busybodies who touted psychology as the answer to the world's problems. In particular, he disdained people like me, clinical psychologists, who charged money for what he said used to be given freely and known as friendship. He urged us to work with people who had real problems or caused real trouble, like pedophiles. I could recite his rant by heart. Clinicians were Freudian wannabes with whining, sniveling clients for whom the best therapy would be the admonition to grow up and get a life, followed by a kick in the butt. A point he once gleefully illustrated in class by hoisting his leg in the air, dislodging a disk in his back that sent him to the hospital for a week.

"Might the children feel differently about these pictures in the future?" I ask. Frank gives me a look.

"They might. I worry about that sometimes. Don't we all hate it when our parents pull out baby photos of us lying naked on a bearskin rug? But it's a chance I'm willing to take. My nieces and nephews love me. These images are hardly the sum total of our relationship. I bathed them, fed them, stayed up with them when they were sick, went to their recitals and soccer games. They know I'm a photographer and that these images are how Aunt JJ makes art. To me, these images are not real children in the same sense that a map is not the territory it depicts. That distinction is lost on some people, particularly my critics. I shouldn't be surprised about that, but I am." She looks around at the gathering crowd. "I should move on, say hello to some other people." She shakes my hand with both of hers. "Nice to meet you, Dot. I hope our paths cross again sometime soon."

"Now what do you think?" Frank asks after JJ is absorbed by the crowd.

"I think her 'map is not the territory' comment is an intellectual rationale for taking the pictures she wants to take, damn the consequences. Or maybe she has exactly the consequences she wants. The gallery is full, the program catalogue is flying off the shelves, and there is a line of people waiting to buy her photos."

"That's pretty cynical."

"You asked."

"Frank." JJ's voice drifts back through the murmur. "Come over here for a minute, there are some photographers I'd like you to meet." He turns away from me without a word.

"Thank you, thank you, thank you. I overheard what you just said and I couldn't agree with you more." The woman talking to me in a whisper is about the only other person in the room my age and one of a select minority without tattoos, piercings, or Technicolor hair. "If this is art, I'll eat my hat." She laughs. "Sorry. That's an old-fashioned saying, isn't it? I feel pretty old-fashioned in this crowd." She looks at me for some affirmation. She's a tall, trim woman with a pleasant face hardened by a bit too much makeup that reveals, rather than conceals, small spidery lines around her mouth and eyes. "So, how are you connected to JoAnn Juliette?"

"My fiancé is her student."

Her face shifts slightly. "Does he take portraits of children, too?"

"I don't know, to tell the truth. He's new at this. He hasn't shown me any of his work yet. What's your connection to JJ?"

She points to Chrissy's pictures. "I'm Chrissy's stepmother." She musses her hair with a manicured hand and then pats it back into shape. "Sorry," she says. "I get nervous when I see these pictures. All these people. You just don't know who's here or why." She shakes her head and apologizes again. "My husband thinks I'm overreacting. Maybe I am." She expels a long sigh and extends her hand. A diamond the size of a sugar cube glints in the overhead lights. "I'm sorry, my name is Kathryn Blazek. And yours?"

"I'm Dot Meyerhoff."

"Are you a photographer, too?"

I hesitate. The minute anybody finds out what I do for a living, I get asked for my professional opinion about somebody's miserable marriage or their drunken nephew. Sometimes I say I'm a ceramicist who fixes crack pots for a living and wait to see if they get the joke. Kathryn Blazek doesn't look like she's in a joking mood.

"I'm a psychologist," I say. Her eyebrows tilt.

"Really? Do you mind if I ask your opinion?" I don't answer because I know from experience it won't make a bit of difference if I do or don't. "Do you think these are wholesome pictures? Is it good for children, safe for them, to be posing like this?" The same question I asked JJ. Only more direct.

"I couldn't say. I don't see children in my practice. I'm a police psychologist." I take a sip of champagne and wait for the inevitable questions. *Remember that cop who shot that girl? Why didn't she shoot her in the leg instead of killing her? I got a speeding ticket when I was only five miles over the limit and there was no one else on the road. Why aren't the police out looking for the real criminals?*

"How interesting. Police officers have such difficult jobs. Your work must be very challenging." She looks around the room again. "Could I ask one more question? If these were your children, would you be concerned?"

This is not a question I should answer. She's asking for my professional opinion. I don't know her, her stepdaughter, her husband, or her husband's ex-wife.

"I'm sorry. I've put you on the spot. I'm not asking for your professional opinion, just your general reaction. As a mature woman."

"Yes," I say. "If these were my children, I think I would be concerned."

"Thank you," she says. "Thank you so very much."

* * *

Frank is quiet over dinner. He gets that way when he's irritated. "Are you angry with me?" I ask.

"Why should I be angry with you?"

"Because I didn't react to JJ's work the way you were hoping I would."

"Your reaction is your reaction. I didn't have any expectations."

I want to hit him with the Vietnamese pancake we're sharing. He doesn't have trouble sharing his opinion about what he calls the important things of life, religion and politics, but the closer we get, the harder it is talk about our differences because we have so much more to lose. Confrontational partners make for a loud, rowdy marriage. One confrontational type paired with a risk-averse partner and you have a seesaw relationship where one side never gets off the ground. Put two risk-aversive people together and problems can go unresolved for years until one tiny unimportant thing—a favorite sweater that should not have been put in the dryer, a toilet seat left up or down—unleashes a torrent of suppressed feelings. That was how it was in my first marriage. Two psychologists who couldn't talk to each other about unpleasant stuff. I'm determined not to repeat the pattern.

"Come on, Frank. I can tell when you're upset."

"JJ is important to me. She gets what I'm trying to do with my photos."

"How important?"

"She's encouraging. Generous with her time. Her critiques are spot on. I'm learning a lot from her."

"I'm happy for you."

"You insulted her with your questions."

"I did not."

"You implied that she is an irresponsible mother. That she put these children in harm's way."

"Apparently, I'm not the only one." I haven't told him about Kathryn Blazek and I don't intend to. It was a brief moment that will amount to nothing.

"She gets hate mail, threats, nasty reviews every time she has an exhibit."

"You said so yourself, her work is edgy. She has to expect that kind of reaction."

"Not from her friends."

"I'm not her friend. You are. I just met her." I pour tea to fill the silence. "She's a serious artist. No question. And there's something very appealing about her. But I think she's defensive about her work and in denial about the consequences of what's she's doing. She's sexualizing children."

"And you're pathologizing her art. Sometimes, Dr. Meyerhoff, to quote one of your heroes, 'a cigar is just a cigar.'"

CHAPTER TWO

I DO A lot of counseling on the hoof, just walking around the police department, casually checking in with people. Funny thing about cops, when you come to them, it's not counseling. Same thing when you're standing up and talking or riding in a patrol car together. But if you're sitting down behind a closed door—doesn't make any difference if it's my private off-site office or my little broom-closet office at headquarters, or even what we're talking about, it could be last night's Giants game or the best place to eat tacos—it's counseling.

I've been hoping Manny would contact me, but he hasn't. I feel pretty certain that he wouldn't hesitate to call me if he was having trouble. On the other hand, my job is a little more complicated than just talking to people with problems; it's my job to spot problems before they happen. Given that the number one problem in the PD is Chief Pence, the person who signs my annual consulting contract, sometimes the issues get complicated. I would have preferred that Pence had talked to me before he appointed Manny to the ICAC task force. But since he didn't do that, the best thing I can do now is try to support the person he chose. Which is why I'm heading over to Manny's office in the sheriff's substation a few blocks from Kenilworth HQ.

The substation, a single-story gray cinder block structure that might once have been a garage or a repair shop, is wedged between a taqueria and a discount shoe store. It was meant to be a local outpost, a place where the largely Spanish-speaking residents of this unincorporated area of Kenilworth could feel comfortable dropping in to talk to local law enforcement. Many of the residents in this neighborhood are undocumented, worried about deportation, and fearful of reporting crimes or acting as witnesses. No amount of reassurance, in Spanish or English, that the sheriff is not interested in their legal status seems to have overcome anyone's apprehension. Frank and I eat and shop in this area a lot. Not once have I seen the door open or the lights on.

I ring the doorbell. A crackling version of Manny's voice comes over the ancient intercom and tells me to wait at the door. An older woman pushing a grocery cart along the broken sidewalk glances at me and then looks away when I smile at her.

"Nobody home, lady." A middle-aged man steps out from the shoe store. He has boot-black hair and is wearing an untucked guayabera shirt with embroidered pleats in the front and back.

"Someone just spoke to me on the intercom."

Manny opens the door. He looks surprised, as though he hadn't recognized my voice. He shakes hands with the man from the shoe store and exchanges a few words in Spanish. "This is Hector. Hector, this is the police department doctor. I think she's here to check up on me." He raises his eyebrows and makes a face. Twirls a finger next to his head, sign language for crazy.

Hector shakes my hand. "Just in time. Manuelo's a hard case, Doctor. I've known him since he was a kid."

A woman with two children walks into his store. "*Hasta luego*. I got to go sell shoes."

Manny opens the door to the substation. The huge open space has been sliced in two by a plywood wall that stops two feet short of the ceiling. The front room is small and furnished with an old wooden desk and some battered office chairs. Lopsided notices are stuck to the wall with push pins. There's nothing remotely welcoming or even slightly related to the Hispanic culture. Manny walks me through the second room, a large hollow space that smells of burnt rubber and grease. The walls and floor are painted gray, with blotches of red showing through the worn spots. There's a short hall with three doors at the back of the room lit by a flickering fluorescent fixture. One door leads to the outside, another to a grungy bathroom I hope I won't need to use, and the third to Manny's office.

He opens the door and gestures me in with a comic bow. "Welcome to ICAC headquarters."

The office is painted a light-sucking institutional green and the walls are bare. There's a black metal filing cabinet, a peeling Formica table, four chairs, three computers, and a pile of unopened cartons. The only personal item in the room is propped on top of a computer. A studio portrait of Manny's baby in a pink dress with painted fluffy white clouds behind her. A lock of her dark hair is pulled up in a little bunch that looks like a small palm tree is growing out of her head. She's holding a toy lamb and smiling at the camera. I flash back to the photo of JJ's daughter, Chrissy. How she was posed. How her face and body invited speculation. There is nothing open to interpretation about the image of Manny's daughter. It's neither aesthetically challenging nor compelling like JJ's portraits. Just a record, a single moment in the life of an ordinary little girl in a little girl's dress holding a little girl's toy. There must be millions of similar photos on mantelpieces all over the world. But only one eye-stopping, heart-grabbing photo of Chrissy.

"Carmela," Manny says. "Her name is Carmela." He opens his briefcase and takes out another picture and sets it next to Carmela's on top of the computer. "And this, as you know, is my Lupe."

"Look at the computers they gave us. Ancient. My computer at home is faster. I can't even make a cup of coffee for you, but we could go across the street for a Mexican Chocolate, if you want." I look at my watch. I love Mexican Chocolate, but it's too late in the afternoon for caffeine.

"I had no idea you volunteered for the task force. I wondered why I haven't seen much of you."

He sits on the edge of the table, facing me.

"At first it was going to be temporary. Just helping out. Somebody on the team got sick. The chief told me to keep a low profile. Work from headquarters until the guy came back. Guess what?" He walks around the table and sits. The chair complains. "The guy got medically retired. So the chief made me an offer I couldn't refuse."

"What do you mean you couldn't refuse?"

"First of all, there's a big pay bump. If I do it for a couple of years, Pence's going to make me Sergeant. I got a kid now, we can use more money."

"How's Lupe like this assignment?" He wrinkles his nose like I've just released something very smelly into the air. He shrugs and pulls at the corners of his mouth, puffing out first one cheek and then the other. My question apparently requires considerable thought.

"She doesn't like the hours. Pedophiles work at night. And she worries too much."

"What does she worry about?"

"That I'm getting contaminated. That the stuff I see is affecting me somehow. I tell her, I'm not getting personally involved. All I'm doing is looking at crime scenes."

"You're looking at real children who are being hurt in real time."

"I'm looking for evidence. Just enough to meet evidentiary standards so I can get a warrant and make an arrest."

"What about pretense calls? You're talking to guys who are prowling the Internet looking for pictures of naked children. Or worse, wanting to meet children to have sex with them. How does it feel to pretend to be one of those creeps?"

"C'mon, Doc, you sound like my wife. This is my chance to do something important. Make a difference in some kid's life. Get a few perverts off the street. Now that we have Carmela, it'd be good for me to know what these creeps are up to. It will help me keep her safe. Plus, to tell you the truth, Doc, I was getting bored with leaf blower complaints and barking dogs. I need a little excitement."

This is the typical progression. In the beginning of their careers cops are so overwhelmed with novelty and newfound power they would work for free. Give them a few years and boredom sets in. They start looking around for ways to restimulate the feeling of excitement and passion.

"It might help you keep Carmela safe, but having Carmela might make it harder for you not to identify with the victims."

"Do you know how peer-to-peer files work, Doc? How people share music or movies over the Internet? You find the site you want, enter a search term, and you can download whatever you're looking for to a computer anywhere in the world. That's how these guys trade images. I could show you if I could get IT to fix this freaking computer." He slaps it on the side. Carmela's picture falls over. Manny picks it up, rubs the glass with a corner of his t-shirt, and puts it back. "What the pervs don't know is that we're watching them. We get an IP address, match it to the owner, get a warrant, and make an arrest. We busted a guy last week. A tweaker. Had fourteen hundred images and three hundred videos on his computer."

"So you never actually look at the videos or the photos yourself."

There's a small twitch at the corner of his eye. "Yeah. I looked at a couple. We had to verify that he was trading porn. The guy was a frigging hoarder. Boxes and crap all over the place. He actually urinates in an empty Gatorade bottle because he doesn't want to take time away from his hobby to go to the bathroom."

"What's your reaction when you look at these videos?"

"There's just not that much to see. You know, just some guy's . . . you don't want to hear this, Doc." Now he's protecting me. This is what cops do, protect other people from the things they see, and in the process, protect themselves from revisiting unpleasant memories. I can tell that if I show any reaction, any emotion, he's going to back off. I wonder if Lupe is doing the same.

"Sorry, Doc," he says, and looks at his watch. "I gotta get back to headquarters. I need to move some stuff over here and bug the IT guy again." He pushes out of his chair sending it squealing into a file cabinet. "Thanks for dropping by."

I stand. I've pushed this as far as I can at the moment. "Would it be okay if I check back with you in a couple of weeks?"

"If it makes you feel better, sure."

"I'd like to make one suggestion before I go." He nods. I pick up the photos of Carmela and Lupe and move them away from the computer. "It might be better to keep these pictures away from your computer screen. Just in case. I have a feeling that it might be important to keep a bright line between work and home."

* * *

I sit in my car outside Manny's hole-in-the-wall office. Here I am in the midst of one of the highest income-producing regions in the country, with the biggest share of America's high-growth, high-wage sectors. A skinny little stretch of land that lays between the San Francisco Bay and the Pacific Coastal Range and accounts for 43 percent of all venture capital investments in the country. Where the hell is the venture capital to buy Manny a decent computer so he can track down pedophiles?

* * *

Pence is hiring new officers as fast as others are retiring in the wake of drastic changes proposed to the retirement system. The citizens of Kenilworth, many of them multimillionaires, are complaining that public safety sector employees retire too young and their pensions are too big. Never mind that most cops, fire fighters, and teachers, let alone clerks and waiters, can't afford to live anywhere close to Kenilworth. It doesn't seem fair to take away a promised benefit. Change the rules for the new hires, but leave the current employees alone. I, on the other hand, as a consultant, have no pension. Only what I can save. The same is true for Frank who is also self-employed. He grits his teeth every time the subject comes up.

"I get it. Cops and fire fighters have a hard job. But so do roofers. More construction workers are killed in the line of duty than cops."

"Cops are murdered. Construction workers fall off buildings."

"Half the cops are murdered. The others fall off their motorcycles."

We've had this conversation many times before. It never goes anywhere.

"How many fires does the average fire fighter fight in a year?"

"I have no idea, Frank."

"Hardly any. But a roofer roofs five or six days a week, fifty weeks out of the year. Climbing ladders, working with hot tar."

"Where are we going with this, Frank?"

"I don't know. You brought it up."

"Let's talk about something else, shall we?"

We're in his living room. It's after dinner. Everything is washed up, put away in its place. We're just filling time until it's late enough to go to sleep.

"Sure, why don't we talk about getting married? We haven't talked about that in a long time."

This is hardly less dangerous than roofers falling into a vat of hot tar.

"Okay."

"So why haven't we talked about it?"

"I've been busy. I have a slew of pre-employments to do. And exit counseling."

"What's that?"

"Sometimes cops have bad experiences they haven't told anybody about. This is a chance for them to process those memories and not take them into retirement. Others need help preparing to go back to civilian life. They're going to miss the fraternity. Sometimes they need a little marital counseling."

"I'd appreciate a little marital counseling myself."

An adrenaline surge sweeps through my body. "What do you mean?"

He leans forward in his chair. "Seems to me you've been postponing talking about this. Have you changed your mind about us getting married?"

Truth is, I already feel married. I rarely go home, except when Frank goes to his photography class. Most of my things are at his house. We've established a routine. We start with a "how was your day" conversation and a drink before dinner, then we cook, eat, clean up, watch TV, and go to bed. On the one hand, it feels a little stifling. On the other, it feels sweet and comforting.

"We're not getting any younger, Dot. I want to be married to you for a long time. I can't unless we get going soon." He smiles. I want to cry. If I had any sense, I'd meet him at the city clerk's office tomorrow with a marriage license in hand. It's what my mother thinks I should do. And all my friends.

Frank looks at me and splays his hands. "We need to rent a place, get a caterer. From what I hear, you have to do that months in advance." He shifts forward in his seat. "I want to settle down, Dot. I'm going to retire in a few years. I need something to do with my time. Someone to be. Something I can say to a person at a cocktail party who asks me what I do. I know now it's going to be photography. But I'm a latecomer and have a lot of catching up to do. I'm the old man in the class. Thirty years older than everyone else."

"What's that got to do with our getting married?"

"I want to get serious about photography. Not wait till the day I hang up my tool belt. I can't do what I need to do to catch up shuttling back and forth between our two houses."

"We don't go back and forth. We're mostly here." Small-minded of me to keep score. "We could just move in together. I'll rent my place out . . ."

"No. I want to do it right. This is not an experiment. It's for real and it's forever." He bends over and takes both my hands in his. "I don't know what's eating at you. You have a bad case of cold feet. Post-Traumatic Divorce Syndrome. I get it, I've been divorced, too. But you're not like my former wife and I'm not like your ex. So what's the problem?"

CHAPTER THREE

FRANK STARTS WORKING day and night to prepare for JJ's annual show of student art. I ask to see his photos, but he's not yet ready to show them to me. Getting ready, he explains, means something different to a digital photographer than it does to a photographer whose output is constrained by the cost of film and developing materials. Frank takes hundreds of pictures every time he goes on a shoot. It takes hours and hours to organize, cull, and edit. Then mat and frame the ones he's chosen. It's an enormous amount of effort just to produce six photos he considers good enough for his first-ever public showing.

We drive past the gallery where JJ had her show toward the flats of East Kenilworth, a working-class neighborhood separated from the hills of affluent Kenilworth by a concrete ribbon of north-south highway. I'm surprised at how nervous Frank is. This is a student show. No reviewers from the *New York Times* or even the *Kenilworth Daily*. He hardly says a word in the car.

The closer we get to East Kenilworth, the fewer white faces we see and the more window signs written in Spanish or Vietnamese. We drive toward the bay past small houses with fenced yards, concrete patios, and mismatched lawn furniture. Luxury homes hidden behind ornate wrought-iron gates lay claim to the waterfront, speculators banking on the future gentrification of the last swath of affordable real estate in the Bay Area. The streets are blanketed with heavy fog. Nothing looks the way it does in the day. Frank's headlights penetrate the mist like the glowing eyes of a nocturnal animal.

We are the only car on the street. Frank pulls a U-turn at the end of a cul-de-sac and stops. He looks at his watch, curses, and pulls his iPhone out of his pocket. He swipes the screen until he gets to the navigation app. He wants me to get this app, too, but every new piece of software I buy comes with a time-sucking learning curve. At least for the present, it's easier to pull over and ask someone for directions. We head back the way we came, slowing at every corner until he makes a sharp right that takes us through a sprawl of industrial buildings, their metal shutters locked and covered with graffiti. Frank lets out a deep sigh of recognition. And relief.

One last turn and we're facing JJ's artists commune. It's a two-story building. Probably a converted warehouse or factory. The outer walls are covered in murals and stylized graffiti. The colors so bright they penetrate the dusky light. Two enormous doors on the ground level stand open. Light spills into the darkness. I hear music. We park the car and walk in. The space is cavernous and filled with people.

Frank looks around. It's hard to see much of anything beyond the crowd and the tree-sized sculptures of glass and metal towering over us.

"I thought this was a photography exhibit," I say.

"It's a multimedia show. Different teachers, different art forms."

Something catches my eye, a floor-to-ceiling tapestry that is crusted and dripping with glittering objects. It must weigh a ton. I tug on Frank's hand.

"That's JJ's, too. She works in several mediums. Amazing, isn't it?" Frank says, pointing at a clump of melted glass hanging on a long cord like a nest of barnacles. "She made the whole thing from detritus. Things she collected off the beach: bottle caps, glass, plastic shopping bags. She picks up tons of the stuff because it's killing birds and wrecking sea life. Buffs them, twists them, melts them. It's stunning. Never saw anything like it. It takes talent and imagination to make something this beautiful out of human garbage." He bends to my ear. "We can come back here later. I want you to see my photos."

* * *

Frank's images are easily the strongest, most vibrant of the student works on display. His series is called "Lumbermen." Individual portraits of six men, each dressed in work clothes, standing in front of a plain white background, looking directly at the camera. They are posed with the props of their trade: a sawhorse, a ladder, a chainsaw, a coil of rope, dirty hands, scuffed boots, hard hats. Their presence is overpowering.

"These are fantastic, Frank. I had no idea."

"I've worked with these guys for years at the lumber yard. They deserve to be seen for who they are. Honorable. Dignified. Men who get their hands dirty for a living don't get much respect in a town filled with brainiacs. I want to change that with my pictures." He looks at me.

"These images are the work of an accomplished photographer. They're moving. Powerful. I'm not a student of photography, but these are as good as anything I've seen in a museum." His face goes red. "I'm so impressed I don't know what to say."

I do know what not to say. That the moment I saw his photos I realized I've been secretly worried he was taking pictures of nude children. Sometimes I am clueless.

The other students' work runs the gamut. There are three giggly au pairs from Norway who love taking pictures of the babies they mind. Privileged children in party dresses. Not exactly hackneyed, better than that, but nothing to sear the eye like JJ's images. There are a couple of nice landscapes, an obligatory sunset, and some interesting travel shots. No other portraits.

"Where's JJ?" I ask.

"She was here a little bit before. I am Anjelika." One of the au pairs takes my hand. "You are Frank's fiancée?"

Before I can answer, JJ appears, materializing like fog out of nowhere. "Sorry. I live upstairs. I wanted to kiss Chrissy goodnight." She extends her hand to me. "Glad you could come." She's wearing a long graceful skirt, a sweater, and a magnificent necklace fashioned from sea glass looped together on a coiled rope of plastic straws.

"What a beautiful necklace."

She picks it up and runs her long fingers over white quill-like beads. "Tampon inserters." She laughs at the look on my face. "Everyone has the same reaction." Her jewelry, like her photography, is edgy, daring, provocative. Everything about her, except her soft voice and unhurried way of moving, has an in-your-face feel to it. She leans over and whispers to me so that none of the others can hear. "He's good, isn't he? It's the artist's job to make the commonplace singular. Frank gets that. He's the kind of student every teacher wants, hardworking, serious, and talented. It's a pleasure having him in class. You're a lucky woman. So am I."

* * *

The door to Manny's office is closed. I knock. No response. I knock again. I can hear voices. I knock a third time and open the door. The room is dark. The only light comes from a string of images flickering across his computer screen. In only a few seconds, I see enough and hear enough to look away. Grunting, then a moan, followed by the sound of a slap and a whimper. I flick on the lights. Manny wheels around in his chair. There are pools of crepe-like bluish skin under his eyes. He blinks for a moment and turns back to the computer. The screen goes black and silent. By the time he turns around he has his game face on.

"Hey, Doc. How you doing? I wasn't expecting you."

"Sorry, I should have called first." This is a lie. I didn't call on purpose because I was sure he'd tell me he was fine, just fine, but too busy to see me. "How's it going?"

"It's going."

There are two more desks in the office since I was here last. One looks unoccupied, the other is covered with an assortment of books, coffee cups, and empty water bottles.

"Finally got some company?"

"Not unless company means a guy who thinks that if you have sex with a girl who's thirteen, you're a felon. But put twenty bucks on the table and she's a criminal. He wanted this assignment because he likes porn and thinks he can spend all his time hanging out at massage parlors."

People have all sorts of reasons to volunteer for this assignment. Exactly the reason there needs to be rigorous psychological screening, stress inoculation, training, on-site supervision, and a whole bunch of things Pence apparently never thought about in his rush to play hero to the tax-paying citizens of Kenilworth.

"Get any training?"

"Pence sent me to talk to a retired guy from child protective services. His only advice was to hang in because it gets easier once you get used to it."

"That's it?"

"I got a couple of certificates about how to get into chat rooms, track online images, that kind of techie thing."

"Nothing about the emotional consequences of doing this work? How to manage the stress?" He shakes his head.

"So, after all these months, is it getting easier?"

"I got a lot to learn still."

"That wasn't what I asked."

His face splits into a smile. He slides forward in his chair and puts his hands over mine.

"You are such a worrywart, Doc. Ever think of seeing anybody about it?" He laughs. I don't. "Not to worry. It's what I want. Something new. Somewhere I can really make a difference."

"Are you making a difference?"

"Let me show you something." He walks me out into the hall. There is a row of photos pinned to the wall. All men. Some of them so dirty and disheveled, I would cross the street if I saw one coming. "This is the wall of shame. I arrested all these guys. Task force territory covers a bunch of counties. We're busy."

"Who's he?" I point to one of the few clean-shaven, wholesome-looking men.

"Funny you should ask. This is Mr. Idle Hands. You're going to hear a lot about him in a day or two. The guy's a lawyer. Beautiful home. Gracious wife. Found his hard drive hidden in a shoebox in his closet, under his Armani suits. Video cams all over the house so he can video himself . . ." A red flush crawls over his face. He pulls at a fingernail.

"You mean masturbating?" He nods. I wonder why he can't say the word aloud. I'm a grown-up, he's a grown-up. The people he's arrested are grown-ups. Is he just being polite? Protective? Deferential? Everything about his job is connected to sex. He has to be able to use exact words when he's writing reports, interviewing suspects, talking to victims.

"He's a righteous pervert, this creep. And now he's in county jail, where he belongs."

"For how long?"

"If we get a conviction? Three to nine months."

"That's all? Seems like a slap on the wrist."

"It's not up to me. If it were, I'd lock the door and throw away the key. We only got him for collecting. If you ask me, 95 percent of these perverts who watch porn have put their hands on some actual kid. But that's the way the law works in this county if all you got is collecting. Like it's a victimless crime to just watch. None of these babies wanted to be on video. Whoever makes these laws should see what I've seen." He stops. His eyes register surprise. Something's slipped out and now he wants it back. He opens his arms like a master of ceremonies introducing a troupe of entertainers. "All these fine gentlemen are in jail where they belong. That's what I mean when I say I'm making a difference."

* * *

The minute Pence sees me at his office door he laughs.

"What have I done wrong now, Doc? Because I know from the look on your face, this isn't a friendly visit. My mother used to say to me, 'Okay, pucker-puss, if you don't wipe that expression off your face, it's going to stay that way forever.'" He stands, walks in front of his desk, and pulls up two chairs.

"Have a seat. Tell me how you're feeling. Isn't that what you shrinks always say?" Pence's efforts at humor rarely rise above sarcasm. I doubt that he knows the difference.

"You're in a good mood."

"Yes, I am and I hope you're not here to ruin it."

"I've just been to see Manny at the substation."

"And?"

"He won't admit it, but I can see the job is wearing on him. People should be psychologically screened to investigate crimes against children and carefully supervised. They should not be dumped in front of a computer in a dismal room, doing a dismal job, with no real training, no supervision, no breaks, and not even a real team."

Pence's good mood evaporates before my eyes.

"When I asked for task force volunteers ten months ago, Manny put in for it."

"How can you volunteer for something you don't fully understand?"

"This isn't rocket science. What is there to know? He's a cop. He knew what he was getting into."

"I'm certain he didn't know how he would react."

"Thanks for your concern, Doc." Pence stands, signaling that my time is up. "I'll check on him myself."

"I don't want you to tell him I talked to you."

"You should have thought about that before you decided to tell me how to run my shop."

"It is part of my job description to identify things that cause stress for the officers. The way you've set up this task force is causing him stress."

"So are you saying Manny is unfit for the job?"

"No. I'm saying you've made a hard job harder and he needs more support. This is about you as much as it is about Manny."

"Is it really? Let's hope Manny agrees."

* * *

Manny leaves a message on my voice mail. He tells me the chief called to see how he is doing. He hopes that the chief's call had nothing to do with my visit. He tells me, once again, not to worry, that he's doing okay. He prefers that I call first before dropping by again. He repeats, just in case I didn't believe him the first time, that he's fine, just fine, and the only help he could use is a new computer. If I could be of any assistance with that, I should go for it.

CHAPTER FOUR

"THINGS LIKE THIS don't happen in Kenilworth. I've lived here all my life." Fran is scraping the griddle with the sheet rock trowel she uses to flip pancakes and eggs. She doesn't see me take a stool at the counter. The fall heat wave isn't giving up and I can see rivulets of sweat trickling down the back of her neck. Fran's Café is the place where most Kenilworth street cops start their day. Fran is like a mother hen to them and as the widow of KPD's only line-of-duty death, she holds a special place of respect.

"All those years working the street, BG never worked sex trafficking or pornography. Not once." A formal photo of BG in his Kenilworth PD uniform looks out over the restaurant from a shelf high above the stove, safe from the grease splatters, surrounded by plastic plants, and the framed, folded American flag presented to Fran at his funeral.

"Are you kidding? He saw stuff, maybe worse, he just never told you." Eddie Rimbauer wipes his hands on his apron and starts clearing the breakfast dishes off the counter.

"BG told me everything."

"That's what you think. There's things us cops see that we never talk about, not even to each other."

The café is quiet. Except for a few retirees with no place to go, the breakfast rush is over. I'm here because I've had two pre-employment screening cancellations. Cops apply to several agencies at once and take the first offer that comes to them. I'd rather they spent time researching the departments they applied to, rather than going for the first offer or the biggest paycheck. On the other hand, most cops like toys, trucks, cars, speedboats. Anything with a motor. And anything with a motor costs money. A better long-term investment would be figuring out which agency fits best for their personality. Some crave the action of a big-city department. Others prefer a quiet suburb like Kenilworth. The consequences of making a bad choice can be disastrous because once you sign up, those golden handcuffs, money, and security make it hard to start over in another department at the bottom of the totem pole, pushing a patrol car on dog watch.

"You don't know BG like I did."

"I know cops. We don't talk about certain stuff. Especially not to our families. You have to have someplace to go that doesn't stink like a sewer."

"Morning, Eddie. Morning, Fran. Sorry to interrupt."

"Hey, crazy lady, when did you sneak in?" Crazy lady is Eddie's pet name for me. He thinks it's funny calling a psychologist crazy. He pours a cup of coffee into a worn porcelain mug and sets it in front of me. "What'll you have?" I order a plain toasted bagel with cream cheese. "You're the shrink. Tell her how cops don't like talking about work, except for the funny stuff."

"What's going on?"

Eddie shoves someone's left-behind newspaper at me. There's a photo of Manny and two others on the front page, all of them smiling, thumbs up. "Our boy Manny and his team caught some upstanding resident of our fine city, a lawyer no less, with a shitload of child porn he bought from a dentist in New Jersey. I knew that kid was bound to do good things because he had a good trainer. Me." He takes a bow, first to the left and then to the right. "Thank you, thank you, hold your applause." He slices a bagel and drops it into the toaster. "Seems the good dentist was offering free services to some kids from poor families, putting them under, undressing them and taking more than X-rays of their teeth. Sticking more in their mouths than—"

"Stop it." Fran turns around. Her face is red and shiny with grease. "I don't want to hear it. It's disgusting."

"See what I mean, Doc? Nobody wants to hear what we do for a living. Half the time they don't believe the stuff we see. My third wife complained when I wouldn't talk to her about work. So I used to make shit up. Something she could understand." He dabs at his jowls with a towel and purses his lips. "I had the best day, sweetie. I caught two bank robbers and saved an old lady from a mugger."

Eddie's been a cop for years until he was put on medical leave to treat his alcoholism. Our relationship is good now, although it hasn't always been. While he was still on the job and I was new to KPD, we fought over the way he was treating a rookie he was training. Then I tried to hit him over the head when he sneaked into my house thinking I was being burglarized because he saw an open window on the ground floor of my condo. Someone had recently broken into my house and when I heard Eddie sneaking up the stairs, I thought the vandal had returned. Last year I asked him to help me unmask an unethical therapist. He took a bullet in the gut for his efforts, which didn't help him get his job back. Fran's been looking after him since he was a small boy. Working for her is part of his therapy.

"One day I got fed up with her whining about my never talking. So, I told her the truth. We're in a Chinese restaurant. She's babbling about something. I'm eating rice and thinking about the maggots I saw on a homeless dead guy. She wants to know what I'm thinking about. So I told her. She walked out of the restaurant. Left me there. By myself."

My bagel pops up. Eddie slathers it with cream cheese like he's texturing a wall. Slices a tomato and a red onion, flicks some capers on top, and hands me the plate with a sideways motion like he's throwing a Frisbee.

"Probably 'cause you don't close your mouth when you eat." Fran slaps his backside with her trowel.

"You're just like everybody else, Fran. You think living in Kenilworth is like living in LaLa land. Nothing bad ever happens here."

Fran whacks the trowel against the stove. The sound of metal on metal reverberates like a shot.

"If anyone knows that bad things happen in Kenilworth, I do," Fran says without turning around.

Eddie drops the pan of dirty dishes he is holding on the counter and shakes his head in shame. "I'm an idiot. That was a stupid fucking thing to say. Sorry."

Fran turns around, her face drained of color, and gives him a slap on the arm with her trowel. "Enough already. Stop your yammering and get to work. What am I paying you for?"

"You don't pay me; did you forget?"

"I feed you, don't I? The way you stuff yourself, you're eating up all the profits." She whacks him again on the backside. "Get those dirty dishes in the back, you big oaf."

As soon as he's out of earshot she leans over the counter. The smell of bacon grease clings to her clothes and hair.

"He didn't mean anything bad, I know that. But can you please, please, please, help him get his job back?" She puts her hands together as though praying. "Not only is he going stir crazy working here, he's driving me nuts."

Eddie comes back with the empty dish pan. "What are you doing for Thanksgiving, Doc?" Fran turns back to the stove, but I know she's listening. My love life is of consummate interest to my friends and my mother. Frank's been asking me for months to go home with him at Thanksgiving. Last year I wiggled out of it by saying my mother would be crushed if I didn't spend it at her house. Nothing could have been further from the truth. She had a gaggle full of her women friends over for cocktails and then we all went out for Mexican food and a movie. If I hadn't been there, she would have hardly noticed.

It's not that I don't want to meet Frank's family. They seem really nice. We Skype together and they send me charming handmade greeting cards on every occasion, sometimes just to be friendly. Now that we are officially engaged, I don't think I can put it off any longer. I don't know why I'm hesitant. Afraid I won't fit in? Afraid they won't like me? Afraid I won't like them? I doubt any of them have ever knowingly had a conversation with a psychologist, let alone a Jewish psychologist. Frank tells me my fears are unfounded. His family is not judgmental. He thinks I'm projecting my concerns onto them. I told him to stick to hammering, that he's not licensed to practice therapy.

"So?" Fran says. "You haven't answered Eddie's question. After all his blubbering, he's finally said something important. Are you going to Iowa for Thanksgiving?"

I put a five-dollar bill on the counter. "Stay tuned," I say, borrowing Pence's phrase. "All will be revealed."

I'm being coy. I know perfectly well I am going to Iowa. What I don't know, couldn't have known, is that, at the same time I'm planning what to pack, someone is planning to kidnap Chrissy.

* * *

That's why, three days after we get to Iowa, Frank and I head back to California. The plane ride is uneventful, largely because we are seated in separate rows, having to settle for whatever seats were available on standby. Thanksgiving is a better day to fly than the day after, unless you're hoping the airline attendants will be cheerful about spending the holiday with strangers. During the interminable wait for our luggage we decide to take separate taxis to our separate houses. We're being rational. Frank wants to go home, put the leftovers his sisters stuffed into his suitcase in the refrigerator, take a shower, and go to JJ's place. I need to do the same and get over to the PD. Neither he nor I want to take on the tangle of feelings hovering between us.

My house smells stuffy and unused. It's cold, not as cold as Iowa, but colder than when I left only a few days earlier. I open the refrigerator. There's nothing to eat and I'm hungry. Amazing, considering the endless calories I consumed in Iowa and the promise I made to myself never to eat again. I'm tempted by a few hours of sleep but determined to go to headquarters first to show my concern. I take a quick shower, pull on some slacks, a sweater, and a jacket. As I back out of the garage, the sky is turning from black to purple.

* * *

The command center at headquarters is blanketed in silence. No talking, no laughing. Being able to laugh is as important to a cop's survival as is a gun. It's a pressure valve that relieves the tension accumulated from controlling emotions and trying not to react to the daily dose of misery and miserable people that come with the job. The only problem is that cop humor doesn't work when it comes to children. There's nothing funny about a toddler who's been neglected or abused. No way to blame a child for being raped, murdered, run over by a drunk driver, or kidnapped.

The command center walls are covered with flip chart paper. An annotated timeline extends across one wall. Suspect sheets are scribbled with notes. It is so quiet I can hear the photos of local known sex offenders flutter every time someone walks by the wall where they are pinned. Chrissy's photo is posted at the front of the room. It's the photo from JJ's exhibit, Chrissy naked, in front of a white background, wearing only a headband decorated with a floppy organza bow.

Manny is bent over a laptop. The ceiling light illuminates his shiny black hair. I hadn't noticed before, but there are tiny wisps of gray along the sides. His face concentrates with effort. I stand in the doorway unnoticed. There is nothing I can do to help him or anyone else. This is a police operation, full speed ahead. At times like this cops need a psychologist like a fish needs a bicycle. There will be room enough for my services after Chrissy is found. If she's ever found. And if she's alive.

I leave the command center and grab a cup of coffee from a vending machine. It's hot and vile. Pence has called a meeting of command staff in the conference room. If he's surprised to see me back early from vacation, he doesn't show it. He raps on the table to start.

"We have a media storm to deal with, people. A frenzy. Every newspaper and TV reporter in the Bay Area is here. We have to play this right. Be transparent without revealing any information that will jeopardize the investigation. Any questions before or after the press conference, refer them to me." He studies his notes. "What I plan to say to the press is the minimum, short and sweet. I'm going to read it to you. If you think of anything I've overlooked, shout it out. I don't want to be blindsided." He stands, notes in hand.

"Thank you for coming. We are dealing with a terrible tragedy. An innocent child stolen from the safety of her bedroom during the night.

"Because this is an ongoing investigation, I cannot release the name of the victim or the family. All I can say is that the mother put her child to sleep in the evening, checked on the child before she herself went to bed, and when she returned in the morning, the child was gone. The mother heard nothing during the night. Thank you for your patience. I will be giving periodic updates on the progress of our investigation as I have them."

He folds his paper and looks at us. His airtight smile gone. He has no love for a voracious press, beyond getting his face in the paper when something good happens.

"What am I missing, folks? Just shout it out."

"Someone's going to ask about a ransom note."

"Can't answer. Too early."

"What about the FBI, Chief? Are they coming in? If I'm asking, they'll be asking."

"They're available to help, should we need them. But I doubt we will. I have every faith in you guys. You know the community, they don't. Anything else?"

"What are you telling parents?" I say. "They're going to want to know if they should keep their children home from school. If you anticipate more kidnappings."

"Good one, Dot. I'll remind them that parents should be aware of their children's whereabouts at all times. Stay calm and continue their lives as usual."

"But the child was at home, asleep in her own bed."

A swath of red blooms on Pence's forehead. He does not like being pushed.

"What about the ICAC team?" My second question sends a flush of red down his neck. I gave up several days of vacation to come back here. Might as well make it worth my while.

"What about it?"

"Some reporter is going to ask if you were aware at the time you assigned Manny to the team that Kenilworth children were in danger from traffickers or pedophiles. And why you withheld that information for ten months."

His lips furl into a tight line showing his extra-white teeth. "I resent the implication behind your question, Dot. I would never . . . have never put the citizens of Kenilworth in danger by withholding information that would lead to their safety."

The room rustles with discomfort.

"I'm not asking the question personally," I say. This is only half-true. "I'm merely suggesting you need to be prepared for the press to ask this question. That's what you asked us to do, isn't it?"

"The community doesn't need reassurance that I'm doing my job. It is because I initiated the task force and have a certified investigator at the ready that we are able to respond to this incident so quickly. It is because I had the foresight to face this problem squarely and not pretend something so loathsome couldn't happen here that I am ready to deal with it. I've canceled all leaves. Removed all restrictions on overtime. Asked the surrounding communities to provide mutual aid as needed and to handle all minor calls for service. The community doesn't need reassurance, Dr. Meyerhoff. I know what I'm doing, because I've prepared." He heads for the door, chest out, spine straight, a soldier heading into battle.

CHAPTER FIVE

I WAIT FOR Frank to call me—and when he doesn't—I leave a message for him. It's been two days since we came home from Iowa. Two days without any contact and no news about Chrissy. I tell myself I'm not personally involved. But I'm lying. How could I not be involved? I open the refrigerator. Nothing there. I prepare my fallback cuisine, popcorn with red wine, preferably pinot noir, and turn on the evening news. With Chrissy still missing and no ransom note, Pence is going to step two, put JJ in front of the TV cameras to plead for Chrissy's return. He has already begun talking from the council chambers podium.

"As promised, I can now give you the identity of the missing child. Her name is Chrissy Stewart, two years old. Chrissy's mother, JoAnn Juliette, is here tonight." There's a low murmur. Reporters are turning in their seats. "She's waiting in an adjoining room; she'll join us in a minute." He pauses, waiting for everyone's attention. "Ms. Juliette wants to make a public statement. I'm sure you'll understand that she is under a great deal of strain and will not take any questions."

JJ steps out from behind a door, a uniformed officer next to her. She is simply dressed in jeans, a boxy black sweater, and flats. A large round basket with leather straps hangs over her shoulder. Her face is bare, no makeup to cover her swollen eyes. A lock of hair has pulled loose from her braid and hangs over her face. She brushes it back with one hand and looks at the crowd of reporters.

Pence moves upstage, dismisses the officer, places his hand on the small of JJ's back, and escorts her to the podium. She moves as though she's walking through frozen slush. Pence tilts the microphone toward her mouth. She looks at it and then at Pence. He nods, smiles, signals her that it's her turn to talk. She takes a deep breath.

"I'm Chrissy's mother. My name is JoAnn Juliette. Friends call me JJ." Her voice is soft. Pence moves the microphone closer to her mouth. "I'm a photographer. I'm better with pictures than words. I don't know if I can express what's in my heart." She takes a deep breath. "I love Chrissy more than anything in the world. I don't have words to tell you what being without her is like, not knowing where she is or if she's safe. She's my life and I'm hers." She licks her lips. Pence offers her a glass of water. She takes a drink and wipes her mouth with the back of her hand. "Chrissy is a happy child, a free-spirited child, very sweet with a wonderful disposition. She loves everybody. You only have to have known her for a little while to see how sweet she is." This is the scripted part of the mother's appearance. Humanize Chrissy. Make her real. The more real she is, the harder it will be for someone to hurt her. That's the theory at least.

"Please. Whoever has Chrissy, please return her. Leave her at any church or fire station. Anywhere safe. Please." She grips the edge of the podium with both hands. Long shiny streaks of tears make their way down her face, bright with reflections from the overhead lights.

She stares straight ahead for a moment and then pulls something from her basket. It is Chrissy's toy dog. The one she dangled with one hand in her portrait. It's soft, plush with button eyes, floppy ears, and a stubby tail. JJ sets it on the podium.

"This is Butterfly. Chrissy sleeps with her every night, takes her wherever we go. It's a dog, but Chrissy named her Butterfly because she loves butterflies." She starts to smile at the memory and her smile twists into a grimace. She presses her knuckles against her teeth. The tendons in her neck flare. Pence reaches out and touches her lightly on the shoulder. He leans in. Mouths some private reassurance. She takes a long, deep breath and releases it slowly. The microphone moans softly in response.

"Chrissy won't be able to sleep without Butterfly." JJ presses her hands together. "Please . . ." Her voice rises slightly. "Do the right thing, whoever you are. End this suffering. Yours and ours. I am a Buddhist. I believe in Karma. Whoever took Chrissy is suffering as much as we are. The Buddha says that whatever we do, for good or for evil, to that we will fall heir. Bring Chrissy home safely. Save yourself from lifetimes of suffering." She touches her hands together lightly at the fingertips and dips her head.

There is a roar of questions from the reporters. "Where's Chrissy's father?" someone shouts.

"Thank you for your questions," Pence says. "But we need to let Ms. Juliette leave." He gestures for the uniformed officer to escort JJ off the stage and waits a minute until she's gone before turning back to the waiting reporters. "Chrissy's father is Bucky Stewart," he says.

"Bucky Stewart, venture capitalist?"

Pence ignores the question.

"Who does the mother think took Chrissy?"

"We don't know."

"Are Chrissy's parents divorced?"

"No comment."

"Has there been a ransom demand?"

"We cannot comment on details of the investigation."

"Is there a custody battle? Could the father have taken the child?"

Pence sighs. "I know it's frustrating but I cannot release any more details."

"What was Chrissy wearing when she went to bed?"

He starts to gather his notes. "Thank you, everyone, we'll give you updates as we have them."

"Why won't you answer the question?" someone yells.

I know the answer to that. The more details Pence releases, the more likely the PD will get a slew of false sightings or confessions. People calling in, tying up the phones. They hold back stuff that only the real kidnapper would know.

"Is this a publicity stunt? A way for the mother to bring attention to her photographs?"

That thought has crossed my mind, too.

Pence stops in his tracks. His face dark with anger. "I won't even dignify that absurd assertion with an answer."

There's a shout from the back of the room.

"No more questions," Pence says. "The conference is over."

Now the TV cameras move to the parking lot. A barrage of reporters run around the corner and are stopped at the gate. JJ darts across the pavement to her car, flinching at each shouted question as though she were being pelted by stones. Someone jumps out of the car, runs around the side, and opens the passenger door, deliberately shielding JJ's body from the press. Even in the dark, with all the people and all the movement, I know it's Frank.

The phone rings. I jump and spill half a glass of pinot on the rug.

"Frank?"

"Pence here. Sorry to disappoint. You coming in tomorrow?"

"Yes."

"Come by my office first thing. I need you to do something for me."

* * *

I get to Pence's office before he does and sit in the waiting room. This is odd. Pence rarely consults me on anything, even when it involves something in my field of expertise, like how and who to select for a specialty assignment to the ICAC task force. I believe he'd fire me if he could think of a way to do it without calling negative attention to himself. My first chief, Baxter, would have loved to have dumped me, too, but by the time I exposed him as an underhanded sleazeball, he was the one who was forced to take an early retirement. My second boss liked me but was in such a hurry to leave after a short, stressful stint as chief that I was unable to dissuade her from recommending that Pence be appointed chief after she retired. So he keeps me around to cover his butt in case something bad happens and he can claim he did everything possible to support his officers, including giving them easy access, no-cost-to-them work-related counseling, like every other department in the modern world. He senses that the cops have grown accustomed to me. They no longer believe I have a video camera in my office that goes directly to his office. And, miraculously, they've come to expect that I'll be around when they need me.

"Sorry I'm late. Long night. Didn't get a lot of sleep." He sticks his hand out to shake mine as though our meeting together was an everyday occurrence and I didn't tick him off less than twenty-four hours earlier. His office is still the same old dilapidated room desperately in need of remodeling. Pence looks overdressed for his surroundings in a three-piece suit with matching tie and silk handkerchief. "We're planning a second TV interview with Chrissy's family. I'm not sure if it's a good idea to have the mother and father do this together."

"You've spent time with them, what do you think?"

"Difficult to say. I've only been with them separately. I don't think they're candidates for the Jerry Springer show, but I don't want any surprises. The father's a bit of a rogue. Thinks he knows more than I do. Did you see his interview last night? Standing outside in front of his house. Looks like a giant spaceship. So big the cameras couldn't get it all in. He's marshaled his own private police force. Announced the 'Campaign to find Chrissy.' Clever, huh? Probably got his PR person on it. He wants the public's help to post flyers, comb the woods, check out all the fleabag hotels. Like he's a cop, for Pete's sake. Look at this." He turns his computer screen toward me and zooms in on a freeze frame of Bucky Stewart's wife, Kathryn Blazek, flashing a large button filled with Chrissy's little face and those big, wonder-filled eyes. The same photo that was on display at JJ's exhibit and is hanging in the command center. Only miniaturized and cropped to show Chrissy's face, as though the photo of her naked body hadn't already spread around the world.

"I want your opinion, as a neutral third party, as to whether we can proceed with them together or put them on-screen separately. The mother's an earth biscuit. Nice looking, but airy-fairy."

I should tell Pence right now that I know JJ, but after that snarky comment I decide against it. First off, he thinks I'm a little airy-fairy myself. Secondly, with his attitude, JJ is going to need someone on her side. Technically speaking, I'm not a neutral third party, but at least I'm not a judgmental sexist.

"I need to ask, is either one a suspect in their daughter's disappearance?" I know they are. Most child abductions are parental abductions. Children have more to fear from warring parents than strangers hiding in the bushes.

He raises an eyebrow. "I can't answer that question except to say that we're investigating all possibilities." Now we're in genuine Pence territory. Ask me to do something but don't give me the information I need to do it. "I don't want you to investigate, Dot, I just want your opinion about whether or not they can cooperate long enough to do a TV appearance together." Pence has not yet forgiven me for inserting myself in last year's shooting incident, although without me, that case wouldn't be solved. "Is that something you think you can do or do I need to look for someone else to help?"

"Is that a threat?"

He smiles. "Not at all. I'll understand if you're not able or willing to help."

"Have them come to my office," I say. "I have some free time later this morning."

"Actually, they're in the building, talking to the public information officer. She's like their minder. Hold on a minute." He picks up the phone, says a few words, and hangs up. "They're almost finished. The PIO will walk them up to the conference room in fifteen minutes." Typical Pence. He wasn't asking *if* I would do this, he had it set up all along.

"That doesn't give me any time to prepare."

"You don't need to prepare. I just want your gut reaction. You know, woman's intuition, that sort of thing."

I'd want to say that, as a psychologist, I rely on science, not intuition, but I wouldn't win the argument. Psychology is a soft science. Doesn't help that in California any peacock feather–waving, hot tub–loving psychologist can hang out a shingle. Pence isn't alone thinking that psychology is common sense combined with voodoo.

* * *

The hallway to the conference room is deserted. Anyone not responding to an urgent call is tied up investigating Chrissy's kidnapping. I walk past the command center. It's running in full gear. Everyone, including Manny, looks as if they haven't had time to go home and change clothes. There's a coffee urn in the corner and a tray of pastries donated by Fran who constantly worries that Kenilworth's finest don't get enough to eat, especially when they're under pressure. I can hear Eddie's voice in the back of the room. Eddie never misses an opportunity to go back to police headquarters. I can see his head bobbing up and down as he walks from desk to desk, slapping old friends on the back. By the time he works his way around to me, he's scowling.

"Out of sight, out of mind. I taught some of these punks everything they know." He looks around the room. "I'm a widget. Nobody wants to know how I'm doing, just when am I coming back to work because they need the help. And they don't even wait for an answer before their eyes glaze over and they go back to their frigging computers."

"They're busy, Eddie. It's not you. They're working the kidnapping."

"I know when I'm not wanted. Except for the donuts." He turns around. "This used to be my family. They were going to watch my back. I loved this job. Too bad it didn't love me back." He pushes the delivery cart down the hall, his feet scraping along the floor as if they are too heavy to lift. I'm proud that he's stopped drinking because I know what an effort that is for someone who's been drowning his sorrows in alcohol most of his life. But not drinking isn't the entire answer. Emotionally he's still unstable, too easily wounded, and too desperate to connect.

Manny straightens up, grips the back of his chair, and twists his back from left to right. He walks stiffly to the coffeepot, pours himself a cup, and pokes through the tray of pastries.

"Bear claws," he says. "My favorite."

"When did you last eat real food, Manny?"

"The chief ordered a bunch of pizzas. Last night sometime. I can't remember."

"How's it going?" When a child is kidnapped, the first forty-eight hours are absolutely crucial to the child's survival. We're way past that deadline.

"Not too good."

"Any contact from the kidnappers?"

"Nope. Not a word."

"Is that unusual?"

He shrugs his shoulders. "We got coppers talking to all the neighbors. There have been a few burglaries in the neighborhood the last month. We're running them down. Opportunistic guy busts in looking for something to steal and takes the kid instead."

"The father lives in a mansion. I'll bet there are alarms and security guards all over the place."

"He does, but she doesn't. She lives in the flats. East Kenilworth in an artist's commune. An old warehouse that's been converted to lofts, artist studios, and galleries. They have an open-door policy."

"I know."

He stops, bear claw in midair. "You do? How?"

"I've been there for an art show. My fiancé, Frank, studies photography with the mother." He looks at me so intensely I back up a few steps. "I've only met her once or twice. She seems nice enough although her photographs are a little controversial."

"You think? About this close to pornography, if you ask me." He squeezes his thumb and forefinger together. "That's why I'm here and not at the substation. We're interviewing everyone who lives in the commune. They're not exactly a police-friendly crowd. Plus, all the father's house staff, anyone he ever fired from his business and anybody who ever had a grudge against the family. Plus, a dozen registered sex offenders who live in Kenilworth. Not to mention the nutcases who write to JJ or post stuff about her online. I got my work cut out for me."

"Looks like you haven't been home in a few days."

"How'd you guess?" He smiles, his eyes blurry with fatigue. "And I won't go home until . . ." He doesn't want to say what *until* means, although we both know. Without warning, his eyes fill with tears. He takes a swig of coffee to cover his face.

"Yuck." He pitches the coffee into the sink and rinses out his cup. When he turns back, he's fully in control of himself. It would never do to show tenderness in front of other cops. Tenderness equals weakness and weakness is the fastest way to get yourself ostracized. No one wants to work with a weak officer. Weak officers are undependable.

"What are you doing here?"

"The chief asked me to meet with the parents. See if they can do a TV interview together. Are they suspects?"

"Sure. We always go there first. There are cops crawling all over where they live, looking for stuff, secret rooms, locked closets, bloodstains, bleach. So far, nothing."

My cell phone goes off. It's the chief telling me that the PIO is almost finished interviewing JJ and Bucky. I don't know about JJ, but I'll bet Bucky doesn't tolerate being kept waiting.

"Got to go. Take care of yourself, Manny. Don't work too hard."

"I'll stop when the bad guys stop." His laugh is a mirthless bark.

CHAPTER SIX

THE CONFERENCE ROOM has a one-way mirror into an adjoining office. I stand there watching as the PIO shakes everyone's hand and leaves.

"How'd it go?" I ask. She's a redhead, sharp as a tack, and very good at finessing reporters' questions, saying a lot and revealing little.

"Nothing new," she says.

"What's your opinion? Do you think they should do this together?"

"Hard to say, I'm not a psychologist, but they seem okay with each other. A little stiff, but no fighting or finger-pointing. I'd take my chances they can stay on topic. Let me know if you think differently. I have to write up my notes. FYI, they're pretty exhausted."

I turn back to the one-way mirror. JJ's arms are stretched out on the table and she is resting her head like a schoolchild taking a nap. There are dark welts under her eyes, and she is wearing the same jeans and sweater she had on yesterday. Her braid has come loose at the base. Bucky is leaning back in his chair, eyes closed, his hands resting on the table in front of him. He's short, balding, well tanned, and muscular. Dressed in pressed jeans, a multicolored pullover, and tasseled loafers without socks, he looks as though he's about to board his yacht for the Bahamas. Kathryn Blazek is rubbing his shoulder. Her eyes are darting from him to JJ and back again.

I enter the room and JJ sits up. "Dot. Thank you for coming. I'm so glad to see a familiar face." She reaches for me with both hands. Her smile is lustrous. And brief.

"Me, too." Kathryn stands and extends her hand. She turns to JJ. "We met at your showing. By accident. We were standing together in front of Chrissy's portrait." She starts to tear up and sits down.

I introduce myself to Bucky and explain how I know JJ, just to keep the playing field even. This is a man who keeps score. Any breach in my neutrality would put him off.

"Why are we talking to a psychologist? We don't need counseling. We need to find our daughter."

"I'm not here to do counseling, Mr. Stewart. Chief Pence has asked me to spend a little time with you to see if there's anything that will interfere with the two of you cooperatively making a plea to your daughter's kidnapper. This has nothing to do with counseling."

"No problem then," Bucky says pushing his chair back from the table. "Ask away."

"It's important that the two of you present a united front. Is there anything that might interfere with that?"

"Not unless you consider that Chrissy's mother, having chosen to live in a commune in a totally unsecured building with unidentified people coming and going all day, might be a reason to harbor some animosity." JJ closes her eyes and shakes her head just slightly. My guess is that she's heard this before. "I give you enough money so that you could afford to live anywhere you want."

"I live exactly where I want to live," JJ says in a soft voice, her eyes focused on me.

"That's your choice. You're an adult, but Chrissy's a baby. From now on, if you want to see her, you can come to my house where she has a nanny, a security guard, and an alarm system on every window."

Kathryn places one hand on Bucky's arm to quiet him. "Please tell the chief that they can do this. Getting Chrissy back is more important than whatever any of us may think or feel at the moment." By anything else I presume she means blame, guilt, crushing disappointments, and devastating betrayals. Thank God Mark and I didn't have any children to complicate our divorce. Our pain was our own. No children were harmed in the process.

* * *

Later that afternoon, after JJ and Bucky's televised appearance, I walk past the briefing room where a small crowd of cops are talking about it. I stop to listen.

"The mother's a looker," somebody says about JJ with her swollen eyes and blotchy face.

"Some creep snatched her kid. Have a little couth."

"The father's rolling in dough. Must be women crawling all over him. Wonder why he didn't marry the mother."

A voice sings from the back. "If you want to be happy for the rest of your life, never make a pretty woman your wife, so from my personal point of view, get an ugly girl to marry you."

"Never know what turns a guy on. Maybe she has other talents." One of the reserve officers makes an obscene gesture with his tongue. The cop next to him spots me and jabs his friend hard in the ribs.

"Hey, Doc," he says. "C'mon in. We got questions about these parents. You got the PhD. Help us out." I step into the room. "The mother keeps saying she's not angry. What's that all about? Some guy touches our kid, my wife would hang his balls on the Christmas tree. Pardon my French."

"I don't even let my wife take pictures of our kid in the bathtub and send them to her mother," someone else chimes in. "That woman's pictures are pornographic. I've seen them. What did she expect would happen to her kid when she put them on the Internet? In my humble opinion, she asked for it. What do you think, Doc?"

They look at me as though my degree equips me to speculate on JJ's motives like those TV shrinks, including my ex, who jump at every chance to offer their uninformed but pathologically certain opinions to the public. Mark would know if JJ asked for it. He'd have an opinion about whether or not she was a good mother even though he never met her and has no specialized training in assessing parental competency. Are JJ's photos of Chrissy pornographic? He'd have an opinion about that, too. I'd make a lousy pundit. If the Supreme Court's threshold test for obscenity and pornography is "I know it when I see it," how am I supposed to figure it out?

* * *

There's a message on my phone from Frank. His voice is reedy.

"JJ's staying at my house for a few days to avoid reporters. Can you come by tonight? Maybe bring us some dinner? I'm too bushed to cook. Miss you."

JJ staying at his—almost our—house for two days? Why didn't Frank ask me first? I go to the bathroom. I need to wash my face and calm down. I look in the mirror, staring at my reflection like the Wicked Queen in Snow White. Here I am worrying about who's the fairest in the land when JJ's world is falling apart. And God knows what's happening to Chrissy. There is nothing more horrible than losing a child. Nothing. It leaves a hole in your heart that can never be fixed. The only thing that could make it worse would be knowing that you were the one responsible for putting your precious child in harm's way.

* * *

JJ looks worse than she did on TV. Her eyes are sunken and rimmed with purplish circles. Her lips are chapped and the skin around her mouth is a raw red. She stands when I walk into the living room, thanks me for my support, telling me how much it meant to have someone on her side at the police station. I start to tell her it wasn't my idea and stop.

"I know they all think this is my fault. How could they not? It is my fault." She tears up and sits on the couch next to a neatly folded pile of sofa-sized blankets and sheets. I feel relieved. Also, small-minded and mean-spirited. "Somebody once said that fame is a prize that burns the winner. They were right. Chrissy, my nieces and my nephews did whatever I asked them to do. If somebody took Chrissy because he thought she was sexy, it's because I posed her that way. Asked her to look directly into the camera. I made her look sultry. The second before and the second after I took that shot, she was giggling, like any ordinary child."

She grits her teeth, biting back tears. "What have I done?" she asks no one in particular, except herself.

Frank takes my grocery bags into the kitchen, puts them down, and gives me a long hug that I wish was even longer. We unpack the groceries. Bread, salad fixings, cheese and eggs for an omelet, my one reliable culinary achievement beyond popcorn.

"Can you help her?"

"Nothing's going to help her until Chrissy comes home. If she comes home."

JJ walks into the kitchen, touching her long fingers to the wall and the doorway for support. She appears to have lost ten pounds in three days.

"Did you just come from the police station? Is there any news?"

I shake my head. "Someone will call you the minute they hear anything."

She looks at the food spread out on the counter.

"I'm afraid I'm not hungry. Sorry to disappoint after you've gone to all this trouble."

"No trouble at all. I'll cook. Maybe you'll be hungry in a little while."

"I won't be hungry ever. Not until Chrissy comes home."

She picks at her food. A mouthful of egg, a forkful of salad. She refuses wine for fear of losing her ability to concentrate and stay alert. I want to tell her that sleep deprivation is the cognitive equivalent of being drunk and urge her to take a nap, but she refuses. Someone may call with news or a ransom demand. I clear the dishes, leaving her a chunk of bread and butter. Just in case. Frank follows me into the kitchen.

"I'll clean up. See if you can get her to talk. Woman to woman. When she's with me, she just sits and stares."

I take my wine and head into the living room. JJ is sitting on the couch, cell phone in hand, her long legs curled beneath her.

"Don't you want to take a shower? Change your clothes?"

"I don't want to miss the telephone."

"We can answer it."

"What if it's not the police? What if it's the man who took her and he'll only talk to me?"

"What man? Any particular man?"

"The police asked me that. No. No one in particular."

"Tell me about yourself," I say. Mostly as a distraction. Partly out of curiosity.

"What's to say? Normal happy childhood. Nothing out of the ordinary until Chrissy came along. She changed my life."

"Were you and Bucky ever married? He and Kathryn seem like they've been together forever. Just an impression."

She laughs. "Married. Me and Bucky? Heavens no." She untangles her legs and shifts to face me. "We met in Hawaii. Bucky was on a business trip without Kathryn. I was on a photography assignment.

We met in the hotel bar. He seemed nice. I was lonely. So was he. We had an affair and I got pregnant. Simple as that."

"Nothing is that simple," I say.

"We stayed in touch after we got back to California. That's how he knew I was pregnant. He's an honorable man. I don't think he's cheated on Kathryn a lot. But he was at a low point in his marriage, bored I guess. Looking for a little excitement. I was younger, pretty. I didn't have a lot of money and he did. So, I got to go to nice places. But it was never anything more than a fling for me."

I wonder if infidelity is inevitable for men. No doubt there is a biological imperative that drives men to spread their endless supply of sperm to as many females as possible in order to propagate the species, while we females zealously guard our spare allotment of eggs. That was true for Mark who now has a baby, maybe more than one, with his young wife when he never wanted one with me.

"Kathryn is apparently unable to have children. So when I got pregnant, Bucky was thrilled. He wanted to leave her and marry me. I wanted to be pregnant, but I have no interest in marriage. Or money, although everyone I knew thought I'd hit the jackpot. Money changes you. It makes you care more about material things than people or the planet."

"He doesn't give you child support?"

"He does. He's very generous. But I only agreed to accept enough money to pay for Chrissy's schooling, cover our living expenses, and buy art supplies."

"And Kathryn?"

"She's been wonderful. Loves Chrissy like her own child. I'm grateful for her support. She's a forgiving person. Not many women would have the generosity of heart that she has."

I certainly wouldn't. Look at me. Relieved to see JJ's linens folded on the couch, at the same time I wonder if Frank put them there to fool me into thinking he and JJ weren't sleeping together. I can't imagine how Kathryn manages to stay calm and collected watching her husband and his ex-lover orbit around their love child, still a presence in each other's lives. Frank's never given me a reason to distrust him. But then again, neither did Mark. Yet there he was, having an affair with Melinda, literally under my nose, while I was too dumb, too besotted, too I don't-know-what, to notice. I'm not proud of that, nor do I take any pride in the fact that I seem to have turned into a suspicious female whose guiding mantra about life and men is, "Fool me once, shame on you; fool me twice, shame on me."

CHAPTER SEVEN

TWO DAYS LATER, the radio alarm wakes me at 6:00 a.m. I was at my office late last night writing reports. Frank was out photographing workers at a night-time road repair project so I went home, poured myself a glass of wine, made a bowl of popcorn, and collapsed in front of the TV watching a stupid cop show where an implausibly beautiful detective in stiletto heels kicks in a door by herself, shoots two suspects before the first commercial, and winds up having vigorous sex with her implausibly beautiful cop boyfriend. I don't know what I'll do to de-stress when Frank and I are living together.

The traffic report screeches to a stop with the announcement of breaking news heralded by a blast of terrible music and a reminder that this is the station informed listeners rely on for the latest updates in their world. I roll over to hit the snooze button.

"The body of a small child has been found in a dumpster in East Kenilworth. It is presumed to be the body of Chrissy Stewart who was kidnapped from her bed less than a week ago. The police are not revealing any information until the child's identity is confirmed and they notify the family. Updates every five minutes." It's Chrissy, who else could it be? I feel like throwing up. This beautiful child, all promise and potential, destined for the best life has to offer, tossed in a dumpster like a piece of garbage. Her parents doomed to a life disfigured by never-ending grief and unanswered questions. Longing for the past a constant ache. I call Frank. He's already heard the news and is rushing over to JJ's. He promises to call me later.

I take a shower, dress for the office, and eat breakfast. It seems wrong to be doing these ordinary things. I wonder what JJ and Bucky are doing. Are they in shock, sedated, suicidal? Screaming, crying, blaming? Humans are meaning-making mammals. We can't abide randomness. In the absence of facts to help us make sense of chaos, we are driven to search for explanations, villains, something or someone to blame. When we find nothing, we blame ourselves. This is a monstrous crime. There's little I can do to help JJ, but there are things I can do to help the cops. A short defusing to acknowledge the impact that crimes against children have on an officer's psyche. Some tips on self-care. Later on, an extended debriefing. After the case is solved. If it ever is.

* * *

There are always one or two cops who grumble about defusings and debriefings being too touchy-feely. Eddie Rimbauer is one of them. Left to his own devices, before he stopped drinking, he'd opt for choir practice, boozing it up in the parking lot with his buddies. Now he's delivering coffee and cookies and giving me advice.

"Don't put out Kleenex. That'll shut them down. If they need to wipe their noses, they can use napkins. I left extra. And don't ask nothing about their childhoods."

"I never do, you know that. This is not therapy. It's a time to talk about what's happened, what to expect, psychologically and physically, and how to take care of yourself and your family."

"You were plenty interested in my childhood."

"You're a special case. Now, if you're finished telling me how to do my job, you can leave. Thank Fran for the goodies and thank you for bringing them."

The door to the conference room opens. A dozen patrol officers and a dispatcher file in. They look exhausted and very grim.

"Don't keep 'em too long. They need sleep. Don't let the chief in here and don't forget to remind them about confidentiality."

"Thank you, Eddie," I say, shoving him from behind.

"The doc is okay." He waves to the group. "Listen to what she has to say, otherwise you'll wind up like me, pushing a coffee cart instead of driving a patrol car."

* * *

There's a certain formality to defusings and debriefings that lends some structure to the conversation. Cops like structure: they want to know what to expect next. The unknown is what gets them hurt. I go over the ground rules—what's said in this room stays in the room, speak for yourself not anyone else, don't sit on your feelings—we've been through this before, most of them know the drill.

I start with the dispatcher as Manny rushes in the door and grabs a seat. Her name is Linda. She took the call from the person who found Chrissy. Young and relatively new with small children of her own, she's not yet carrying the extra pounds many dispatchers accumulate from sitting for hours attached to a console by a cable that reaches no further than the nearest tray of cupcakes. Cops can run, jump, and yell to spill their stress. A dispatcher is forced to stay calm no matter what she's hearing on the other end of a 911 call.

"The call came in about four thirty a.m. from a janitor. He was emptying garbage into the dumpster behind the building he cleans.

He thought she was a doll wrapped in a blanket. He was very upset. When he turned her over, she . . ." Linda releases a long sigh that whistles through the room. "She was made up like a woman—lipstick, eye shadow, and false eyelashes. He said it was grotesque."

"Did he describe the blanket?" Manny says.

"Pink with green butterflies."

Something shifts in Manny's face. His eyes, his skin color, in this light, I can't tell which.

"Got an address for this dumpster? I just got in, went home to get a little sleep."

"Manny," I say. "I need to remind you and everyone else that this is a psychological, not a tactical, debriefing."

He turns his head and stings me with his eyes. "And I need to remind you, Doc, that we have a dead baby and we don't know who killed her. Once again," he says to Linda, "where was the dumpster?"

She hesitates and looks at me. "Okay to say?"

It never works for a civilian to argue with a cop in front of his buddies. Even if the cops hate each other, they'll team up and turn on the outsider.

"Sure," I say. "It's not a secret."

She takes a deep breath. "In East Kenilworth. Outside some artist's commune."

Before I can react, there is a commotion in the hall, loud voices, the sound of someone throwing something against a wall. Everyone goes on alert, our bodies stiff with adrenaline.

Manny steps to the side of the door, his hand on his weapon. The other cops scatter. Someone tells Linda and me to get under the table. The door flies open while I'm still on my feet. Bucky Stewart, his face florid, eyes popping from their sockets, screams into the room.

"Where is she? Where is her body?"

Pence is right behind him and behind Pence is a line of cops.

Bucky turns around, nose-to-nose with Pence. Pence pushes him into the room, gently but firmly, until he is up against the table. Three cops follow.

"You need to calm down and listen. I have no options here. The law requires me to have the medical examiner do an autopsy in any circumstance when someone, including a child, has died in a violent or suspicious manner or when we don't have a clear cause of death. The medical examiner will work as quickly as possible to release Chrissy's body for a funeral. Do you understand?"

Bucky leans against the table. He's breathing hard, staring as though Pence is talking in Chinese.

"How long?"

"How long what?"

"How long will you keep her?"

"I don't keep her, she's at the medical examiner's office."

Bucky slams his fist against the table.

"I know that, you just told me. How long will the medical examiner keep her?"

"I don't know. I will ask him and get back to you. He will want to perform a number of tests. This can take a while." He speaks slowly, sweat dripping off his nose and chin. "It may not be necessary to keep Chrissy's body until the test results are available. But again, I would have to ask the medical examiner." He reaches his hand out to touch Bucky's shoulder. Bucky throws it off and moves out of reach. "I will ask about the waiting list. We have one medical examiner. Sometimes there's a queue."

"The fuck there is." Bucky's face goes florid again and he pushes against the table so hard it screeches across the floor. "My daughter is not waiting in line. I'll hire my own medical examiner before that happens."

"Before anything happens, Mr. Stewart, the medical examiner needs an identification. To make sure this is your daughter."

"Who else's daughter could it be? Jesus, Mary, and Joseph. What a bunch of fucking Keystone cops." Bucky pushes Pence with two hands, sending him backward, and races out the door.

"Want me to go after him?" someone asks.

Pence shakes his head. "No harm done. Let him go. The poor guy's hurting way worse than I could ever imagine."

* * *

Frank and JJ are sitting side by side on hard wooden chairs staring at an arrangement of landscape paintings. Decorating a room that is barely ten feet away from a half-dozen dead bodies places limits on the kind of art being displayed. Anatomical drawings of the human form, however close to the medical examiner's essential mission, would hardly be appropriate.

JJ reaches out to me with a bony hand; her touch is light as a sparrow.

"Thank you for coming."

"I'm so sorry."

"At least it's over. I know where she is and she's not suffering."

"We don't yet know if it's Chrissy." Frank is pale as a ghost.

"It's Chrissy," JJ says. "I can feel her."

The door to the waiting room bangs open. Bucky charges into the room. Kathryn following behind.

"Where is she?" Bucky's voice splinters the unnatural stillness.

"They haven't called us yet," JJ says.

Kathryn's eyes are bloated with tears. She starts to say something to JJ and then drops her head. JJ stands, taking both of Kathryn's hands in her own—they are still as statues, except for the tears running down both their faces. An interior door opens and a middle-aged woman wearing a dark business suit walks toward us. Her steps are slow and deliberate, giving us time to adjust to the inevitable. She has ruddy cheeks and teased hair the color of cotton candy that has been left out in the sun. She introduces herself as a medical examiner's investigator. As soon as she says her name, I forget it.

"Who is here to identify the child?" Her voice is soft, with a practiced, pastoral cadence.

Bucky, JJ, and Kathryn stand.

"I'm sorry, but I just need the child's biological parents." Kathryn sits down.

Mrs. What's-her-name, I presume she's married from a wedding set on her left hand, looks at me and Frank. "And you are?"

"Friends," Frank says. Mrs. What's-her-name asks us to take seats across the room. Kathryn grabs my arm the minute I sit down. "I loved her, too, no less than they do," she says in a watery voice, cupping her hand over her mouth.

The investigator motions Bucky and JJ to sit. She sets a chair in front of them and lowers herself slowly as though she were starting a Japanese Tea Ceremony. She lays a blue folder on her lap, places her hands over it, and takes a slow breath.

"Our procedure is not to ask you to view the child's body, but rather to identify her from a photograph."

"No photograph. I want to see her."

"I'm sorry, Mr. Stewart. I understand that you want to touch her, but this is our policy. If this is your daughter, we will release her body in a matter of days. And then you'll be free to touch her."

"Now. I want her now." Bucky scoots to the edge of his chair until his knees touch the investigator's legs and they are almost nose-to-nose.

"When there is no obvious cause of death, we need to run a battery of tests. The results of these tests can take up to six weeks, sometimes longer."

Bucky clenches his fists.

"Please understand. We don't need her body for six weeks. We can release her in a day or two."

JJ touches Bucky's arm. He pulls it away as though he's been burned, hesitates, and sits back. The investigator remains motionless—only her chest rising and falling in rapid respirations betrays what is beneath her calm.

"Testing is a matter of standard policy and government regulations. The tests are necessary to determine the cause of death when it is not obvious."

Now JJ moves to the front of her chair. "Was she beaten or raped? Can you at least tell us that?"

"The results of the tests will be released to . . ." The investigator opens the blue file and looks at her notes. Her every movement slow and deliberate. "Officer Manuelo Ochoa."

"Why not to me? I'm her father. Or to her mother?"

"Because this is an open homicide investigation. Our policies are mandated by law. Within a month, we will also convene a child death review system involving the police, child protective services, county mental health, the district attorney's offices, myself, and possibly one of the doctors from our office. In addition to discussing the cause of death, we will be considering the welfare of other children in the home."

Bucky jumps to his feet, knocking over his chair. "There are no other children in the home. Chrissy was my only child." He leans over the investigator. "If you think one of us did this to Chrissy, you're crazy."

The interior door opens and a uniformed officer walks in the room, summoned by some secret code or button. It's obvious he and the investigator have encountered this kill-the-messenger reaction before.

Kathryn leans forward. "Bucky, please, sit down. You're making things worse."

JJ stands. Towering over Bucky. "Kathryn's right. Please sit down. I'd like to get this over with. Chrissy's at peace, Bucky. What's happened has happened. I just want to go home."

He turns on her. "You don't have a home, you have a fucking commune."

The uniformed officer steps further into the room.

"Please, Mr. Stewart, let's all sit down again." The investigator places her hand on Bucky's arm and guides him into his chair as if he were not only brokenhearted, but blind. "If this is your daughter, we will need your help to understand the circumstances of her death. That's all you can do for her now. And the first step is to make a proper identification so that the police can start their investigation." She removes a small black-and-white photograph from the folder she's been holding on her lap, and carefully lays it on top as if she were showing a precious object to a potential buyer. I can see from across the room that all traces of makeup have been removed. Bucky glances at it, moans softly, and starts to rock. His moaning bounces off the walls like a caged bird looking to escape. Kathryn pushes out of her chair, tries to stand, and then sinks back, collapsing against my shoulder. JJ picks the photo up and holds it, her long fingers tracing Chrissy's image over and over again. She presses it to her chest. "May I take this with me?"

The investigator gently pulls the photo from JJ's hand. "I'm so sorry, but that's not allowed. The photo is evidence. Once your daughter's body is released you, of course, may take as many photos as you like."

* * *

After Frank and JJ leave, I need to use the bathroom. When I open the door, I hear Bucky and Kathryn arguing in the hall.

"This is bullshit. I'm getting a lawyer. I'll get my own goddamn autopsy. I don't care what it costs, I'm not waiting any six weeks."

"Six weeks is just for the test results. That's how long it takes for the results, no matter who does it. Please don't do this, Bucky. There's nothing to be gained by it. Let the police do their job. I don't care if I never know the results. The idea of an autopsy destroying Chrissy's little body is more than I can take."

Bucky's howl is beyond human.

"You see what I mean? Another autopsy will cause you more pain than you already have. Our hearts are broken. Please don't do anything to make it worse. We need to grieve together and to plan her funeral. Let's not let anything else get in the way."

* * *

Frank calls me at eight p.m. He's at home, exhausted.

"I just left JJ. Been there all day."

"I can't imagine what she's going through. And what you're going through trying to be supportive."

He makes a kind of coughing, choking sound. I hold the phone and wait until he speaks again.

"I have never felt so helpless in my entire life. What do you say to someone whose child has been murdered?"

I haven't a clue. Psychology isn't about morality or good and evil. It's about understanding behavior. It can be illuminating, but it is rarely comforting at a time of intense grief.

"The place is lousy with people. Too many. Everyone who lives in the commune is milling around. Lots of hugging and crying. The phone rang all day. She doesn't want to talk to anyone. I spent most of my time making coffee and sandwiches for people while JJ was in her bedroom weeping. Such agony. It was hard to listen to. She came out around five, refused any food, and told us all to go home because 'It is what it is.' God, I hate that expression. What does it mean? Roll over, forget it? Move on."

"What happened after she said that?"

"She went into her studio to meditate. She's been there ever since. I went to the store, bought some groceries, made her a pot of soup, and waited around. About six thirty a guy came looking for her. We sent him to her studio. Somebody said he was the Buddhist teacher from JJ's spiritual center. I stuck around another hour until I got tired of waiting and went home."

"Sometimes all you can do is show up and be present for people. You did that. I love you for it. I'll get in my car and come over. You could probably use a little support yourself. I can stop and get something to eat if you're hungry."

"Thanks, but no thanks. I'm not fit company for anyone."

CHAPTER EIGHT

CHRISSY'S BODY IS released by the medical examiner within the week. The cause of death is listed as "pending." Further testing is required on tissue and body fluid samples that were retained during the autopsy. Estimated findings regarding the cause of her death could now take as long as eight weeks, possibly longer.

There are two funerals scheduled. The first, at Bucky and Kathryn's place of worship, is private, family only. The announcement is accompanied by an obituary in the local paper and a picture of Chrissy, smiling and happy. She is seated in an upholstered chair in front of a fireplace, wearing a red velvet dress, patent leather Mary Janes, and white socks trimmed with lace ruffles. I think back to JJ's so very different portrait. That poor child led two parallel lives. Both of them far too short.

Frank and I are invited to what JJ insists is not a funeral but a celebration of Chrissy's life and a rite of transition. At the commune, in the large gallery. I'm on my way to talk to Pence. No doubt there will be cops at the celebration, scanning the crowd for suspects. If that's how Pence finds out that I have a personal relationship with JJ, I'll be in a lot of trouble.

I catch him in his office before the staff meeting. I haven't seen him since the day Chrissy's body was found. He looks exhausted. Bloodshot eyes ringed by puffy dark circles. Pence is not one to get emotionally involved with cases, but who isn't thunderstruck by the murder of this innocent child, her face a painted mockery of God-knows-what happened to her before she died. Whatever I think or feel about him is beside the point. This is happening on his watch. The buck always stops with the chief.

"Rough week?" I ask.

"The worst." He drops his briefcase on his desk. Stares at it lying there unopened.

"Coffee?" His secretary has been in early and started the coffeepot. "Black, cream, sugar?"

"Black."

The mugs on the tray next to the coffeepot are cobalt blue with gold KPD insignia. I fill one and hand it to him. Both of us silently surprised that I, of all people, am serving him coffee.

"These are nice."

"My wife bought them for me. Trying to add a little class to my office." He looks around. "I told her, it's going to take more than that." He takes a sip. "What can I do for you, Dot?" He sounds resigned, none of the usual irritation or impatience in his voice.

"I need to tell you something."

He lets out a long sigh, as though I'm about to deliver another one of the hundreds of dead-end tips that have come in over the tip line.

"Shoot."

"You should know that I have a personal relationship with JoAnn Juliette." There's a twitch in one of his eyebrows. Nothing more. "My fiancé, Frank, studies photography. He's part of a small group of people who study with JoAnn Juliette at her studio, in the commune where she lives. Besides having talked to her here at headquarters before the TV interviews, I've been to a photo show she put on at a local gallery and an exhibit of her students' work at the commune. I was also present when she and Bucky went to identify Chrissy's body."

Pence opens his mouth to say something and then closes it again.

"Frank has grown close to JJ. After Chrissy was kidnapped, JJ stayed at Frank's house for several days to avoid the press. I had dinner with the two of them one evening. Actually, JJ wouldn't eat. And she's invited us to Chrissy's funeral."

He looks at me. His face unreadable. "Anything else?"

"I know a little about JJ and Bucky's relationship."

"And you're going to tell me that you can't tell me about it because it's confidential. Is that it?" The Pence I know is finally waking up.

"No. I'm not going to say that. JJ is not my client. She's also really not my friend, more like an acquaintance. She's Frank's friend and an important person in his life."

"Does Frank take nude pictures of little kids, too?"

"No. He takes photos of people at work. Most of his portraits are of construction workers." Pence nods. "I should also tell you I've talked briefly with Chrissy's stepmother when JJ had a show at the gallery."

"And Chrissy's father?"

"You asked me to interview him and JJ to see if they could cooperate for the TV interview. And then I saw him again when he crashed into the conference room demanding Chrissy's body be released. As I said, I was also present at the coroner's office when he and JJ went to identify Chrissy's body. No other contact."

Pence drums his fingers against his desk for a long minute. "Do you have any information relevant to Chrissy's death?"

"No."

"What's your opinion about JJ? Is she off the charts? Is she a pervert?"

I shake my head. "No."

"What about this cult she belongs to?"

"What cult?"

"They sit around on pillows. Burning incense. Chanting."

"I think she's a Buddhist. Buddhism is not a cult."

"It is in my book. Unless you're Chinese." Pence is either incredibly ignorant or he's baiting me. I choose the latter and don't bite.

"What I'm really asking is do you think the mother did this?"

"You mean murdered her own child? No. Definitely not. Some might call her eccentric. But I think her grief and despair are genuine. So does Frank who knows her better than I do. And I trust his opinion."

"Good thing if you're going to marry him. What about Bucky or the stepmother?"

"The father's like a loose cannon. But according to JJ, both he and the stepmother adored Chrissy. They were concerned about her living in a commune. And about the photos."

"No shit. Glad somebody has some sense." He takes another sip of coffee and swallows loudly.

"I know parents are the first suspects in a child abduction, but even if Bucky and JJ were fighting over custody, why would either one of them kill the very child they were fighting over?"

"If I can't have her, neither can you. Happens all the time."

I don't know about *happens all the time*. I'm a psychologist, not a criminologist. "What about the makeup, the lipstick, and the eyelashes? Doesn't that suggest pornography? Isn't that what you've been worried about? The whole reason you started the task force? Maybe Chrissy was kidnapped by a pornographer who saw JJ's photographs. Maybe he thought he could use JJ's famous photos as a come-on to his own pictures of Chrissy." The very thought makes me nauseous.

"Interesting theory. What are you now, an FBI profiler? The big mistake amateurs make, Dr. Meyerhoff, is to fit the facts to the theory rather than let the facts create the theory. I believe psychologists call that deductive rather than inductive reasoning." He swings his chair around so that the sun coming in the window puts him in silhouette, and I can't see his face. "I will continue to order my officers to investigate any and every lead," he says as though he's back at the podium, talking to the press. "I've asked Manny to head up the investigation."

"This is a homicide. Manny's not a homicide detective."

He swivels his chair back to face me.

"First you objected when I appointed Manny to the ICAC team. Now you think putting him in charge of this investigation is a bad idea. What is it with you and Manny? And does Frank the Fiancé know?"

I ignore the implication. Manny is young enough to be my son.

"It's the principle," I say. "When you give people responsibilities without the proper training or screening, it creates stress. That's part of my contract, to identify sources of organizational stress."

"I pay you big money to screen and train my employees, to insure they won't fall apart on the job. Manny's a good man. A capable officer. Credentialed to investigate crimes associated with child pornography. Which, as you have suggested, is a distinct possibility in this case. He can handle whatever I give him. Stop babying him."

"I'm not babying him. I'm trying to apply behavioral science to making wise employment decisions."

"Well then, how about employing some behavioral science to your friendship with Chrissy's mother? That would be a lot more useful. Instead of digging around in my business, dig around in hers."

My father's voice rises up in my head. He would have called Pence a Nazi. Warned me not to cooperate, railed that a Jew doesn't turn her friends over to the enemy.

"But she's a friend."

"I thought you said she was only an acquaintance."

"Whatever. My relationship with her is personal. I'm not going to dig around in her life."

"I don't care if you think she's Mother Teresa. You work for me. If you withhold information pertinent to this case, I can charge you as an accessory to Chrissy's murder."

I have no idea if this is or isn't legal, but it certainly feels threatening.

"Are you asking me to play undercover cop with my personal associates? You have forbidden me to get involved in police investigations. In no uncertain terms and on multiple occasions."

Pence grins. Invigorated by our little fencing match. "I've changed my mind. It's a man's prerogative as much as it is a woman's. You are in a position to be helpful, rather than interfering. It's probably a once-in-a-lifetime opportunity, so I'm going to take it."

"How I can be helpful?"

"Keep your eyes and ears open. If you hear something, anything, that might be relevant, bring it to me or Manny. We'll decide if it's useful."

"And if Frank hates me for spying on his friend and teacher?"

"I can't help you with that."

"And if the person who killed Chrissy tries to kill me?"

Pence stands up, walks to my side, and gives me an avuncular pat on the shoulder. "Do let me know about that. Preferably before it happens."

* * *

The morning of Chrissy's celebration and rite of transition is gloomy. JJ has requested mourners to wear white. Anything white that I own is stuffed with my summer clothes in a plastic bag under my bed. The best I can come up with is a gray silk shirt the color of the sky and dark gray pants. When Frank picks me up, I see the same is true for him. We drive together, silently, two people dressed in gray with moods to match.

The doors to the commune gallery are open and draped with garlands of white flowers. There are candles burning everywhere. A low chant vibrates the air. The front of the room is dominated by a large altar surrounded by floor cushions and a circle of chairs. Almost every seat is taken. Frank and I find two chairs in the back, off to the side. I see Anjelika and others of JJ's young students sitting cross-legged on the floor cushions, eyes closed with their hands resting on their spread knees, palms up. Anjelika's face is streaked with tears.

JJ is seated next to the altar on a large cushion, her body wrapped in meditative posture, still as the statue of Buddha next to her on a low table. This is not the fat, happy Buddha, his hands in the air that oversees my mother's garden, but a slender, contemplative figure of carved wood. JJ looks positively ethereal in flowing white pants and a loose gauzy top, a row of white flowers fixed to her long braid. Her face is washed clean. The scorched red skin around her mouth and eyes has healed and there is fullness back in her cheeks.

The now famous portrait of Chrissy, naked, wearing only a floppy bow on her head, sits on the altar, surrounded by flowers and colorful butterflies. She looks out at us from her frothy white world with curious eyes as though wondering why on earth this room is full of somber-faced adults who look so sad.

A tall, slender man with graying hair steps forward and positions himself next to the altar. He is wearing white pants and a matching long-sleeved shirt. A red string is tied around his left wrist. He closes his eyes, puts his hands together in the prayer position, and bows slightly, first to the statue of Buddha, then to JJ, then to Chrissy's picture, then to all of us.

"Welcome," he says. "My name is Gordon Feinstein. I am the founder and main teacher of the Kenilworth Meditation Center. Welcome, everyone."

Feinstein? My father's voice thunders in my ears. *Jew-Bu. Traitor.* He would have spat the words. *Abandoning your people for a tribe of do-nothing cowards who pretend sitting on a pillow is going to right the wrongs of this world.* The memory makes me wince. My father was a torment of contradictions. One day, rejecting religion as an illicit, oppressive authority designed to camouflage the sins of the villainous rich behind a facade of holiness. The next day, railing at anyone, no matter how desperate or life-threatening their circumstances, who hid their Jewish roots.

"Dot." Frank nudges me in the ribs. "You're talking to yourself."

Feinstein raises his hands and bows again. "We are gathered today in the Buddhist tradition to celebrate Chrissy's short life, to remember how she enriched our lives while she was here, and to wish her well on her journey. If you are not of our tradition, please feel free to contemplate Chrissy's life in whatever way works for you. It is also our tradition to chant, read poems, and to make statements directly to the departed or to the assembled group. We will start with a recorded chant. Please join in if you know it. For those of you who don't understand the ancient Pali language, what we are chanting is roughly interpreted as: *All things are impermanent. They arise and pass away. Having arisen, they come to an end, their coming to peace is bliss.*

The chant starts softly and builds, rolling over and then through us. The vibration thrums my body like a pulse, touching something beyond conscious thought. I drift in a current of sound sensing all the others drifting with me. When the sound fades, I feel lost.

The teacher gently breaks the silence. "JJ has asked that I conclude our ceremony by reading from a book titled *No Death, No*

Fear written by Thich Nhat Hanh, the great Buddhist teacher and poet. It expresses our beliefs about life and death.

"*This body is not me; I am not caught in this body, I am life without boundaries, I have never been born and I have never died. Over there, the wide ocean and the sky with many galaxies. All manifests from the basis of consciousness. Since beginningless time I have always been free. Birth and death are only a door through which we go in and out. Birth and death are only a game of hide-and-seek. So smile to me and take my hand and wave good-bye. Tomorrow we shall meet again or even before. We shall always be meeting again at the true source, always meeting again on the myriad paths of life.*"

I watch as tears slide from under JJ's closed eyelids.

Feinstein bows again. "If there is anyone who would like to speak directly to Chrissy or to our gathering, now would be the time."

JJ doesn't move. Several people walk silently to the altar and bow in front of Chrissy's portrait, speaking words intended only for her ears. I sense movement behind me and to my left. Manny, dressed in a dark suit and tie, walks across the back of the room and stands by himself in a corner scanning the crowd. He spots me, gives a quick nod, and continues to run his eyes over the gathering. I wonder if he expects Chrissy's murderer to show up with a bright red M drawn on the back of his head.

When the last person sits down again, Feinstein introduces another chant followed by a cello solo so wrenching I am close to tears. He closes the service with a dedication of merit and goodwill to Chrissy and to the welfare of all living beings.

"The members of the commune have prepared food for us in the garden outside," he says. "Or, if you are so inclined, you are welcome to stay here and sit with JJ in silence."

Frank heads for the garden and I head for the bathroom. There's a tug on my sleeve. I turn around expecting to see Manny. It is

Kathryn Blazek, dressed all in black. Shiny rivulets of tears striping her cheeks.

"Could I talk to you for a minute?" she asks, and without waiting takes my hand and leads me down a short hall. We stop in front of an empty woodworking studio. The door is closed and the light is out, but I can see through a window that opens to the hall. The floor is littered with shavings, long curls of wood that look like Chrissy's tumbled hair. "JJ needs support. I wanted Bucky to come with me, but he wouldn't hear of it. He blames JJ for Chrissy's death."

"And you don't?" I ask.

Kathryn sucks on her lips. "She did a lot of things that were unwise. But no mother would murder her own child. She loved Chrissy every bit as much as we do. I don't blame her. She is suffering. We all are."

"Dot? Everything okay?" Frank calls to me down the hall. He is holding two small plates of food.

Kathryn hoists her bag on her shoulder. "Will you tell JJ you saw me? I just want her to know I was here." She looks around. "I guess I expected to sign a guest book. And I sent flowers." She pats my arm. "I'm sorry. I didn't mean to put you on the spot. As they say, it's the thought that counts."

Before I can reply, she gives a nervous chortle and skitters down the hall.

* * *

Manny is waiting for us in the parking lot. He looks as tired as I've ever seen him. I introduce him to Frank.

"It's Sunday. You should be home with your family," I say.

"You sound like my wife."

"Pence could have sent someone else."

"He doesn't know I'm here."

"Who are you looking for?" Frank asks. "What do you think happened to Chrissy?"

Manny steps back. Sizes Frank up. He's used to asking the questions, not answering them. People are walking to their cars. Manny waits until they pass.

"The mother paraded this kid around in the nude. What did she expect? That's like waving a red flag at a bull thinking it won't hurt you because you're a vegetarian." He moves closer to Frank. "You know her. The doc told me you study photography with her. What do you think of those pictures?"

"They're beautiful. Unique. As good as anything you'll see in a museum."

"What about the content? Don't you think it's a little strange, a little risky, to put nude photos of your child, any child, on display?"

Frank's mouth pulls down at the corners. He takes a few breaths. "I know JoAnn Juliette. I have never seen any indication that she would do something to jeopardize her daughter. She is totally professional. Her photos are works of art. Nothing else."

"I don't know about works of art, but I do know a lot about pictures of nude children and what happens to them. Sorry to say bad things about your teacher, but in my opinion she is either the most naive person in the world or she's got you fooled. She can sit up there all spiritual, but sooner or later I'm going to find some pervert in a chat room offering Chrissy's pictures for sale. The ones she took and the ones he took." He looks at his watch. "I gotta get going. Nice to meet you. Sorry to bad-mouth your teacher." He leans in toward Frank and lowers his voice as more people walk past. "Just in case you learn anything that can help me, or you meet someone who gives you the creeps, maybe someone in your class, give me a call." He pulls a business card out of his wallet and hands it to

Frank. "You, too, Doc. Anything or anyone that seems out of place, let me know." He sticks his hand out to Frank, and for a millisecond I think Frank is going to refuse to offer his in return.

As soon as Manny is out of earshot, Frank rips up his business card and drops it on the ground. "Son of a bitch, who does he think he is, asking me to report on JJ?"

"Parents are always at the top of the list of suspects in a child kidnapping. Manny has to suspect everyone until he finds the person who did this. He's just doing his job. He didn't mean to be offensive."

"I don't know what he meant. But I didn't like it. He needs to slow down. Stop jumping to conclusions."

Frank opens the car door for me and walks around to his side. He slides in and turns the key. The engine rumbles. "You do what you think is right, Dot. I know you like this kid Manny a lot. But if you ever spy on JJ for the cops . . ."

"He didn't ask me to spy on JJ, just to report anything that seems strange or out of order."

"Call it what you will, sounds like spying to me."

CHAPTER NINE

THE WEEK AFTER Chrissy's so-called celebration we are about to eat dinner at my house—grilled salmon, arugula salad, and a friendly sauvignon blanc from New Zealand—when JJ calls on Frank's cell phone. It's barely more than a month since Chrissy's murder. He walks out of the kitchen into the living room. I stand at the stove trying to figure out what to do. If I put our plates on the warming griddle, the salad will get hot. If I don't, the salmon will get cold. Frank would know what to do—he's a master at making everything turn out at the same time. I scrape the salad into a bowl, put it in the refrigerator, and heat the plates. Dinner can wait. This is JJ's first Christmas season without Chrissy.

"Are you sure?" Frank listens for a few minutes, says, "See you then," and hangs up.

I reassemble the plates and bring them to the table.

"Class starts right after New Year's. JJ says she's ready. I hope she's right, because I have stuff to show her and I need her feedback."

"Seems a little premature, but sometimes reestablishing normal routines can be healing."

"She thanked me for my support and said to tell you the same. She is asking all her students not to talk about Chrissy in class or ask questions. It is her intention to maintain her—and I quote—'equanimity, attitude of forgiveness,' and something called 'metta.'"

"Metta means loving-kindness or goodwill." I've taken a few classes in Buddhist psychology.

"Beats me why she wants to have goodwill toward the bastard who killed Chrissy."

"It's not for him, it's for her. So her life is not consumed by loathing."

Frank raises his glass. "If she can do that, she's a better person than I am. If it was me, I'd want to kill the son of a bitch with my bare hands."

* * *

The week between Christmas and New Year's is slow for therapists and contractors. It's a good time to get away. Last year Frank surprised me with a trip to Big Sur. A whole week hunkering down in a B & B, reading books and drinking wine in front of the fireplace while rain pelted the roof and scratched at the windows. This year is different. The PD is on high alert looking for Chrissy's killer. All holiday leaves are canceled. Pence doesn't order me to work, he doesn't have to. Showing up when I'm not expected is a way to demonstrate my dedication to the team. Fran keeps everyone supplied with Christmas cookies. Eddie hangs around hoping someone will ask him to do something besides keep the coffeepot going. Frank makes a traditional Christmas dinner for some of our friends. My mother goes out for Chinese and to the movies with her women's group. And Manny drops by my office at headquarters to tell me he's in the doghouse with Lupe because he didn't have time to help decorate their tree. Then he missed Midnight Mass and wasn't home in time to watch Carmela open gifts.

"I don't know why Lupe is so upset. Carmela's too young to know about gifts. She likes to play with the wrapping paper." He's lost color in his face and his clothes look baggy.

"Anything new on your end?" he asks.

I tell him what Frank made for Christmas dinner. That we decided not to exchange presents, but to give each other a rain check for a weekend away.

"I mean anything new with JJ?"

"We haven't seen her since the celebration of Chrissy's life. But I know she's going to start teaching again, right after New Year's."

"So she's over her grief? That was quick. Guess that meditation stuff works. When you see her next, you might want to tell her that while she's been sitting on her pillow, there's a dozen guys who didn't get to spend Christmas with their kids because they've been working overtime trying to find the creep who killed hers."

* * *

"What kind of thugs do you work for?" Frank slams the door and throws his camera bag on my couch. He sits down, no kiss, no hello, no nothing.

"First night back at class didn't go so well?"

"It was going fine until your pal Manny barged into the middle of the class, told everyone he was going to confiscate our hard drives, and dragged Anjelika down to the police station. She can't be more than twenty-one years old. What in hell could she have done? She was absolutely terrified."

I remember her from the student art show and the funeral. Meditating on a cushion, her eyes swollen from crying. "Young girls do a lot of things they shouldn't," I say. He glares at me, walks into the kitchen, pours himself a drink, and brings it back into the living room.

"I don't think she understood what was going on. Her English isn't very good." He swigs his drink. "Right in front of everybody. She was in tears. JJ tried to stop them, but he threatened to arrest her. Maybe instead of shrinking heads, you should teach your favorite cop and his buddies some better techniques." He sits down with a thud. "She's a nanny, for God's sake. A nanny. There's three of them in class. They're friends from Denmark or Norway. All they want to do is practice their English and take pictures of adorable babies."

* * *

Manny is in the command center drinking a Starbucks latté when I go to headquarters the next morning. In Silicon Valley, cops prefer espresso to coffee and croissants to donuts with the occasional vegan-schmeared five grain bagel. Nobody has the heart to tell Fran.

He stands up when he sees me and raises his drink in salute. "Morning, Doc."

"You look better than you did the other day," I say.

"I think we got our man or I should say our girl." He makes air quotations with his hands around the word girl. "I'm not being sexist; she really is a girl."

"Nice looking one, too," someone mutters just loud enough for me to hear.

"I guess you know that we detained the Stewarts' nanny last night at her photography class. We had interviewed her along with the rest of their house staff. She was conveniently out of town when Chrissy disappeared. We took a look at her hard drive. She's got photos of Chrissy all over the place. Probably got a boyfriend somewhere who did the snatch. Told him about the layout of the mother's commune. She's been there a dozen times at least, picking Chrissy up, dropping her off."

"Anjelika was the Stewarts' nanny? I didn't know that." I wondered if Frank did. If he did, why didn't he tell me?

"Don't feel like the Lone Ranger. She's a secretive girl. The Stewarts didn't know she was studying photography with JJ on her nights off. She's in the same class as your fiancé."

"I know. I met her at an exhibit of student artwork." Manny's eyes widen.

"You knew she was Chrissy's nanny?"

"No. Never came up."

"Frank didn't tell you?"

"I doubt he knew. He would have told me."

Manny's jaw waggles, chewing on this new piece of information.

"Were the images you found on Anjelika's computer pornographic?" I ask.

"Depends on your point of view. Some in the bath, naked. Some naked in the pool." I want to say that lots of people take pictures of their toddlers in the bathtub, but it's not the time to argue.

"Why did you detain her?"

"We got a phone call."

"From whom?" He's making me pull this out of him, detail by detail.

"The father. He caught her packing a bag. With her passport in her purse. She still has months to go on her contract."

"Bucky Stewart is too careful to not have thoroughly vetted Anjelika and anyone else who works for him."

Manny shrugs. "That's what he says, too. Says her references were golden."

"Where is she now?"

"Right now she's in the lobby, waiting for you."

"Me?"

"Yup. Doesn't want a lawyer. Only you. Shall we go?"

* * *

Anjelika is sitting on a bench across from Kathryn and Bucky. Bucky's eyes are closed, his head tilted back, arms slack as though someone has siphoned out his insides, leaving only a wilted exterior. Kathryn sits rigid as a pole, clicking the lock on her handbag. The noise bounces off the walls of the empty lobby like distant claps of thunder. The minute she spots me, Anjelika jumps to her feet. Her hair is wet and spiky. She's wearing running tights, short boots, and a sweatshirt emblazoned with a Norwegian flag. "Thank you so much for coming for me. I love Frank. He's the best man ever. So nice. He loves you. Says you are the best psychologist. That you know how police think. Please help me make them know I'm honest girl who never hurt a baby. Please." She says it over and over.

Kathryn slides next to Bucky and whispers in his ear. He opens his eyes and for a split second looks confused until he remembers where he is. He shifts forward, places both hands on the bench, and pushes himself to stand. Kathryn stands with him, her hand hovering next to his elbow.

"Does she need a lawyer?" Bucky's voice is thready and hoarse.

"I don't need a lawyer. I don't do nothing wrong." Then hearing the vehemence in her voice, Anjelika softens. "So nice people, Mr. and Mrs. Stewart. So sad. I cause too much trouble."

"Just talk to the police," Bucky says. "Tell them whatever they want to know."

"I'm good person. In my country, Norway, I'm good student and athlete. I love children." Her eyes gloss with tears.

Manny opens the door to the interrogation room. He's smiling, a warm, friendly spider-to-the-fly grin. "Anjelika." He extends his hand. "Come in, we're ready for you. You, too, Doc."

* * *

Anjelika has been holding my hand so tightly and for so long that I can't feel my fingers. I've drunk two bottles of water and urgently need to pee. Manny doesn't appear to be close to stopping. There's a pile of soggy tissues on the table. Anjelika's eyes are more red than blue.

There's no apparent logic to Manny's interviewing technique. His questions come fast and furious, spinning and swirling from past to present, from California to Norway. I feel like I'm watching Jackson Pollock create a painting. And then suddenly he drops back to his same monotonous insistence that Anjelika must have a boyfriend somewhere. That she's been taken in by this evil American boyfriend who forced her to help him kidnap Chrissy from her billionaire employer and promised her they'd run away together with the ransom money. Then he swerves again, asking about skiing and did she ever take her evil American boyfriend back to Norway to meet her family. Dizzy from going around this track a hundred times, I inject a question.

"A ransom note? Has there been a ransom note?"

In an instant, Manny shuts down the interview and allows Anjelika to go to the bathroom under the watchful eye of the red-headed PIO. As soon as she's out of the room, he turns on me. "I'm the one who has to ask the questions, Doc. Not you."

"Manny, I'm not your enemy here. I'm your friend." For a minute his face relaxes and then hardens back into his bad cop persona. He's a man on a mission and nothing or no one is going to get in his way.

"You're here to help us establish rapport. Make her comfortable. Get her to talk. Not to ask questions."

If he's going to play it like this, so can I. "Is there a ransom note or not?" I don't care if he kicks me out, I need to pee and I think I need to tell Anjelika to get a lawyer.

The door opens and Anjelika comes back.

"Can I go now? I'm so tired. I loved Chrissy. I would never hurt her. I have a heartbreak that she's dead. I told you. I have no boyfriend. Not even in Norway."

Manny leans over the table. He's apparently been building up to this moment, wearing Anjelika's defenses down to a nub.

"Maybe you and your boyfriend kidnapped Chrissy, but you didn't mean to kill her. Could have been an accident."

Anjelika's hands knot into fists. "No accident. Never. You're terrible man. You have terrible thoughts."

Manny and Anjelika are both on their feet, face-to-face across the table.

"Then who, Anjelika, if you didn't, who took Chrissy?"

"You hate. Your heart is full of hate. Now I'm full of hate for you. You're a terrible man. I want a lawyer. And I want my passport back."

"Sorry. No can do."

"You make me arrested? Mr. Stewart says if you don't, you must give my passport back to me."

* * *

As soon as Anjelika leaves, Pence appears.

"Hey, boss." Manny gives him a limp salute. He's sprawled in a chair, depleted of adrenaline and venom.

"How'd it go?"

We answer simultaneously. Manny says "Good." I say "Not so good." Pence laughs and pulls up a seat.

"Which is it? You first." He turns to Manny.

"She's hiding something. Someone. She isn't capable of doing this on her own, but she's involved. There's a boyfriend someplace who smells money. Maybe she's shagging the old man and he put her up to it so he can ditch his responsibilities and they can run off to Ibiza. He's coaching her, told her that unless we arrested her, we couldn't keep her passport."

"She asked for a lawyer," I say.

Manny straightens in his chair. "She'll come around when she realizes I'm not backing off, lawyer or no lawyer."

Pence turns to face me. "You have a different perspective?"

"I think she doesn't have a clue about what happened. She never wavered from her story even though Manny was more than vigorous in his questioning. She seems genuinely distressed over Chrissy's death and the pain it is causing the family."

Manny snorts. "She's playing dumb." He raises his hands in the air, fingers curled and his pinkies outstretched. "I don't know anything. I'm just the nanny," he says in a child's singsongy voice.

"She's not dumb and she's telling the truth," I say.

Pence turns to face me. "And you know this how?"

"Anjelika was incredibly emotional, weeping, angry, all over the map. When a person lies in a high-stakes situation and only pretends to feel genuine emotions, the corrugator muscle in the face doesn't move."

"The what muscle?" Pence sits up in his chair.

"The corrugator supercilii, a little muscle close to the eye. It's the frowning muscle, the principal muscle in the expression of suffering."

"Come on." Manny shoves back in his chair. "I'm tired. I need a break."

"I took a class in grad school. Detecting high-stakes lies by observing facial, nonverbal, and verbal behavior." Professor Charles Randall pops into my head with his roly-poly body and wild thatch of gray hair. Always late to class, flustered and red in the face.

Wearing the same clothes he wore the day before; nothing laced, zipped, or buttoned.

"When was that? A hundred years ago?" Manny mutters under his breath, just loud enough for me to hear. "You going to listen to her or me, Chief?"

"I'm going to listen to both of you," he says in a surprisingly conciliatory move. "You're both tired and you're both on edge. I suggest we call it a day, go over it again tomorrow. Good work, both of you."

Manny walks out. I start collecting my things. Pence holds the door open for me and waits.

"Do you see?" I say.

"See what?"

"How Manny is changing. He's turning into a bully. He's angry, hostile, sarcastic. That's not him."

"Of course. He's under a lot of stress. And he's not getting enough sleep. What do you expect? That's a copper's life."

CHAPTER TEN

"WHAT HAVE YOU done?" I say the minute I walk through Frank's front door. So much for my intentions to stay calm and reasonable. Frank is in the kitchen wearing a denim apron that says "Kiss the Cook." The house smells sweet and spicy.

"Just a little something I whipped up for my sweetie. Duck confit with oven-fried potatoes, and green beans with mushrooms."

"I'm not talking about dinner. I'm talking about Anjelika, the girl in your photography class. Did you know she was Chrissy's nanny? That she worked for the Stewarts?"

He looks puzzled. Dries his hands on a towel. Takes a sip of wine and offers me a glass. I tell him I'll pour it myself. He checks the food and turns down the oven. I sit at the kitchen counter. The motion-activated outside lights wink on and off in a brisk invisible wind.

He sits on the second stool. "No, I didn't know. Is that what's got you so upset?"

"Remember the evening she was arrested? Although it turns out she wasn't really arrested. You told me that you didn't want to get involved."

"I didn't. I don't."

"Manny interviewed her today. And she asked for me specifically to sit in on her interview. Was that your idea?"

He gets up, walks to the stove, and pokes at something burbling in a saucepan. "Want a salad?"

"What I want is an answer to my question. Did you tell her to ask Manny to let me sit in on her interview?"

"Do you really think I would do that without your permission?" He looks at me, his eyes like blue ice, cold and sharp. "If you do, you underestimate me."

"So how come she knows I work at KPD in the first place?"

"We talk on breaks. The whole class talks on breaks. She asked if I was married. I said I was engaged. She asked what you did and I told her. That was months ago when the class first started."

"Well, you shouldn't have. How do you think this makes me look? She's a potential baby murderer, for God's sake. What else did you tell her about me when you were getting cozy with each other?"

"What do I have to do, ask your permission to talk to people?" He stands up. "You want to eat or not?"

I never turn down anything with duck in it. Or potatoes.

Frank plates up the food, carries it to the table. I bring in the wine and refill our glasses. We eat in silence. The food is delicious.

"Are you going to tell me?"

"Tell you what?" I say.

"About the interview." His voice drops to a deep bass. "Did she do it?"

"I doubt it, but I could be wrong."

"And Manny? Does he think she did it?"

"He's not finished with her. I'm certain about that."

"Okay, then. That's all I need to know." He starts to clear the dishes and stops. "I'm sorry that my relationship with Anjelika or JJ upsets you. I've never given you any reason to doubt my intentions. The fact that you do bothers me."

"It's happened to me before."

"I know. You've told me. And I've told you that I'm not like your ex. I'm sorry for what he put you through, but you are going to have to get over it someday. There is a statute of limitations. You only get so long to blame your ex because you're scared of commitment. After that, if you push me away, it's on you."

* * *

Manny is waiting for me the next morning as I drive into the parking lot at headquarters. It is cold and windy, but he stands in his shirtsleeves, watching me try twice to back into a parking space, give up, and drive to where there is enough room to park an eighteen-wheeler. I can feel his eyes on me as I bend to retrieve my briefcase from the trunk, my backside in the air, feeling clumsy and old.

"Morning, Doc. How are you this fine morning?"

The truth is I spent a very restless night at home. Frank invited me to stay but given the frosty air between us I opted to leave. Bad move on my part. The minute I got into bed I couldn't stop seeing the hurt on his face and hearing the anger in his voice as he skewered me about the statute of limitations. "I'm fine, thank you, Manny. And you? Did you get some sleep?"

"Not so good, actually."

"Why is that?"

"Our little Norwegian angel has flown the coop."

"What do you mean?"

"Gone. Vanished. Vamoose. I called her early this morning to set up a second interview. When Bucky went to her room to get her, the room was empty and her clothes were missing. I checked the airports, all the flights to Norway. Seems she took a late-night flight to Oslo. My bad. I should have arrested her and kept her passport."

"Did the Stewarts know she was planning to leave?"

"I'm about to find out. They'll be here in twenty minutes."

"I'll be right back. I want to leave my briefcase in my office."

"You're not invited to sit in on this one, Doc. The chief has changed his mind. He asked me to tell you that as far as you're concerned, anything to do with this case is strictly off limits."

* * *

I find Pence in his office, sitting at his desk, swiveled around with his back to the door staring out the window at the rain that is coming down in large, sloppy drops. "What's happened?" He doesn't turn around.

"Our prime suspect has fled the country."

"That's not what I mean. Manny just told me that you told him I can't have anything to do with this case. Is that true? And if so, why? Yesterday, you thanked me for my help."

"That was yesterday. I didn't have the whole picture until Manny and I spoke this morning." He turns his chair to face me. He doesn't get up. I don't sit down. "Did you ask him about a ransom note in front of the suspect?"

"Yes."

"Putting an interrogating officer on the spot is very poor judgement as is revealing information in front of a suspect with whom, I understand, you were holding hands."

"She grabbed my hand and wouldn't let go. She's a kid, she was scared."

"She is an adult, over twenty-one. Traveled to a strange country where she knew no one, didn't speak the language, and got herself a job. Children don't do that." I want to grab him by his lapels and shake him.

"You thought my personal relationship with JJ could be helpful in the investigation. You asked me to keep my eyes and ears open. So did Manny."

"It may have been a mistake to put you in the middle of this. My apologies if it was. From now on, if you accidentally discover something that may be related to Chrissy's case, do not pursue it or get directly involved. Bring it to me or Manny."

* * *

I don't know who to be mad at first. My choices are legion: Anjelika, the flying angel; her mentor, Frank; her employers, Bucky and Kathryn; her nemesis, Manny, or my nemesis, Chief Pence, whose moods are as changeable as the weather, which is now sunny. Of course, I could be mad at myself for misjudging the situation and everyone involved. I have four clients and two pre-employment screening interviews this afternoon with just enough time to go to the drugstore for Tylenol and grab lunch at Fran's. I drive out of the parking lot and pull up to the corner stop sign. A sleek gunmetal-gray Tesla sedan crosses in front of me and pulls into the visitor's parking space facing the front door of headquarters. Bucky and Kathryn are early for their interview. A parking space across the street opens up. I pull in and tilt my rearview mirror for a good look. To hell with lunch, this is way more important.

As soon as he stops the car, Bucky turns toward Kathryn and starts waving his hands in the air. I don't need to hear what he's saying to know he's upset about something. Kathryn never looks at him, just stares out the front window and dabs at her eyes with a white handkerchief. Bucky pounds the steering wheel with both hands. I can see her jump every time he does. He slumps forward resting his head on his hands. He could be crying, I can't tell. Kathryn touches his shoulder and says something. He shakes her off. She looks out the side window toward the front of the police building. Bucky slumps against the seat, his head on the back rest. A moment later, he looks at his watch and opens his door. Kathryn pulls down the mirror-backed visor, opens her purse, and takes out a small compact. Bucky steps out of the car and straightens his jacket. Even from this distance, I can see his eyes are red and puffy. Kathryn powders her face, applies lipstick, and waits for Bucky to open her door. He does, but makes no effort to help her out. She stands, smoothing the front of her dress, one of those knit numbers with a matching jacket favored by women in politics. They stand for a moment as though gathering their wits and then walk, arm in arm, toward the front door.

* * *

Lunch at Fran's is hurried. Eddie serves me a bowl of soup without spilling a drop, which leads me to think he might actually make a life for himself working here. He is, as usual, full of complaints about his current work status, looking to me for any shred of hope that Pence will give him his job back. I tell him that, at the moment, Pence and I are not on the best of terms.

I call Frank on the way to my main office to ask if he knew Anjelika was planning to return to Norway to escape potential prosecution. My imagination, he says, is working overtime. He tells me he won't be available for dinner before his photography class. And since he can't be any more irritated with me than he already is, I inquire if he wouldn't mind asking Anjelika's two Norwegian photo-shooting nanny friends if they know where she went, why she went, and how to get in touch with her.

* * *

Professor Charles M. Randall still lives in Berkeley, about an hour's ride north of Kenilworth and then across the Bay Bridge. It's a glorious morning, sunny and bright. Not a shred of fog or smog. Everything rain-washed and saturated with color. The newly built east end of the bridge is blazing white in the sun. A graceful rebuke to the old steel bridge that wasn't worth rebuilding after the Loma Prieta earthquake shook loose a sagging section of the roadway.

It's the day after New Year's. Out with the old, in with the new. Anjelika is new. JJ is new. I'm old and, to be honest, starting to sag a bit myself.

Dr. Randall's house is high in the hills, one of those iconic Berkeley brown shingle craftsman-style cottages, all angles and ivy. The steps to his front door meander down a sharp slope crowded with plants and stones. A worn teak bench sits in front of a miniature waterfall that drops into a pool studded with floating hyacinth where a metal egret stands on one leg peering into the water. Before I can knock, the door is opened by a dark-skinned woman wearing slacks and a loose sweater the color of plums. I'm a bit startled. Dr. Randall existed in an academic bubble. I never gave a thought to whether or not he was married, single, straight, or gay. His life outside the classroom was of no interest to me. He never brought it up and neither did I.

Yet here he is with a wife. Her name is Bette with a silent E. Her handshake is warm and firm. She guides me into a small living room crammed with throw rugs, book-lined shelves, baskets, and masks from all over the world. She makes a sweeping gesture with her hand. "Always bring an empty suitcase with us when we travel. For souvenirs. Every one has a story. Don't get him started."

These aren't souvenirs. She's being modest. It's a fabulous collection. Each object carefully chosen for its beautiful handiwork.

"Tea? Coffee?" I decline both. "Charles will want some. It's his midmorning break." She notices my expression. "He's up at five every morning. But then again, he goes to sleep at seven thirty in the evening. Not much of a party animal anymore. Although he is immensely pleased at your visit. So am I." She disappears into the back of the house.

Something squeaks and thumps, squeaks and thumps. Then voices, then more squeaking and thumping. Dr. Randall pushes into the room leaning on an aluminum walker. He's grown thin and his gray hair has turned entirely white. His wardrobe is still the same and so is his smile. He opens his arms and gives me a hug.

"Dot Meyerhoff. What a pleasure to see you. Sit down, sit down." He motions me to the couch and bumps his way across several throw rugs to a large wing chair next to a folding table. He turns, one hand on his walker, the other on the chair, and sits heavily, pulling the walker over on its side. I move to pick it up. "Damn thing, always in the way."

"If you sat the way they showed you at the hospital, that wouldn't happen," Bette says from the doorway holding a tray in her hands. "Never marry a man older than you are," she says to me and kisses him on the forehead.

"She doesn't need a lesson from you, she already did that." He looks at me. "Didn't you marry Mark Edison? If you had asked me, I would have advised against it. Smart as a whip, but no staying power. Too much preening and too little teaching in front of his students."

"We're divorced."

"I'm not surprised."

Dr. Randall pulls a pair of glasses from his pocket, cleans them on his sweater, and puts them on. A tuft of white hair sticks out from one earpiece. "I've gotten old," he says, "but then so have you."

Never one to mince words. He bangs his leg. “I had a little stroke a few years ago. I’m weak in the leg and one arm. Got a little foot drop. But no damage to the old brain.” He taps his head.

“Or to your big mouth,” Bette says, handing me the coffee I didn’t want. “Don’t let him wear you out.”

* * *

The morning passes quickly into afternoon. Charles—he insists I call him Charles—no longer teaches, but continues to write, and while he doesn’t travel easily anymore, he Skypes with law enforcement agencies around the world. He’s dictating another textbook. Bette is transcribing it although she’s a poet and thinks academic writing is turgid and constipated. Can’t say as I disagree. Mark and I used to argue about our books. I wanted to write like I talk. He was a slave to the dictates of the American Psychological Association’s style manual. When I tell Charles this, he laughs. “I always thought Mark was far more interested in form than substance.” My face goes hot with embarrassment at missing something so obvious to the people around me.

“Not that I was analyzing him. My field is detecting high-stakes lies and pedophilia. Mark wasn’t either. He most likely meant everything he said to you at the time.” Charles takes a sip of coffee and wipes his mouth on the back of his hand. He asks me about my work. I tell him about Chrissy’s murder.

“Tragic,” he says. “Absolutely tragic. You know, the mother consulted me about her photos before she agreed to show them publicly. Wanted to know if she was endangering the children. I’ve been meaning to get Bette to write a note of condolence. No one can read my handwriting.”

“Your impressions?”

"I thought she was being extremely diligent coming to see me. She's very talented. Not to mention beautiful. I thought her photos were breathtaking. Never seen anything like them before. Are they provocative? Of course. She's gotten a great deal of hate mail over the years. All great art pushes the boundaries. If not, it's merely decoration. Today's world seems to be filled with people who want to control what we read, what we say, what we do in our bedrooms and with whom we do it. Even in the Republic of Berkeley." He laughs. It's an old joke.

"What about pedophiles being aroused by the content of her images?"

"It's virtually impossible to predict who will be aroused by what, and what they'll do after. Some research suggests the majority of pedophiles do not molest, but instead spend hours looking at child pornography. I would call them passive abusers because children were victimized to make the material they find so compelling. Other studies estimate that seventy to ninety-five percent of those who view and collect child pornography are active abusers." He shifts awkwardly in his chair and leans forward. "If we tried to avoid every possible danger in the world, no one would get out of bed in the morning. But what I think you're really asking is do I regret downplaying the danger." His eyes drift upward as though the answer to my question is written on the ceiling. "If I had known there was a pedophile lying in wait to kidnap and murder Ms. Juliette's child, I would have told her to grab her daughter and run as fast and as far as she could. But to live in fear of a possibility is to turn your life over to the fearmongers who want to sell you guns and alarm systems and lock up anyone who looks vaguely suspicious, particularly if they don't look like us." He's breathing hard. A sheen of sweat spreads across his forehead. "So, yes. I regret telling her not to worry as much as I regret not having X-ray vision and a crystal ball. I hope you can help her more than I did."

Bette sticks her head in the doorway. "Everything okay in here? Anyone need anything?"

Charles asks for water.

"What is your interest in this, Dot?"

"JoAnn Juliette is a friend of my fiancé. And the department I work for has jurisdiction over the case. I thought you could help me help the investigators. Especially since you've met her."

Bette walks back in with a carafe of water and two glasses on a tray.

"Don't trust anything Charles says about JoAnn Juliette. He was absolutely mesmerized. Besotted. Couldn't stop talking about her for days. If you want my opinion, she was a bit too nice, too spiritual, to be believed."

"Thank you, Bette, for the water and the opinion. Only one of which I asked for. Now, can Dot and I get on with our consultation?" He peers at me over his glasses. "So, do the police have any suspects?"

"Too many."

"Always the case. Investigating is a process of winnowing down. I'd be happy to talk to the police. I would think they'd have contacted me already. Unless Ms. Juliette never mentioned she had consulted me about her photos. Even if she did, they're likely too busy running down other, more significant, leads. Where I think the police can use your help is figuring out who is lying and who is not, based on evidence, not intuition. Among your group of suspects, one or more of them will be lying, giving you the opportunity to compare one to the other in terms of facial and verbal clues. Forget body language. There's nothing significant in body language although the amateurs would like you to believe that there is something deeply meaningful when a person crosses his arms over his chest. Ditto for avoiding eye contact or hesitant speech. Total garbage. People have idiosyncratic styles of communication. Words and face, that's what counts. I have to warn you, though, facial expressions are hard to read. You're better off looking for leakage, little micro-expressions, that betray the true content of a contradictory verbal message. Someone says they're happy and you see tears in their eyes." He turns to the door. "Bette, where the devil did you go?"

She's at the door almost the moment he calls to her, hands on hips, smiling. "What now?"

"Run off a copy of the chapter on 'Detecting High-Stakes Lies.'"

"I haven't finished editing it."

"Do it anyway. Dot doesn't care about your poetic edits. What she needs is the content." She looks at me, shakes her head, and walks down the hall. "It's important to remember that this theory works only when the stakes are truly high. Which they appear to be in this case. Liars are clever. Deception requires significantly more cognitive resources than truthful communication. And remember, there are all sorts of ways people evade the truth. Bald-faced lies, omitting material facts, equivocation, changing the subject, offering indirect responses."

Bette returns and hands me a sheaf of papers held together with a large metal clip. "Don't blame me, dear, if you can't read this. It's a slog."

"You're not the only one in this house who can write, you know." Dr. Randall turns to me. "She only thinks she is. If you ever decide to marry again, don't pick a poet." He gives her a light whack on her rear as she leaves.

I start to get up. I've been here for nearly two hours and I can see Dr. Randall is beginning to fade.

"Not so fast, young lady, I'm fine," he says, but I can see he is having trouble enunciating his words and one side of his face is sagging slightly, giving me an in vivo example of what he means by behavioral leakage. "You've got more reading to do." He hands me one of his books. The title is *Pedophilia: Monsters in our Midst.* "Pedophiles are everywhere, Dot. They look like normal people. They have normal jobs. They're married and have families. Some of them are prominent citizens. Even when they don't act on their impulses, they most likely indulge in child pornography, supporting an industry that brutalizes children. But as horrible as pedophilia is, murder is worse. Certainly, not all pedophiles are murderers. Be careful, Dot. A person who would murder a child wouldn't hesitate to murder you."

* * *

It's midafternoon before I start for home. Commuter traffic jams the road, trapping me in my car alone with my thoughts. I start to cry. Blubber actually. In full view of a busload of people who are all looking at their iPhones and couldn't care less if I suddenly opened my car door, dashed across the road, and jumped off the bridge. Charles and Bette, in full crotchety detente, can't hide what they really feel toward each other. I wonder if Frank and I will ever reach that same level of love and respect. And if we don't, will it be my fault?

By the time I get home, a dismal dusk is covering my townhouse development. I pull into my garage, go inside, turn on the TV and every light on the first floor. Anything to fill the empty space. I pick up the telephone to call Frank. A stutter tone signals that I have a message. This makes me happier than it should considering the number of robo-calls I get from people trying to sell me everything from fake free vacations to electronic pendants for old women who live alone and need help when they fall.

The message is from Frank. "I talked to Anjelika's two nanny friends. They didn't know she left town and they don't know where she might have gone. They're all from Norway, but they didn't meet each other until they got to the US." Click. No hello, no goodbye, and no how-was-your-day. I call him back and get voice mail. "This is Frank. Can't come to the phone. When the tone sounds, you know what to do."

What I want to do and what I know to do are two entirely different things. I want to get into my car and drive to his house. What I do instead is hang up without leaving a message.

CHAPTER ELEVEN

I HAVE A poster in my office at headquarters that reads, "If you think it's tough being a cop, try being married to one." It's my not-so-subtle way to remind everyone that the job follows them home even if they don't think it does. A cop isn't going to tell his buddy that he can't sleep because he's having nightmares and he checks the locks on the doors three times a night. But his wife knows, and his kids know. While I wish it were different, he isn't going to tell me either because he's scared I'll tell the chief that he's unfit to work. Families have enough to do just dealing with the extra hours, the worry, and the public scrutiny. They're not psychiatrists. It's unfair to ask them to deal with a traumatized cop by themselves without giving them any help to do so. Chrissy's abduction and death is a unique and catastrophic event that has touched everyone in the department. That's why I'm holding a family meeting to talk about trauma, how to recognize the symptoms, what to do about it when you see it, and how to get help for yourself and your loved one. Forewarned is forearmed. And, seeing that the one book I authored by myself, not with my ex, is about supporting police families, I try to practice what I preach.

Fran and two of her friends, Irma and Lil, all veteran police spouses, are helping me with the meeting, just like they have before. They're kind and generous women, sharing their years of experience in the hopes that young wives can avoid the mistakes they made when they were starting out. Fran, in particular, is living proof that even if your worst nightmare happens and your husband is killed in the line of duty, life still goes on. Pence isn't fond of this program although he pays it lip service.

We're gathering in the cafeteria at headquarters. Fran has brought a tray of small sandwiches and an enormous sheet cake. An urn of coffee bubbles on the counter. Irma is putting tiny bouquets of dried flowers on all the tables. Lil is welcoming the arrivals, giving each a name tag and directing them toward a table of handouts with information sheets about PTSD, vicarious trauma, and a list of warning signs that signal the need for professional help.

Eddie carries a second tray of sandwiches into the room. We're expecting twenty-five, and Fran's supplied enough food for three times that many. Eddie's breathless with the effort and sweating.

"Am I old or out of shape, Doc? Maybe both?" He wipes his hands on his apron. "What are you going to tell these ladies about the creep who killed Chrissy? How do you explain that kind of evil shit? Could be anyone, you know. These ladies probably think it's some tatted-up parolee who lives in a trailer park. You better tell them it could be their neighbor or their kid's Little League coach. What are you going to say when they ask how anybody could hurt a baby? Most of them have babies. They're gonna ask."

"I've asked Police Chaplain Barnes to join us."

"The God Squad?" He slaps me on the arm. "Smart move, Doc. Because priests sure as hell don't know squat about molesting little children."

I'm not religious. Whatever I am is complicated. My heritage is Jewish. My father was raised in an observant Jewish family, immigrants to the United States from Eastern Europe. His distrust of Gentiles—all of whom he suspected were anti-Semites—was matched only by his distrust of every rabbi he ever met. He left the synagogue in an anti-Semitic rage of his own after his father was barred from attending services on High Holy Days because he didn't have enough money to buy tickets for the entire family. My mother, on the other hand, was raised in an assimilated southern Jewish family without any of my father's paranoia or combative tendencies. Her spiritual beliefs range from Pilates to macrobiotic cooking. She is very ecumenical, loves everyone and everything equally.

I've kept my distance from all religious studies except for those episodic forays into Buddhist psychology. I only met Chaplain Barnes when I started working with KPD. I see how the cops relate to him without any of the apprehension they seem to feel when talking to me. And they're grateful for his help delivering death notifications, one of the worst tasks a cop has to do.

The hum in the room dies down as Barnes stands to deliver a benediction. He's African-American, the color of oak. Tall, slender, and athletic, he's dressed in a class-A uniform with a clerical collar. Sharp, shiny, and official. "Let us begin." Heads bow, hair shining under the ceiling lights. I see Manny's wife, Lupe, sitting by herself at a table in the back. "In your own way, according to your own spiritual beliefs, take this moment of silence to express your gratitude for the opportunity to be together, to comfort yourselves in the face of tragedy, and to learn how, in this New Year that has barely begun, we can be of service to each other. Amen."

He stays on his feet. "I expect that the question on everyone's mind is—how could somebody harm a child? And how could God allow it? I'll let the doctor deal with the first question. I'll try to deal with the second." He closes his eyes for a moment. "This is my belief. God does not cause these terrible things to happen. God is not a puppeteer, up in heaven, pulling the strings, deciding who gets to live and who doesn't. God's work is to help us get through the terrible things that we do to each other. He laughs with us at times of joy and cries with us when we are suffering. I believe he is here now, in this room, encouraging us to reach out to each other in peace and friendship. God bless us all." He sits down.

I move to the front of the room. "Thank you, Chaplain Barnes. Glad you could be with us tonight." I turn to the group. "Our purpose tonight is to talk about how you can support your officer and yourselves during this crisis. Mandatory overtime puts a strain—"

A woman with hazel eyes and short curly hair stands up before I finish the sentence. "My husband is so concerned about traffickers he won't let our child play on the front lawn. I'm a psych nurse. He keeps asking me how anyone could do this horrid thing to a child and why. I don't know what to say. We get sick people on my unit. Not perverts." A murmur runs through the group and then silence. All eyes are on me. I'm not exactly sure what other horrid thing, aside from kidnapping and murder, she's talking about. We're barely five weeks out from the day Chrissy's body was found. The autopsy results are not in yet and details about the way Chrissy's face was made up have not been released to the public.

"This is not my area of expertise, but I'll tell you what I know and it's not a lot. Psychologists have been studying pedophiles for years without coming up with any definite ideas. What we know is that some child abusers were themselves abused when they were younger. Others seem to have an inbred fixation with children. There is even research that suggests that pedophilia results from atypical wiring in the brain."

"Can you cure a pedophile?" someone asks from the back of the room.

"Unfortunately, at this point in time, there is no cure. There have been a lot of things tried. Chemical castration to reduce the sex drive. Behavior therapy similar to how we treat addiction. But no real progress has been made and there is no reasonable way to study what's effective. As you can imagine, pedophiles are reluctant to voluntarily seek help because it's a reportable offense and they would be arrested."

"Once a pedophile always a pedophile. They ought to be locked up and have their dicks cut off," a heavyset woman in a business suit says loud enough for everyone to hear. There's laughter and a smattering of applause.

"Actually, some pedophiles never act on their impulses while others are able to restrain their impulses until their life circumstances become so desperate that they have nothing left to lose."

"Bullshit," the heavy woman says. "I work corrections. Nothing cures these assholes."

A small, very pregnant woman raises her hand. "My husband is suspicious of every man we meet, including my daughter's play school teacher and our neighbor's son."

"That's not an uncommon reaction. Has anyone else's husband grown more suspicious since he became a cop, less trusting of anyone who isn't in law enforcement?" Every hand in the room goes up.

* * *

The rest of the evening is pretty pedestrian. Questions and answers. Some advice from Fran, Irma, and Lil. A few more words of wisdom from Chaplain Barnes and me and then it's over. Everyone seems to think the evening was well spent. I gather up a sheaf of anonymous evaluation forms that we asked the women to complete and carry the leftover food to the dispatch center before driving home to an empty house and an empty refrigerator. I should have bagged a few sandwiches for myself. I change into my bathrobe and settle on the couch with a glass of wine and a bowl of microwave popcorn. It's too early for the nighttime news and too late for anything else. I pick up the evaluation forms. The ratings are uniformly positive, not glowing, but positive, between 3.5 and 4 on a scale of 5. There is only one handwritten comment. It is from Lupe. "Call me on my cell, please, I need your help."

* * *

Lupe is sitting on the front steps of my private office, holding two cups of Starbucks coffee. It's seven a.m. I rarely see clients this early, I'm hardly awake myself, but it was the only time I had available. After talking with her on the phone last night, it was clear that something is seriously wrong at home.

I unlock the front door and we walk up the stairs to my office. Lupe hands me the coffee and fumbles in her jacket pocket for packets of sugar.

"I hope you like cream in your coffee. I took a chance."

She's a tiny woman with long, streaked chestnut brown hair and eyes that look everywhere but at my face.

"Nice office. Where do you want me to sit?"

I point to the couch and we settle in, sipping our coffee in silence. I like my office. The vibe here is good even if the building itself is nothing like the charming antique-filled Victorian I once shared with my ex. When we divorced, I mourned for months as though the office and the furniture were a stand-in for my collapsed marriage. Now I'm happy with my clean, contemporary look. It's hardly different from thousands of other therapy offices, except that it's mine. I chose it and I paid for it. It is what it is, a place to meet and talk. Not a restoration project to shore up a failing relationship.

"Are we waiting for Manny?" Lupe's mouth puckers like a drawstring purse. She shakes her head.

"He's not coming. Says he has to work. He never stops."

"The murder of a child takes precedence over everything, including sleep. It's very hard on families."

"It's not Chrissy. This has been going on since the first day he started on the task force. It's just gotten worse since Chrissy. Way worse. He's on the computer all day and all night. Perverts like to do their business at night. So he bought a laptop. It's faster than the computer they gave him at work. He has it fixed so that whenever somebody goes into a certain chat room, he gets a warning signal. Then he gets out of bed. Sometimes he doesn't come back for hours. I can't fall back to sleep."

Now I can see what I didn't notice at the family meeting when she was wearing makeup. Dark purple filling the hollows under her eyes.

"I want him to go back to the street. I feel bad asking him. If anyone was hurting my baby, I'd want someone like Manny on the job, but the chief won't let him. Says there's no one to replace him. Plus, he's earned all those certificates. And now, since Chrissy, he doesn't want to. He says perverts like fetishes. They use the same poses and props over and over. He watches every video ten times looking for some blanket. He won't tell me why, except he thinks he saw it before on a video and if he finds it, he can keep another baby from being murdered. It's like he's obsessed."

And that's all she can manage to say. Whatever brave face she's been faking at home crumples into a noisy, watery mess.

Nobody calls a cop or a therapist when they're having a good day. Cops sometimes get to fix things. They can restore calm, put bad guys in jail, and separate warring parties. Not so for a therapist. It's not my job to fix things, and I can't take anyone's pain away. All I can do is witness it, contain it, share it. This comes at a cost. If you have an ounce of empathy or compassion in your heart—if you don't you shouldn't be a therapist—other people's pain sticks to you. Like secondhand smoke, it seeps into your pores and clings to your hair. I count my breaths as I wait for Lupe to let go of the emotions she's been holding in. At thirty breaths, her weeping slows. At forty-five breaths, she sits up and mops at her face.

"I thought I could wait it out, but I can't. No way. This job is destroying him. And us. My daughter needs him. I need him." She bites down on her lip. "I want to have more children before Carmela gets too old. Manny doesn't want another baby. He says the world is too dangerous for children. He never thought like that before. Never. He wanted four kids. The job has changed him and now it's changing us." Something zigzags across her face, pulling at the corners of her mouth. "I try to be a good wife. I know he needs to talk. I read your book."

I give her a weak smile. Books don't cure problems; at best, they explain them. Providing little more than cold comfort for the suffering.

"I know what he sees. Babies being raped and tortured. I used to listen to his stories, but I can't anymore, not after I had the baby. He's disappointed in me, I know. He doesn't say it, but now when I ask how his day is, all he says is 'fine, just fine.' He doesn't talk about his work to anyone. Says if he did, he'd freak everybody out like he freaks me out. My family thinks he has a regular police job. So does his family. He needs to talk to you." She blows her nose, excuses herself, and does it again.

"He doesn't even have a supervisor. Started out it was just him and one other guy. Now it's four guys. They sit in a room together watching videos and making fake phone calls, pretending to be as perverted as the men they're trying to catch. They try to help each other. But they're guys. They don't talk about how they really feel. All they know how to do is make bad jokes and drink."

"Manny, too? Is he drinking?"

She looks out the window. It's a gray spare-the-air day. A soupy mix of fog, smog, and who knows what.

"I think so. Sometimes I can smell alcohol on him. I don't say anything because I know he needs to unwind. They all do." Now her eyes are full of worry. Worry that she's said too much, betrayed a trust, gotten her husband in trouble. "He's never drunk. And he never drinks on the job." She checks my face to make sure I understand. "Thing is, he doesn't even like the taste of alcohol."

Cops drink. Men drink. But when a man who doesn't like the taste of alcohol starts to drink, it's a warning sign that he is under some serious stress. I can't imagine what it feels like to believe, even if it's not true, that you alone are responsible for preventing an innocent child from being murdered.

"Will you talk to him? Please."

"I can't promise anything," I say. "Except that I'll try."

CHAPTER TWELVE

I get to my office early again. The sun is just beginning to warm the tops of the trees outside the window. It takes a minute for my computer to boot up. The first e-mail in my inbox is from my mother. She wants to know how Frank and I are doing. She's no longer interested in me for myself, only me as half of a couple. She thinks Frank is wonderful. She thinks marriage is wonderful. She only hopes we tie the knot before she dies. She's healthy as a horse, but that doesn't stop me from worrying that when Frank and I finally do tie the knot—a metaphor I find distinctly unappealing—she'll drop dead on the spot because my staying single seems to be the only thing keeping her alive.

The second e-mail is from my women's group about our upcoming meeting. I've known these women since grad school. They suffered through my divorce and now they're suffering through my ambivalence about marriage. I hope they never team up with my mother.

There's an invite for me to join the AARP, some fund-raising appeals, and a slew of newsletters from various organizations. The last e-mail is from Lupe. She thanks me for talking to her yesterday and hopes I talk to Manny soon because she forgot to tell me about his nightmares and he had another really, really bad one last night.

* * *

Manny is unshaven and can hardly keep his eyes open. He apparently doesn't have the energy to be angry at me for showing up at the substation unannounced, once again. I look around. The formerly barren walls are decorated with the half-dozen photos of registered sex offenders I saw pinned up in the command center.

"Suspects?"

"Some are, some aren't." He wheels his chair around to face them. "Number one's in jail, number two is dead, three moved to Arizona, four has a preference for prepubescent boys, and I'm still looking for five and six."

"Where are they? Aren't they supposed to report in?"

"They're criminals, Doc. They don't always do what we ask."

He swivels back to face me.

"What can I do for you?"

"I just stopped by to say hi. How did the interview with Bucky and Kathryn go?"

"Okay. The father thinks Anjelika got scared and ran. Made a big deal about how thoroughly he checked her background before he hired her. Stepmom thinks the nanny's guilty. Wants me to contact the authorities in Norway. Get them to interview her. She's convinced that if someone speaks Norwegian to her, she'll confess." He yawns.

"What did Bucky think about that?"

He yawns again.

"Didn't sleep well last night?"

"The baby woke up at three o'clock. I couldn't get back to sleep."

"Lupe sent me an e-mail this morning. Said you had a nightmare."

"Shit. She watches me like a hawk and it's making me nuts. Now she's running to you."

"She's worried about you."

He tilts back in his chair and puts his feet up on the desk so I am looking at the soles of his shoes. In some countries this amounts to a supreme insult. I doubt that Manny knows this.

"She worries too much. Thinks you have to be sick in the head to do what I do. If you're not a pervert when you start, you'll be a pervert after you stop."

"Do you agree?"

"It's a dirty job, but somebody has to do it. Who's going to protect kids if we don't? I like my job. I was bored before. I'm not bored now. I like the money and I like working with the team."

As if on cue, the door opens and Manny's team members walk in, each one carrying a cup of coffee from a local restaurant and one for Manny. I wonder if they've been listening at the door.

"We interrupting anything?"

"Yeah. The doc is here to check up on me before I go postal."

It's a weak joke, but we all laugh just to be polite.

* * *

I've copied a page from the appendix of Dr. Randall's text on pedophilia and made one for each member of the team. It speaks volumes about Dr. Randall that, in an academic text, he would think to include a section speaking directly to the men and women who investigate pedophiles. Since they're on a coffee break, I ask permission to read his suggestions aloud. Manny speaks before the other men have a chance.

"Go for it, Doc. Couldn't hurt."

I take Randall's book out and show them the cover. For a minute, I think about standing to read but stop myself. There's already enough resistance in the room. Standing up like a schoolteacher will only make it worse. I put on my reading glasses. I'm the only one in the room who needs them.

"Investigating pedophiles requires infinite and careful attention to one's self-care in order to avoid absorbing the pain inflicted on these helpless victims. Scrupulous attention to one's own reactions is the surest way to prevent the investigator from being consumed by compassion fatigue, cynicism, and paranoia. Please consider the following suggestions.

"#1: Put a bright line between home and work. No viewing images or making enticement calls for the first and last hours of your shift.

"#2: Create a home-to-work, work-to-home transition. Select a song that prepares you for work and play it on the way to the office. Pick a different song to play on your way home. Restore some goodness back in your life before you spend time with your family. Watch cartoons or pleasant movies."

A big guy with a shaved head laughs. "Cartoons. Sweet."

"It's better than going to a bar," I say.

Manny gives him a shove. "Let her finish."

"#3: Hang a note on the visor in your car reminding you that when you are home you are a husband, a father, and a friend. Not a police officer.

"#4: Avoid engaging with the victim's story. Your job is to collect evidence. The more you think about the victim and not the evidence, the harder your task becomes. Staying on task stimulates the thinking part of your brain and minimizes the impact on your emotions.

"#5: When you feel yourself tensing up or getting emotional, relieve your stress with exercise or deep breathing.

"#6: Reduce the sensory impact of the images you see. Turn off the sound. Shrink the size of the image, turn the computer on its side. Change color images to black and white."

One of the team members spins around in his chair and pitches his empty coffee cup in the wastebasket. "Are we done here? I have a phone date with a guy who likes little boys with freckles on their you-know-what."

"Almost there. I just have two things to add to Dr. Randall's suggestions. First, fix up this office. It's depressing. Don't wait for your departments to give you the money. Spend a little of your own if you have to. Paint it a different color. Something cheerful. Bring in some plants, pleasant pictures. A bird cage. A fish tank.

"Secondly, pace yourselves. There are too many pedophiles in the world and too many vulnerable children. You can't lock them all up, no matter how hard you work. Give yourself credit for what you can do and leave the rest behind. Your efforts matter to some child, somewhere in the world. Never let anyone tell you they don't."

* * *

"What in hell is going on?" Pence is leaning on the door to my office at headquarters, drinking coffee from one of his special order cobalt-blue coffee mugs. "Did you just go to the ICAC office and give Manny and his team a little lecture on stress management? Who gave you permission to do that?"

I don't bother asking how he knows this. Gossip moves through a police department faster than a speeding bullet.

"I don't need permission. It's part of my job to identify stressed employees before they fall apart."

Pence steps into my office and closes the door.

"Manny's teammates don't work for me. So they got a little free advice? No big deal. What I really need to know is about Manny. Is he falling apart? Do I have to replace him? I don't want to do that, but I will if I have to."

"He will if he doesn't get some sleep and a few days off. He's exhausted. I've told him that. But it doesn't mean much coming from me. I'm not his boss. It would be a lot more meaningful if it came from you."

"That's all? Not a problem." He looks at his watch. "He's coming in for a press briefing. I promised the media that he would be here to answer questions. He can go home after that. Take a few days off."

"He's sleep deprived. If you put him in front of the press, chances are he'll embarrass himself. And you." Pence's right eye starts to twitch.

"Dr. Meyerhoff, there's something you need to understand. Whatever you may think about me, I care deeply about the welfare of my officers." He starts to leave and turns back again. "By the way, do you or your boyfriend have any idea where JoAnn Julliette has gone? We've been calling her for days and she doesn't answer her telephone. I sent a unit to her commune. Apparently she's decided that now, right in the middle of our investigation into her daughter's murder, would be a fine time to go to a spa. Makes you wonder, doesn't it?"

* * *

"JJ's not at a spa," Frank says. "She's on a retreat. Something called healing from grief, using art to mend a broken heart."

"Doesn't look good leaving town in the middle of the investigation. A lot of people at the PD think she's responsible for Chrissy's death. This only increases their suspicions."

Frank folds his dinner napkin, pressing his fingers down on every crease.

"What about you? What do you think?"

"If I was JJ and the police already suspected me, I wouldn't give them more reasons to be wary."

"She just wants to move on. She's very forgiving."

"A little too forgiving in my opinion. You said it yourself, you can't understand why she isn't more angry."

"Well, maybe I'm learning something from all this. Hostility only makes for more hostility. It's like drinking poison and expecting the other person to die. Wasn't it the Buddha who said, 'When seeking revenge, first dig two graves'?"

* * *

One week later, the investigation is still stalled, the autopsy report is still pending, and Frank and I are still walking on eggshells around each other. I want to ease the tension between us, so I agree to go with him to see JJ's new creation, something she started working on at the retreat to honor Chrissy's birthday. To be perfectly honest, I don't want Frank to be alone with her. Petty of me, under the circumstances. The poor woman has just lost her child. On the other hand, grief creates a vacuum that drives some people to fill it with anything they can lay their hands on: booze, food, compulsive travel, other people's fiancés.

JJ guides us down a long hall. She is wearing flowing russet-colored pants and a loose, hand-crocheted ivory sweater. Her feet are hidden in the folds of her pants, giving her the appearance of gliding like a Russian folk dancer.

"The galleries and the workspaces are on this floor. The apartments are on the second floor. He climbed the fire escape, you know, the man who took her." Her eyes shift inward, downward, backward, looking at something I can't see. It is a minute before she blinks back into the present.

The building is quiet. Cooking odors from upstairs waft down to the first floor. Someone is playing the guitar. We walk over old wooden floors, varnished to a high sheen. Paintings line the white walls, each one carefully lit. Whoever restored this building did so with love and good taste.

The door to JJ's studio is painted the color of an angry sea. She takes a key from her pocket and unlocks it. I remember Bucky's accusations about the building being unsecured. Every door in this hallway has a lock. She turns on the light. Frank and I both gasp.

Hanging from a steel frame is an unfinished tapestry of Chrissy. It must be thirty feet high and twenty feet wide. I step back. It's hard to focus in the low light. What looks like embroidery is actually a collage: dolls, stuffed animals, pacifiers, baby bottles, diapers, and children's clothes—shoes, hats, tiny socks, all sewn or glued together to form Chrissy's likeness.

"It's okay to touch it," JJ says. "I want people to touch it." She brushes her fingers across an assemblage of pink quilted onesies that form a ruffle. "I asked Bucky to give me some of Chrissy's things to incorporate, but he refused. Told me I was being morbid. I think it's beautiful. Chrissy would have loved it." She turns to Frank. "What do you think?"

He opens his mouth. No words come out. His hands are turned, palms up, like a supplicant. He takes a breath. "I don't know what I was expecting, but it wasn't this. A photo montage, maybe. But this? This is alive, moving, it's almost supernatural."

JJ smiles. "And you, Dot? What do you think? It's far from finished."

I stifle the first thought that comes to mind. *You'll never finish it because this is how you're keeping Chrissy alive.*

"Come on," she says. "I can take it. Lord knows I've had enough criticism in my life."

"It's beautiful," I say. "I've never seen anything like it." Tears thud behind my eyeballs. I turn my head so neither JJ nor Frank can see my face.

JJ puts her hand on my arm. "What is it?"

It takes me a moment to find the words and a second moment to dare to say them aloud. "Every stitch, every scrap, done with such care. It's overwhelming. Heartbreaking." Tears roll down my face despite my efforts to hold them back. Frank looks shocked. JJ looks pleased.

We sit together quietly while JJ boils water for a pot of tea. "As I said, I'm far from done. Look at all this stuff I've collected." She turns to a worktable piled with boxes, trinkets, and bolts of fabric. She pulls something from a pile of cloth and shakes it loose. It's a blanket. Pink with green butterflies.

"Where did you get that?" I ask.

"I bought it. Chrissy loved butterflies. She had cutouts of butterflies all over her room, on the walls and the ceiling. They glowed at night. Made her feel safe. She even had a butterfly farm. We watched the larva grow until they burst their cocoons and then we released them in the garden. At first she was so happy for them and then she got very sad when they flew away." She smiles at the memory and hugs the blanket.

"Do the police know you have such a blanket? Did you tell them where you bought it?"

The teapot screams in the background.

"No. Should I have?"

I take a deep breath. "You do know that Chrissy's body was wrapped in a blanket just like that one?"

"I do."

"That's why it may be important to the investigation to know where you bought it. If you'd prefer, I can tell them."

"Would you? I'm not comfortable talking to the police. They're working hard, but I know they think I'm responsible for what happened to Chrissy. They don't say it out loud, but I know that's what they think. If I were them, I'd be thinking the same thing." She turns off the stove.

"It's just that details like this sometimes help the investigation."

She turns. Starts assembling a tray of handmade mugs for the tea.

"I got it at the Dollar Store. In East Kenilworth. I bought it for the butterflies. I was going to cut them out and sew them on the tapestry."

"Did Chrissy ever have a blanket like this?"

"Not that I know of, unless her father bought her one. Although I doubt that Bucky shops in Dollar Stores. It made me feel better to know that when she died Chrissy was wrapped in butterflies. That whoever took her had a little shred of humanity left in his heart. Don't take that away from me. Please." She turns her back and begins the business of pouring tea.

"Are you seeing anyone? Like a grief counselor?"

"I went to one meeting of the Families of Murdered Children. I felt great empathy for their losses, but I couldn't relate. They were all consumed with anger."

"And you're not?"

She shakes her head. "Everyone expects me to be. People think I should be camping out on the steps of the police department complaining that they're not doing enough to catch her killer. As you know, I'm a Buddhist. I try to hold compassion in my heart. Only a tortured soul would hurt a child. Chrissy was love. If I'm bitter or angry, I destroy my life and dishonor her memory."

* * *

The Dollar Store in East Kenilworth is on the main drag, between a carniceria and a place to send money back to Mexico, safe, secure, and guaranteed. At least that's what I think the sign says, given my tourist-level Spanish. I don't know what I'm doing here except to get my facts straight before I talk to Manny or Pence. That damn butterfly blanket may or may not be a link to Chrissy's murder. There's only one way to find out.

A buzzer sounds when I open the front door. The place is stacked, floor to ceiling, with an assortment of plastic junk. A tiny dog runs at me from nowhere, yapping and growling.

"Chispa, *calmate*." A command emanates from the back of the store. "He's a nice dog. Don't be afraid. But don't pet him."

No worries. I'm not about to put my hand anywhere close to the little beast's mouth.

The voice from behind the curtained doorway belongs to a tiny human, barely as tall as my shoulder. A toy-sized man with a toy-sized pet. "How can I help you?" He steps behind a low glass counter. Only the top of his body is visible over the case of batteries, cameras, and cheap watches. So precious they need to be kept out of the way of thieving hands.

"I'm looking for a baby blanket. One that is green and pink with butterflies."

He purses his lips. "Popular item," he says and scurries away. A minute later he's back, dragging a stepladder. He climbs, reaches for a cardboard carton, and nearly falls off the ladder under its bulk. I grab one end, and we set it on the floor. He goes up again, this time dragging a large plastic bag from behind another box. It falls to the floor with a soft thud. He gestures at the bag. "What one you want? I got bears, ducks, kitty cats, puppies . . ."

"Butterflies, I want butterflies."

"*Mariposas*, everyone wants *mariposas*."

"What everyone?"

He's on his knees, pawing through the stack of blankets. Bits of fluff float in the air.

"Last week, I had one hanging in the window. A white lady with a long braid bought one. Wouldn't take the one in the window. Said it was faded. This from China. What does she expect?"

"One person. That's what you mean by everyone?"

He stands up holding a pink and green blanket with one hand and massaging his back with the other. This man could use a lesson in product placement. His popular items should not be hidden on a high shelf behind a box.

"This the one you want?" He shakes it out. More fluff flies in the air.

"Yes."

"That'll be $5.99."

"I thought this was the Dollar Store. Everything a dollar."

"You want a blanket for a dollar? Go to the Salvation Army." He starts to shove the blanket back in the bag. I take it out of his hand. "I got something here for a dollar." He shoves an oversized pair of joke sunglasses at me. I open my wallet and hand him a twenty. He gives me a dirty look, then digs in his pocket and pulls out a wad of bills.

"You're like that other lady. Wants to give a credit card. I don't take credit cards. What did she think I am, Bloomingdales?"

"What other lady? The one with the braid?"

"No. Another woman. In a business suit. She doesn't need to shop at my store, I can tell you that."

"When? When did she buy the blanket?"

He lets out a big sigh. "Why you want to know?"

"It's important."

"So's my time." He eyes the change that's lying on the counter.

I push it toward him. "Will this help?"

He puts it in his pocket and heads toward the back of the store, little Chispa following, his tiny toenails tapping on the floor. A minute later they return, shuffle and tap, shuffle and tap. He lays a wall calendar, decorated with a picture of the Virgin Mary, on the counter and flips through the back pages. "It was this date. Maybe a day after or a day before." He points with a smudged finger. "I remember because it was before the holiday. I had a lot of customers and she wanted to examine every blanket like she was swaddling the baby Jesus."

"So it was Christmas?"

"No, lady." He turns the calendar so I can see the page. "Turkey day. Thanksgiving."

My stomach drops. Chrissy was kidnapped the day before Thanksgiving.

"You're absolutely sure of this?"

"Wait a minute. I'll get the surveillance tape."

"You have a surveillance tape?"

"In my head." He taps his skull. "Isn't that right, Chispa? I remember everybody who bought anything from me. You remember this lady, too, don't you?" He looks at his dog who immediately starts to pant and wiggle. "She was afraid of Chispa. Imagine being afraid of a dog so tiny. Wanted me to put him in the back. I didn't do it, did I, *perrito*?"

"What did this woman look like?"

"Tall. Taller than me." Everyone but the dog is taller than he is. Even me.

"I don't look at white women too close. They gonna sue me. Hispanic women, that's another story."

I fold the blanket.

"You want a bag? Ten cents unless you got one of your own."

I'm not giving this creep another dime. I pick up the blanket and my purse and head for the door. He follows after me. "Why you so interested? What'd she do?"

What indeed? That's the sixty-four-thousand-dollar question. The sixty-five-thousand-dollar question is what am I going to do with this information?

CHAPTER THIRTEEN

First thing next morning I'm in Manny's office. He doesn't look any more rested than he did on Friday. His eyes are sunk deeper in their sockets and his warm bronze complexion has faded to the color of day-old coffee with cream.

"Somebody, a woman, bought a baby blanket, exactly like the one Chrissy's body was wrapped in, at the Dollar Store in East Kenilworth a few days before Chrissy was kidnapped." I dump the blanket on his desk.

He doesn't move a muscle. No giveaways. No tells. "And you know this how?"

"The proprietor remembered her because she wanted to use a credit card and she was afraid of his dog."

"Did you just wander into the Dollar Store on a whim?"

"No. Let me back up. JoAnn Juliette has the same blanket. She bought it to use in an art piece she's making in Chrissy's memory. Frank and I were at her studio. I asked her where she bought it and she told me. The store owner remembered her from only a few days ago. And then he remembered that some other woman had bought the same blanket. The woman who tried to use a credit card."

"Okay. And you concluded what?"

"He didn't have a very detailed description, but it didn't sound like the nanny."

He smiles. "I'm not interested in the nanny. Never have been. I only wanted the family to think I was so they'd relax. When suspects relax, they make mistakes."

My first reaction is to demand to know, if Anjelika was never a suspect, why he felt it necessary to put her through that tortuous hours-long interrogation. Scaring her so much she ran back to Norway. My second reaction is to ignore my first and stay on topic.

"If you think someone in the family killed Chrissy, doesn't that suggest that the person who bought the first blanket was Kathryn Blazek?"

"Could be Lady Gaga, too. What we need is physical evidence to connect Blazek to the blanket and the same blanket to Chrissy. I doubt the Dollar Store has exclusive rights to sell baby blankets. The world's a global village, Doc. You can probably buy that same blanket in thirty-five countries." He shifts in his seat and winces. "Recycled chairs. Killing my back. Let me ask you a question. You give this guy any money?"

"For the blanket, yes."

"That's it?"

"I let him keep the change from a twenty for his time. What's with the questions? You've been looking for that blanket for weeks. What are the odds that I found it here, literally at our front door, and it doesn't have anything to do with Chrissy's death?"

He cocks his head. "It's interesting. I grant you that. Worth looking into. But this mystery woman might have bought the blanket for somebody else. Maybe the proprietor sold ten blankets just like it to ten other people and didn't tell you because he thinks you're a mark and wants you to keep coming back to pay him for more bogus information."

Manny's starting to sound more and more like Eddie. Cynical and suspicious.

"Kathryn has money," I say. "Why would she buy a blanket that won't make it past the first washing in a run-down store that specializes in selling crap to poor people?"

"Maybe she did it for her husband. The woman's a regular Camilla Parker Bowles. Hangs on year in, year out, while her husband makes whoopee with Princess JJ."

He has a point. I've had that thought myself.

"Too many maybes, Doc. If someone in the family did this, my money's on Bucky. He's a powerful man who buys whatever he wants. First he wanted his wife, then he wanted JJ, and now he wants Chrissy, full-time, total custody. He admitted as much to me when I interviewed him."

"If he wanted custody of Chrissy so badly, why would he murder her? That doesn't make any sense."

"That's why I'm still looking at registered sex offenders."

He stands up, pushing out of his chair like a middle-aged man. "Let's go, Doc. We need to tell the chief about the blanket."

* * *

"Let me get this straight," Pence says, counting on his fingers like he's the teacher and I'm a child. "JoAnn Julliette showed you a blanket that matches the one her dead baby was wrapped in." I nod. "You asked her where she bought it, she told you, you went to the store, the store owner verified that sale from last week and told you another woman had bought an identical blanket days before Chrissy was kidnapped, and you suspect Kathryn Blazek was that woman." I nod again.

He turns to Manny. "You've seen this blanket?" Manny nods. "It matches?" He nods again. "Did either parent buy a blanket like that when Chrissy was still alive?"

Manny's cheeks flush red. "I don't know."

Pence's face is even redder.

"You don't know? Guess that means you didn't ask. Your job, let me remind you, was to ask both parents, the stepmother, the nanny, and the family dog. If they even twitched at the question, you should have dug deeper. Basic police work. As of now, we have nothing. No threats, no ransom requests, no disgruntled employees, no similars, and no possible 290 sex registrants. All we have is the family. And the blanket."

"We don't know if the person who bought the blanket was Blazek." Manny's face has gone from red to purple. As if things weren't bad enough in his life, now I've humiliated him in front of the chief.

Pence stands and looks at his watch. "Let's find out then, shall we?"

* * *

"We'll take your car," Manny says. "I don't want to go in a patrol car, not in that neighborhood."

"First I need to get something out of the trunk." Manny peers over my shoulder into the abyss. Flashers, battery cables, eight rolls of toilet paper, a six-pack of water bottles, and a bag of protein bars long past the expiration date. This is California. We have to be prepared for an earthquake. Nothing worse than being stuck on the road without toilet paper and something to read. I rummage through a pile of newspapers I saved after Chrissy was kidnapped and find one with a photo of Bucky and Kathryn on the front page. The headline reads "Prominent businessman's infant daughter abducted from her bed." It's a posed picture from a fund-raising event a year before Chrissy's death. The Bucky I know today is a gray specter of his former self, all the pluck and brashness of a man totally in control of his world leached out of him. Kathryn looks about the same, courtesy of a pound of makeup and an unchanging hairstyle. I show the paper to Manny.

"Bring it along. We'll start there."

The minute I touch the door handle of the Dollar Store, Chispa, the miniature menace, is on her feet barking. Not the same for the proprietor who is nodding off over a magazine and appears none too pleased to be awakened. How he makes a living in this dump is beyond me.

"Now what?" he says using his best customer service manners.

"Is this the woman who bought the first blanket?" I lay the newspaper on the counter. The proprietor looks at Manny, then at me, and turns on an overhead light. Bends over the photo as if he were studying the Lost Sea Scrolls. I start to put a twenty on the counter. Manny stops me and pulls out his badge.

"*Respuesta a la pregunta de la señora.*"

The proprietor backs up. "*Policia,*" he says and picks up his dog.

"Answer the question," Manny says. "Is that the same woman who bought a pink and green baby's blanket decorated with butterflies?"

The proprietor bends over the newspaper and whispers into the dog's ear. "What do you think, Chispa? Is this the same lady?" He puts his ear to the dog's mouth and then kisses it on the nose. "Maybe yes, maybe no. My eyes not so good."

Manny lays a six-person photo array on the counter. The proprietor takes off his glasses, pulls a rag out of his pocket, and wipes his lenses. Apparently never getting them clean enough because he does this three times before Manny hits the counter with his fist and yells at him in Spanish, causing Chispa to run into the back.

"This one," the proprietor says, putting his finger on one of the photos. "Most definitely."

Even upside down, I can tell it is Kathryn Blazek.

"Was she alone?" Manny has snapped into enhanced command presence mode. His voice drops half an octave and he appears to have grown two inches.

"Yeah. Nobody in the store with her."

"What about outside? In the parking lot?"

The proprietor raises his eyebrows, shapes his mouth into an upside-down "U."

"*No sé.* It was a while ago."

I pull the twenty out of my pocket, slam it on the counter, and give Manny my version of command presence, a searing look that tells him I have my ways and not to stop me.

"Now that you ask"—the little man smiles as he pockets the money—"I was curious to see what kind of car she drove. I was expecting Mercedes or Lexus. *Qué sorpresa.* She was in a white pickup truck. Old and banged up. Ladders, shovels, lawn mower in the back bed."

"Anything painted on the truck, like a sign or the owner's name?"

"Let me think." He curls up in a poor imitation of Rodin's *The Thinker*. I pull out another twenty and dangle it between my fingers.

"Now that you mention it, it did have a sign. Maldonado and Sons. Maldonado, ugly like the guy driving it."

"There was somebody with her?" I say.

"You don't think that rich lady knows how to drive an old truck, do you? She couldn't get it out of first gear."

"So Maldonado or one of his sons was driving?"

"What do you think, lady, because I'm Mexican I know every landscaper in Kenilworth?" He looks affronted. His alter ego growls from behind the rear curtain.

Manny leans on the counter. "Did she get into the truck willingly or was she forced?"

"Let me think," he says again and rubs his head. I feel like I'm playing twenty questions with a developmentally disabled extortionist.

"No. Not forced. Not happy either."

"Do you know the man who was driving?"

"Wasn't Maldonado. He retired and moved away. I don't know where. Everybody knows that old gas guzzler truck of his. Maldonado loved that truck better than his wife. That's why she left him." He laughs, his face animated by gossip.

Manny isn't amused. "Was one of his sons driving?"

"Maldonado don't have sons. Only daughters. They too fat and ugly. Never married, so no sons-in-law. Made him feel more manly to call his business Maldonado and Sons." He taps his head to indicate that Maldonado wasn't all that mentally stable.

"Did you get a license number?"

The little man shakes his head and looks at Manny with a "what for" expression.

"The guy who was driving was maybe thirty. Very skinny. *Muy flaco*. Kind of hippie type. And, he was *guero*."

"*Guero*? What's *guero*?"

"You know. Gringo. A white guy."

I pocket the twenty and we leave.

* * *

I roll down the windows of my car and look at Manny. It's unseasonably warm and the car is stuffy. "So, what do you think?"

He laughs. "I think you may have just been flim-flammed out of a twenty by a creep who would sell his mother for a dime. He told us what we wanted to hear. Bad witness. His testimony wouldn't stand up in court—that is if he hasn't split for Mexico by the time we need him. He's probably on the phone right now buying plane tickets."

"Then who is the skinny white guy? And what does he have to do with Kathryn? A woman like her doesn't ride around in a filthy truck on her own volition."

Manny's cell phone rings. He looks at the screen, presses a button, and says, "Yeah, Chief." His face skids through a parcourse of emotions starting at neutral and winding up in a mix of anger and despair. "I understand and I appreciate . . ." He gives me the stink eye. "I know she thinks so, but . . . I'm with her now. We may have a lead on the blanket. You don't? You sure? Okay, you're the chief." He clicks off and stares out the front window.

"Apparently, the chief thinks—thanks to you and some conversation the two of you have had behind my back—that I am a bona fide stress case. He was uncertain at first, but after that fiasco this morning when, again thanks to you, he discovered I had overlooked this blanket business, he is ordering me to take two weeks paid R & R. Says it's a good time since the ME's report won't be available for at least two more weeks and we don't have any new leads."

"The skinny white guy is a new lead. The blanket is a new lead."

"This is a wild goose chase. I know it and the chief knows it. We could have stood there all day throwing twenties at that guy, and he would still be stringing us along. Let's go. What are you waiting for?"

If Manny's face were any longer, his chin would be on the floor of my car.

"Look, Manny. Maybe time off isn't such a bad idea. You could use the rest and you and Lupe could use some time together."

"Thanks a lot, Doc. You're a ton of help."

* * *

"If you're finished having your way with me, I need to get to sleep." Frank rolls over, facing me. "It's nearly midnight. I'm a working man, you know. I get up early." He looks handsome, his hair and beard silver in the low light. "I love you. Now turn out the light. I can't keep my eyes open."

I lay in the dark, listening to his breathing start to settle.

"Frank? Have you ever run across a man, a landscaper or gardener, named Maldonado? Drives an old beat-up white truck."

"Sure. Sergio Maldonado. He landscaped a couple of houses I worked on. Drove a 1965 Jimmy with two gas tanks. A clunker of a truck. Never wanted to part with it."

"Seen him recently?"

"He retired. Why are you looking for a landscaper? Your condo association takes care of the landscaping." He sits up and flicks on the table lamp. "Does Maldonado have something to do with Chrissy? I know you, Dot. You wouldn't be asking unless he did."

"Not so much Maldonado as his truck. Somebody who may or may not be related to the case was seen in his truck. Do you think you could call him? Find out who he sold the business to?"

Frank flicks off the light and scoots back down under the covers. A moment later he sits up again and twists around to face me.

"I don't ask you to help me remodel houses, please don't ask me to help you solve crimes."

He slides down on his back. We lay there, both of us stiff as boards, listening to each other breathing. Whatever balm our lovemaking produced now evaporates.

"Forget I asked," I say. "Let's just go to sleep."

* * *

That old saying about never going to bed mad is true. Frank and I barely say a word to each other in the morning. I go to my office. I have a slew of appointments with hardly a break until midafternoon when my office mate, Gary, knocks on the door.

"Just ran into Frank downstairs. He dropped this off for you." He hands me an envelope.

"Why didn't he bring it up himself?"

"Said he was in a hurry. Looked a little stressed. How you guys doing?" Gary takes an avuncular interest in how our relationship is progressing. "Set a date yet?"

"Not yet," I say and kiss him on the cheek. "Not to worry. You and Janice will be the first to know."

"Better get on it. Neither one of you is getting any younger."

"Thanks for stating the obvious. You haven't been talking to my mother, have you? She keeps asking me the same question. So do all my friends."

"Well then." Gary pulls his ever-present pipe out of his pocket, getting ready for his ritual smoke on the patio. "What does that tell you?"

As soon as he leaves, I open Frank's note. Maldonado sold his truck for cash to a skinny white guy with long hair by the name of Buzz. There's a license plate number, a phone number, and a warning not to call before nine or after eight.

A woman picks up the phone.

"*Digame.*"

I ask to speak to Maldonado. I can hear her yelling at someone in Spanish. A younger-sounding woman gets on the phone.

"Who is this?" I give her my name. Tell her I'm a friend of Frank Hollis and I'm looking for a landscaper. "Sorry," she says. "My father is retired. He doesn't do landscaping anymore."

"Did someone take over his business?"

She asks me to wait a minute and puts down the phone. A minute later Maldonado picks up.

"You are Frank's friend, yes? He told me you might call. I sold my truck and my tools to a man named Buzz. But I can't recommend him."

"Why is that?"

"He doesn't know anything about landscaping. Said he wanted to learn. But I don't think so."

"Why not?"

"I know a meth addict when I see one."

"You loved your truck. Why did you sell it?"

"Who wants an old truck that's not worth anything and eats gas? I can't fix it up, I got a bad back. Nobody wants it but Buzz. And he pays me way more than it's worth."

"How would I get in touch with him?"

"Big mistake. I gave him the pink slip to the truck, and he didn't transfer the title. He never pays his parking tickets, so now DMV thinks I still own the truck and I should pay hundreds of dollars in fines."

"Do you know his last name?"

"He only has one name. Like a musician."

"Do you know where he lives?"

"The address he gave me doesn't work. Nobody there heard of him."

"What about the parking tickets? There's always a location on the front of the ticket. Can you look for me?"

He fumbles with the phone and his daughter picks it up.

"You want the location where he got the tickets? It's going to take me a little time to find them. Give me your number. I'll call you back."

* * *

"Maldonado said he talked to you." Frank is cooking tilapia for dinner and I'm chopping vegetables.

"He called you?"

"Yep. Told me not to let you go looking for this Buzz guy by yourself. Are you planning to look for him?" I shrug. He moves away from the stove, fish turner in one hand, pot holder in the other. "You are, aren't you? Will you at least take Manny along?"

"Manny's on vacation, a little R & R."

"In the middle of a murder investigation?"

"Well, they're stalled. And they're waiting for the ME's report, so it's just as good a time as any."

"I don't believe you."

"What do you mean, you don't believe me?"

"What don't you understand about what not believing you means? It means I think you're not telling me the truth."

"About what?"

Frank bangs the fish turner on the counter. "I don't know. About everything. About Manny. About Maldonado." He takes a step in my direction. "You're going to look for this guy, aren't you?"

"I'm just gathering information. Trying to be helpful. Don't worry. I won't put myself in harm's way."

CHAPTER FOURTEEN

IT IS BARELY still light out when Frank and I get to the commune for the celebration of Chrissy's birthday. The doors to the main gallery are open. The sound of a soulful string quartet floats out to greet us.

The minute we step inside it is as though the air is being sucked from my lungs. I put my hand on Frank's arm to steady myself. Chrissy's sweet face dominates the room, looming over us, bigger than life. Is this what JJ is trying to tell everyone? That Chrissy and her memory live beyond time? I move closer. JJ is standing in front of the tapestry. Her hair falling over her shoulders. She's wearing a flowing top over wide-legged pants and a striking necklace made of chunky sea-washed glass.

She walks across the front of the room, moving like water itself, and picks up a huge bamboo fan. She waves it in the air. Once. Twice. Three times. A soft breeze ruffles the tapestry. Chrissy's face, once frozen by her mother's camera, begins to pulse. Her head sways. Her lips move in silent speech. Her eyes float over the room, left to right, right to left. Looking for something. Or someone.

There's a commotion at the back of the room and shouts for a doctor. A woman is lying on the floor. Someone is saying, "Stay back, give her room, she needs air." People always say that when somebody faints. Never mind that we're in a huge open space with high ceilings.

Kathryn Blazek sits up, covers her mouth with one hand as if she's going to throw up, and with the other tugs at her twisted skirt to cover her exposed legs. Someone helps her to her feet and hands her her purse. Someone else brushes off the back of her jacket. Her face is pale under the layers of makeup. An older man offers to get her a chair. She refuses, pauses long enough to thank several people for their concern, and then heads for the door. I follow her out into the cold night air.

She threads her way through the incoming crowd. I wait until she reaches her car before I call out.

"Are you okay, Kathryn?"

She turns. Her eyes wide.

"Are you okay? Shall I find Mr. Stewart?"

She shakes her head.

"It may not be safe for you to drive."

"I'm fine." Her voice is barely stronger than a whisper. "Just a little dehydrated." She backs up against the rear of her car and leans on the trunk. It's cold and she's sweating.

"What was she thinking? I can't look at it." Her face crumples, all the perfectly made up parts twisted in pain.

"Let me find your husband."

"He's not here. He told me not to come. I should have listened. She's going to release balloons, like a party." Tears are carving little roadways through her powder. "I loved that child. I didn't have to give birth to her to love her." She closes her eyes. Bites her lip. "I try to be a good friend to JJ. Chrissy deserved to be surrounded by a loving, calm family. But JJ sees only what she wants to see. She could never see how she was endangering Chrissy with those photos. I want to be clear. She would never hurt Chrissy on purpose, but if she was living in a proper home, not a commune, none of this would have happened. If she had told the police about her secret stalker, none of this would have happened."

"Secret stalker?"

"I told her to go to the police. She refused. Thought I was making too much of nothing. But she was the one who told me about it. I begged Bucky to go the police, but JJ talked him out of it. Said the man was only an overzealous fan and the publicity would be bad for her."

"And you?"

"Bucky forbade me. Believe me, I'll regret it the rest of my life."

"So Bucky listened to JJ and not to you." A small twitch beats under her left eye. She puts her finger on it and presses down.

"Everybody wonders about our unusual friendship. This is modern-day California. Traditional families seem to be a thing of the past. Maybe that's progress. JJ's not the first, nor will she be the last, of Bucky's affairs. There are some things that women in my position"—she hesitates as though she's about to reveal a state secret known only to followers of the Kardashians—"take as a matter of course. After a certain age, it hurts less than you might imagine. JJ is different. She gave us the child we couldn't have. And she wanted nothing in return. Some women would have come after Bucky or his money, not JJ, because she believes in taking only that which is freely offered. We offered her plenty and she didn't want it." She looks at her watch. "I need to go. Thank you for your concern." She pulls out her car keys.

"Thank you for your candor." I touch her on the shoulder. "At the risk of being intrusive, may I ask you another question? By chance, do you ever shop at the Dollar Store in East Kenilworth?"

"The Dollar Store? Why would I shop at a Dollar Store?" Her voice pitches high and tinny. She takes a few steps and turns back. "You know"—she spools her words out slowly—"now that I think of it, I could have been at that store." She moves back until there's barely two inches between us and lowers her voice. "This is embarrassing. Bucky doesn't know that I still smoke. Especially when I'm under stress. I may very well have stopped at the Dollar Store for a pack of cigarettes. How mortifying. You must think I'm terrible, sneaking around like a teenager."

"Might you have bought a blanket while you were there buying cigarettes?"

"Heavens no. When I buy blankets, Dr. Meyerhoff, I go to Nordstrom's."

* * *

The next morning, I swing by the Dollar Store determined to get the proprietor to validate his identification of Kathryn's photo. It's early, but I presume he and the dog live on the premises. The lights are out. I knock hard, hard enough to rouse Chispa to a barking frenzy. No response. I knock again. A small group of schoolgirls pass me on the sidewalk. They're dressed in the uniform of the local Catholic school, pleated plaid skirts, white shirts, navy sweaters, and knee socks. The tallest girl, her hair in braids and blue ribbons, taps me on the shoulder. She points to a sign in the window written in Spanish. *Ido a México. Tienda cerrada hasta nuevo aviso.*

"I don't read Spanish. What does it mean?"

"Gone to Mexico," she says. "Closed until further notice."

I want to call Manny, tell him his prediction was right on the money, but he's on official leave. Anyhow, he's so angry at me that I doubt he'd take my call. I could tell Pence, although it's clear he doesn't, at this moment, give a rat's you-know-what for my opinion. He certainly isn't under pressure to pursue the case until Manny gets back and the autopsy report is available. But then again, he doesn't know about JJ's secret stalker.

My stomach growls. There's nothing in it but coffee. Across the street is a small restaurant attached to a grocery store. When in doubt about anything, my default position is to eat.

There are five tables, each one covered with a brightly colored cloth protected by a plastic cover. I'm the only customer. I choose a table in the back. The waitress hands me a menu and a basket of chips with a dish of salsa. I order chilaquiles, eggs scrambled with fried tortilla strips, and a glass of fresh orange juice. I check my e-mail. None. I check my voice mail. None. I look around for something to read. The only thing available is a crumpled Spanish-language newspaper and a glossy real estate magazine. There's a huge flat-screen TV on one wall tuned to a Spanish-language talk show. A second wall is covered by a large hand-painted mural of two women in native dress, each carrying a large basket on her back. Bent forward under the weight of their burdens, they are walking up the side of a steep volcano as it spews lava and ash into the sky. The waitress sets a steaming platter of eggs, refried beans, rice, and tortillas in front of me. I keep staring at the mural.

"Is okay?" she asks when I don't immediately start to eat.

"*Si. Gracias.*" I pull my eyes away and dig into the food. Everything is delicious, better than restaurants that cost five times as much. I make a note to tell Frank that we have to come here someday for dinner. Although if I finish this I won't want to eat again for a week. I savor the fresh ingredients, the thick handmade tortillas, but I can't stop thinking about the mural. Only now, when I look at it, I don't see two peasant women walking into an active volcano when they should be running in the opposite direction. I see JJ and Kathryn. Both of them trying so hard not to be afraid, that they won't allow themselves to see the danger that lies ahead. JJ, all grace and goodness, intent on forgiveness and abiding by the principles of her adopted spiritual tradition, blind to the world's evil and to the depth of her grief and her fury. Kathryn, loathing her barren, aging self, clings to her sham of a marriage, pretending to herself and everyone else that her husband's infidelities aren't killing her and her love for him.

* * *

The rest of my afternoon drags on interminably. Eager applicants, all shiny and bright. Street-worn guys nearing retirement, tarnished and bruised by police work yet terrified of losing it. By the time I finish with my last client, the sky is dark and the street lights have come on. Frank is making dinner for us at his place, something special, a new recipe he wants to try. I haven't the heart to tell him I'm still full from breakfast.

He greets me at the door as though he hasn't seen me for a month. I envy his lack of inhibition, his ability to wear his heart on his sleeve. He's like my mother with her bighearted embrace of the world. I'm like my father, cynical, skeptical, too cautious for my own good.

"Give me your coat, take your shoes off, let me get you a drink. You'll never guess what I'm cooking." He dashes into the kitchen.

"Come in," he calls. "Try this." He hands me a glass. "Tequila, cucumber, chili, mint, and simple syrup." I take a sip. The mix of sweet and piquant cools my throat.

"Delicious. What is it?"

"My own recipe. Like it?"

"I love it."

"Good, because it goes with dinner. JJ assigned us to shoot still lifes. I bought a beautiful string of chili peppers, and when I was done photographing, I couldn't throw it out. So we're having Mexican food. Red posole and tortillas I made by hand."

After dinner I can barely move. I managed to eat a bowl of posole with all the trimmings, cilantro, radishes, onions, and chips but I refused Frank's offer of Mexican Chocolate with a sugarcoated cookie the size of a salad plate. I'm lying on the couch in front of the fireplace, and Frank is rubbing my feet. Our after-dinner conversation has understandably turned to Mexico.

"We could get married in Oaxaca or Guanajuato."

"Do you think your family would go to Mexico? They rarely leave Iowa. They're scared of strange people and strange food."

"We could elope."

"Your sisters would kill you if you didn't invite them."

"Where do you want to get married?"

I pull my feet from under his hands and force myself to sit up. I feel like a Bobo doll, so bottom-weighted, that if someone knocked me down I would bounce right back to standing.

"Can we put this aside for a minute? I have something I need to talk about and you're the only one I can talk to about it."

"Okay." He settles back against the cushions.

"Did you know that JJ had a secret stalker?"

He sits up. "No. Where did you hear that?"

"From Kathryn Blazek, Chrissy's stepmother. We talked at Chrissy's birthday celebration. She could have made it up. I don't want to pass rumors. But, I need to tell someone at the police department about this while Manny's on leave. This looks really bad for JJ, not reporting a stalker. I don't know what to do."

"I do," says Frank. "Before you go to the police with an unverified rumor from a woman with an unknown agenda who has plenty of reasons to make her husband's lover look bad, why don't we ask JJ directly?"

He gets up from the couch, calls JJ, and invites her for dinner tomorrow night. She's absolutely delighted.

* * *

JJ is her usual ethereal self in flowing garments and giant jewelry. She starts for the couch, hesitates a moment, and sits in an armchair. "I remember sleeping on that couch. Horrible days."

Frank offers her a glass of wine. She asks for water instead. He sets out a tray of homemade hummus and pita chips and goes back to the kitchen. JJ dips the corner of a chip in the hummus and nibbles at it. Savoring it slowly, mindfully.

"Thank you both for inviting me over. I don't have too many social events these days. I think people are afraid to talk to me. What do you say to someone whose daughter has been kidnapped and murdered? There aren't any social guidelines for such conversations. I understand, but still, I'm grateful to you both for your hospitality. And your thoughtfulness."

"So many of your friends came to see Chrissy's tapestry," I say.

"It's easier for people to see me when there's a crowd around. Our conversation can't get very deep. As for the tapestry, many people liked it, but I know others thought it was grotesque. Bizarre. Exploitive. My work always elicits a very mixed reaction. You either love it or you hate it." She takes a sip of water and another bite of hummus.

"Did someone actually say that to your face?" Frank brings in the wine and sits down next to me.

"Never to my face. No one's got the nerve. I get letters. And someone in the commune told me there's a lot of tweeting and Facebooking going on about it. I don't look at social media."

"These letters," I ask. "Are they threatening? Do you ever feel afraid?"

She laughs softly and shakes her head. "I never read beyond the first sentence. I can tell immediately where the writer is going. As I said, my work is controversial, always has been. Better that people express their anger in writing than act on it."

"If you don't read the letters, how do you know they won't act on it?"

She looks at me, then at Frank, and sets her water glass on the table. "Is there something the two of you are trying to tell me? If there is, out with it, please. After what I've been through, there isn't much that can hurt or frighten me. What more do I have to lose? I've already lost the most precious thing in my life."

We sit like dummies.

"Come on, Frank. Come on, Dot. What's happened?"

Frank is first to find the courage to speak. "I want to ask you about a rumor. Ask you to verify if it's true or not."

She stiffens ever so slightly. "What rumor?"

"That someone has been stalking you. Is that true?" Frank keeps his voice neutral.

"No, it's not true. Who told you that?"

"I can't say . . ."

"Why not?" Now that we're down to brass tacks, all the softness runs out of her face.

"Because I heard it thirdhand. I don't know the person who started it."

I lean forward, gripping my wine glass with both hands. "He heard it from me, and I heard it from Kathryn Blazek."

JJ flops back against the chair and laughs. "Good God, not that one again. Nobody's stalking me. It's just an ardent fan who fancies himself a little in love with me as well as my work. He's not dangerous, just deluded."

"Why haven't you told the police about him?"

"Why should I get the poor man in trouble? He wasn't a threat to me or to Chrissy."

"How do you know that?"

"I'm a portrait photographer. It's my stock in trade to read people's faces. To bring what is hidden into the open. That's what people don't like about the images of my nieces and nephews. They want to think all children are like sexless cherubs."

I'm tempted to ask JJ if she knows that Freud's theory of childhood sexuality has been largely discredited. That his notion of screen memories, constructed memories masking forbidden sexual impulses, was later thought to be recollections of actual sexual abuse.

"So the rumor's not true?" I ask.

"No, it's not. I don't have stalkers." She takes a drink of water and another pita chip. "But I do have spies."

Frank and I look at each other. "What do you mean, spies?" he asks.

"Sometimes Bucky sends people to check up on me. I guess he wants to be certain that the place is clean and Chrissy is being properly fed. He saw her every week—if I was starving her or forgetting to bathe her, you'd think he and Kathryn would have noticed. His minions skulk through the commune, stumble into my studio pretending to be lost, making sure I'm not letting Chrissy play with scissors, or something."

"Are you sure of this?"

"I haven't seen any of these people since Chrissy died. No need to check up on me anymore, is there?"

"This is bizarre," I say.

"Not if you know Bucky. He can be refined and well mannered. That's because Kathryn has schooled him properly. But his roots are much rougher. He's like a junkyard dog. Half his family are in prison. He didn't get wealthy being nice to people. Although he can be charming when he wants something. That's how he got to me. But cross him, and you'll see the real Bucky."

I remember him bursting into the police station, wanting to see Chrissy's body, almost assaulting Chief Pence.

"Is he violent?"

"Not to me. Just loud. I walk away. But it upsets Kathryn when he yells."

"So you've all been pretending to get along peacefully?"

"We try to for Chrissy's sake. Every child deserves to feel safe and loved."

Safe and loved. Those were Kathryn's exact words.

Frank's face is a mask. "I don't know how you define a stalker, but if Bucky was sending people to spy on you, that fits my definition of stalking. You should have told the police. You need to tell them now."

"I never felt threatened. I knew what was going on. Bucky likes to play games. I wanted to keep the peace. So I pretended not to know who they were and what they were doing."

"And now?" I say. "There's no reason not to tell the police now."

"What's the point? Chrissy is dead. Nothing is going to bring her back."

"But her murderer is still out there. And he's still dangerous. Pedophiles are addicted to children."

JJ winces. "Let me be clear. Bucky can be a hard man. A foolish man. I know I've told you this before. When I got pregnant, we were both overjoyed. Bucky wanted to divorce Kathryn and marry me. But I didn't want that. He was a fling. All I needed was Chrissy and my work." She takes another sip of water. "Understand me, please. Chrissy was Bucky's heart. He is a difficult man, emotionally stunted, but there is no way on earth that he would have harmed

Chrissy. As a matter of fact, if he finds the man who did this before the police find him, I fear for what he'll do."

"If you don't go to the police, I have to," I say. "I can't keep this information to myself. They need to know about the threatening letters and about your stalkers."

"What's done is done. The police can do what they want. I take my comfort and my guidance in Buddhism. Do you know Buddha's Five Reflections?" We shake our heads. "The Five Reflections are the Buddha's daily contemplations on the fragility of life and our true inheritance, which is not money, although Bucky thinks it is." She scoots to the edge of her seat, her spine straight.

"I am sure to become old. I cannot avoid aging. I am sure to become ill. I cannot avoid illness. I am sure to die. I cannot avoid death."

This is Buddha's enlightenment? I know this every time I look in the mirror.

"I will be separated, parted from all that is dear to me." A small pulse beats under her jaw. "The fifth reflection is the one that guides my life. 'I am the owner of my actions, heir of my actions. Whatever actions I do, good or evil, of these I shall become heir.'"

"Are you talking about Karma?" Frank says.

"We become what we are. I choose not to live with bitterness or seek revenge. If I want a life of grace and joy, I must become grace and joy."

"And the guy that killed Chrissy?"

"He is heir to his actions, too. His suffering will be great. He is doomed to endless lives of relentless misery."

"So it's enough for you that the only punishment this guy gets for murdering your daughter is that he spends his next life as a cockroach?"

"Frank, I wish I could make you both understand. This is the heart of my spiritual practice. I won't dishonor Chrissy's love of life by making my life about the search for her killer."

She stands up, clearly ready to leave. "Perhaps we should stop here and have dinner some other time when we're less agitated."

Finally, she's said something I can agree with. Having dinner together would be agony. It would be all I could do to keep from reaching across the table to wipe that Mona Lisa smile off her face.

"I'm still going to the police," I say.

"Do whatever you need to do, Dot. And thank you for your concern and your kindness. I hope you understand where I'm coming from."

"I don't and I doubt I ever will. I think you're hiding behind your religion. Going to the police isn't about revenge. It is about justice."

Later that night in bed, we pick the evening apart. Frank is as radical in his anger about religion as my father was. He rants for ten minutes about how religion is the source of the world's misery and oppression of women. He can't believe a modern woman like JJ could believe in reincarnation. And then, having vented, he falls asleep, leaving me to toss and turn as the conversation with JJ runs wild in my brain. I listen to his breathing grow deeper and more even as I feel tears trickle out of the corners of my eyes. How much happier and easier would my life and my mother's life have been if, instead of living every day drowning in bitterness, my father had been able to let go of his past and forgive his tormentors?

CHAPTER FIFTEEN

FRANK IS OFF to work before I've finished my first cup of coffee. He gives me a quick kiss and tells me he slept like a log. Wish I could say the same. I call Pence. His secretary answers and tells me he's away for two days and can't be reached.

"Can't be reached? In the middle of a murder investigation?"

"He's having oral surgery. He's put it off as long as possible and he's miserable. He can hardly talk. You want to talk to his second in command?"

The idea of explaining all this to someone who is only familiar with the rudimentary aspects of the investigation is not appealing. I pour myself a second cup of coffee and check my voice mail. I have a message from Lupe. Her voice is shaky.

"Manny is going crazy at home. It's worse than when he's at work. I told him now is a good time to make an appointment with you. But he won't. Do you make house calls?"

* * *

Manny and Lupe's small house in East Kenilworth is a plain, one-story 1950s ranch-style building with a detached garage and a low front deck, white with dark green trim. There's a large playpen with net sides in the front yard. Someone's been digging a planter bed along the deck and under the living room window. I knock on the door. Lupe answers with Carmela in her arms. Her eyes are swollen and red. She is in stocking feet, jeans, and a sweatshirt. Shoes are lined up under a small bench in the front hall. I offer to remove my own, but she stops me. She shifts Carmela to her hip. Carmela is a beautiful child with her parents' warm skin tones and a head of curly, glossy, black hair. She looks at me and starts to cry.

"Sorry, she woke up early from her afternoon nap and she's cranky." Lupe turns to the back of the house and shouts something in Spanish. Manny steps into the doorway between the kitchen and the living room. If it's possible to look any worse than he did the last time we talked, he does.

"Dr. Meyerhoff. What are you doing here?"

"I called her. Asked her to come to our house because you are too stubborn to go to her office." Manny glares at Lupe and says nothing. "Sit down, please. I'm going to try to get Carmela to sleep some more." She looks at Manny. "Ask her if she wants some coffee or water. I'll be right back."

Their living room is sparsely furnished with an Ikea couch, two chairs, and a coffee table. No art, no books, no fancy sound system, only scattered toys. All that a young cop with a stay-at-home wife and a child can afford in Silicon Valley.

Manny takes one of the chairs. "I'm going crazy staying home. I'm trying to do stuff around the house, but it doesn't help. I dug up the front yard, the side yard, the back. Lupe had to stop me before I dug up stuff she already planted. I thought exercise was supposed to relieve stress."

"It does. Unless you're already so stressed exercise won't make a dent."

Lupe comes into the room. "Did you offer her coffee?"

"Forgot." He shakes his head. Lupe turns on her heels and walks into the kitchen. "I'm in the doghouse. Again. I can't do anything right and staying home is making things worse."

Lupe comes back into the living room with a tray holding three cups, a coffeepot, a bowl of sugar, and a carton of milk. We pour our own and settle into silence, waiting each other out to see who will speak first. Manny looks at Lupe. She looks at the floor.

"You called the doc. Say something."

"He's supposed to be resting not working. He's on the computer all the time. Or making phone calls. I need him to help out."

"I am helping out. I've been doing yard work."

"You know what I mean. You need to spend time with your daughter."

"Working, Manny? What are you doing?" I ask.

"He's looking for that damn blanket. When he finds it, if he finds it, it will probably be in Russia and the video will be forty years old."

"I do it when you're asleep or taking a nap. It doesn't bother you. Why do you care?"

"You're here but you're not here."

"What are you talking about?"

"Your body may be in the same room as me and Carmela, but your mind is thousands of miles away."

Manny starts to protest and Lupe cuts him short.

"Tell her why you won't bathe the baby. Go on, tell her."

His lips press into a hard line. He starts to speak and then stops, takes a sip of coffee and sets it down on the coffee table. "I've told you. It's not that I don't want to. I can't."

"Why can't you? Tell her."

He looks at his feet. "I keep seeing other stuff. It's like somebody's switching pictures on me. First there's Carmela, all happy in the tub, and then there's some other baby in a bath, screaming. It's just better if I don't."

"He won't let anybody near her but me. My father wanted to change the baby's diapers. Manny had a fit. It's her grandfather, for God's sake. He loves her."

Manny shakes his head, slowly, from side to side. "That's what they all say. All full of love and making nice. That's how it starts."

"It's my father, Manny. My father." Lupe's voice is shrill and tears muddle in her eyes.

"That's who does this kind of stuff. Not always strangers." He looks at me. "See, she doesn't understand. Her life is full of normal people. I talk to these creeps every day. They could be doctors, lawyers, anybody. I tell them, 'I'm ten years old, want to see a picture of me naked?' They should be horrified, but they're happy. They can't wait to meet me, buy me ice cream and pizza. They're grooming me, setting me up to trust them."

"I've heard this a million times. I can't listen anymore. My father would never do anything like that. Neither would any of our friends."

Manny's hands harden into fists. "I told you. I can't take the chance."

Lupe stands. "Fix him, Doc," she says. "I'm giving him one more month to finish this case and get out of ICAC or I'm taking the baby and leaving. We don't have friends anymore because he doesn't want anyone coming to the house. He won't let me hire a babysitter, so I can't go out with my girlfriends. I'm supposed to be proud of him because of what he does? The way his mind works, he's just as sick as the people he's trying to catch." She walks out of the room.

Manny sinks back against the couch, his face turned upward, as though he's counting the ceiling tiles. "I know things I wish I didn't know. But I can't unlearn them." He wipes his arm across his face and I realize he's crying.

"I don't want to lose her, Doc. Or Carmela. But I can't quit in the middle of this investigation."

"Why not?"

"Because I'm not a quitter."

"Let me make sure I understand. You won't quit your job for your family, but you are willing to quit your family for your job."

"That's not what I'm saying. I'm just asking Lupe to hang in with me until this case is solved and then I'll go back to the street."

"But what if it's never solved?"

"That's what's killing me. I need to be working. The longer this guy stays out there, the weaker our chances of finding him. The more he's likely to think he can take another baby and get away with it. I can't live with that."

Lupe sticks her head through the doorway. "You're obsessed. Like a maniac."

"Why should I have to choose between you and my job?"

Lupe disappears into the kitchen without saying a word.

I tap the table to get his attention. "And why should your family have to choose between your job and you?"

Carmela starts to cry. Manny gets to his feet, but Lupe is already opening the door to the baby's room. Carmela's cries grow louder, then softer. In a minute there is nothing but silence.

Manny's face goes slack. "We've been around this track before. Nothing changes. Nothing I say helps."

"That's because you have to do something, not just talk about it."

He sighs, long and deep. "I need a break. What's going on at the department? Anything new?"

"The chief is having oral surgery today."

"I mean in terms of the investigation."

"You're not supposed to be working, remember? Put some of that energy into your family. Take your daughter to the park. Pay attention to her instead of looking for child molesters. I'd better go. I want to say goodbye to Lupe."

"You know something, don't you?" He is reading me, looking for telltale signs that I'm lying. Unfortunately, I have a face like an open book. Never could master that neutral screen business they pressed on us in grad school. I turn away. "You do know something. Tell me." I walk toward the door. "The best thing I can do for my family is to find this bastard before he hurts another child. If I don't, I'll be stuck with this for the rest of my life. And so will they." I put my hand on the doorknob. "Understand something, Lupe wants me to find this guy as much as I do. The quicker I can do this, the better it is for her."

"Let somebody else do it. You're not the only one capable of finding him."

"I've put hundreds of hours into this. No one else. C'mon, Doc, tell me what you know, even if you think it doesn't matter."

"And if I do? What do you give me in return?"

Lupe is standing behind him, Carmela fast asleep, curled on her shoulder. Manny senses their presence. He takes Carmela into his arms. She murmurs softly, opens her eyes once, and falls asleep, settled against his chest.

"I swear on the baby"—he looks at Lupe—"that if we don't close this case by February, I'll quit the ICAC unit and go back to the street."

"A deal is a deal," I say. "Make no mistake. I'm going to hold you to this. So is Lupe."

"Understood," he says and hands Carmela back to Lupe. "Now, Doc, sit down and tell me what you know."

I start by telling him that he was right about his prediction. The proprietor of the Dollar Store has closed his shop and gone to Mexico. I expect Manny to gloat a little, but he only asks me if there's any word on the autopsy. When I tell him as far as I know it's still pending, he asks me what else I'm holding back.

"The chief doesn't know this yet. I could get in trouble."

He flicks his hands and shrugs. "So tell him, I don't care. I don't hide anything from him."

"You're hiding the fact that you're working when you're supposed to be on leave."

"No I'm not. If he asks me, I'll tell him. You can tell him. What's he going to do? Give me two, maybe three more days on the beach with no pay? I'm already on the beach."

I tell him about Kathryn Blazek letting slip that JJ had a secret stalker during the same conversation when she confessed to being a secret smoker and buying her cigarettes at the Dollar Store. I tell him Frank knew how to find Maldonado and Maldonado had a bunch of parking tickets belonging to the guy he sold his truck to. Manny grabs a piece of paper and starts taking notes. When I describe Frank's and my conversation with JJ, he goes almost rigid with excitement.

"Let me get this straight. She doesn't have a stalker but she has spies, people Bucky sends to check up on her. And she gets threatening letters that she opens but never reads past the first line. And no word on the autopsy? You're sure about that?" I nod. "Be right back." He walks into the kitchen and comes back holding a wireless phone. "I'm going to call the chief."

"I told you. He's not there."

"Too bad. So sad." He punches in the chief's number and when Pence's secretary answers he tells her that he's working from home at the chief's suggestion and asks if the autopsy report, which should be addressed to him, is in yet. "It is?" he says. "Would you be so kind to fax it over to my house? And tell the chief I hope he feels better real soon."

* * *

Lupe isn't happy with me. She bundles the baby into her stroller, stocks it with toys, a bottle, diapers, plastic bags filled with cereal and fruit, and heads for the park. Carmela does not travel light, even to go around the corner.

Manny sets the autopsy report on the coffee table and starts to read. He stops, flips the paper over, and rereads the previous page. The whole of his face seems to be fighting with itself, eyebrows, nostrils, lips, all moving and twitching. He finishes and shoves the report across the table to me.

"What do you think?" I say.

"I don't know what to think. It's not what I expected."

I push the report back. "I can't. I don't want to." There are many things I'm willing to do to prove to the cops that I'm tough, but I draw the line at autopsies. "Just give me a summary."

He picks the report up, flips to the back page, and shakes his head. "Death from terminal arrhythmia."

"Terminal arrhythmia? A heart attack? Babies don't have heart attacks."

"No signs of physical or sexual abuse. No bruising, no burns, no blunt force trauma, no vaginal penetration, no anal penetration, no traces of semen anywhere on the body. Nothing. Just makeup, a blanket, and some flecks of meth"—he swallows hard—"caught in her eyelashes."

"Not raped? Not molested?"

"You can't tell anyone about this. Not a word. The family are still suspects, and now I got a crap load of new leads to follow up. None of this can get out. You understand? It's the details that trip the bad guys up. If I ask a suspect why he raped Chrissy and he says she wasn't raped, I ask how he knows that. If he says someone told him, I don't have any leverage."

He puts the autopsy report in a folder and places the folder in a large manila envelope.

"Do you have that guy Buzz's address with you?"

"There's not one address, there's a bunch." I give him the list. "They all seem to be in the same neighborhood."

"Piece of cake. I think I'll go for a drive in the country. It'll be relaxing. Care to go on a ride-along?"

I don't know if he's asking me because he thinks I can help or because it's the best way to keep an eye on me so I don't call *Good Morning America* with details about the autopsy report. I don't care which it is, I'm going.

* * *

Maldonado has ten tickets with ten different addresses, all in the same area twenty miles south of East Kenilworth. We head out in Manny's Prius. The terrain is flat and dotted with small broken-down ranches. The gentrification that is creeping from Kenilworth to East Kenilworth hasn't infiltrated this far south. Small pens of horses and sheep butt up against the roadway. Compared to the lush irrigated farms and orchards of the Central Valley, this area has been ravaged by drought. Manny consults his GPS and turns off the freeway. We drive another ten minutes. The area around us is all hard-packed soil and field rubble. Goats roam empty backyards, content to eat whatever garbage they find. Driveways are jammed with cars in various states of disrepair, held up by concrete blocks or jacks. Hard to imagine why the mysterious Buzz has gotten a lot of parking tickets. The place is littered with abandoned cars.

"My guess is that the sheriff's department is hassling him. They know he's good for something. There." Manny hits the brakes. "Over there. That's Maldonado's truck in the driveway."

He points to a small clapboard house with a sagging deck. There are curtains on the front windows, all closed. The small yard is partly paved and what little grass that remains is scorched brown.

Manny pulls to the side of the road behind a pickup truck and puts his iPhone on the camera setting.

"How long are we going to be here and what are we looking for?"

"Hard to say. This is police surveillance, Doc," he says. "Just lean back and relax."

* * *

Two hours later, dusk is settling over the fields and the sky is murky red thanks to pollution and dust. As always, I could use a bathroom, especially after all the coffee I drank at Manny and Lupe's house. We've been sitting here looking at nothing but each other and a murder of crows that have been screeching at us from the tops of telephone poles. The collective noun of murder is apt, considering what we're doing and why we're here. I ask Manny if he knows that some people consider crows to be the smartest birds in the world, smarter even than dogs. He sticks his hand out and hushes me as the front door to the small house opens. A skinny white guy with long hair comes out backward dragging a wire laundry cart with a bent wheel down the front steps. Something falls off the top of a jumble of unfolded clothes and sheets. The man curses, kicks the basket, and bends over to pick up what's fallen.

Only when he stands can I see Buzz's face. His bottom lip is cracked and bloody. He shudders and begins to scratch his bare arms violently, leaving long angry red welts. The skin on his face and neck is rubbed raw in places and pocked with eczema. Manny takes a picture. Buzz yells something back at the house. A skinny woman comes to the door wearing a tank top and tattered jeans. She could be anywhere from twenty-five to forty-five. Whatever her age, it's apparent she hasn't had an easy life. Manny takes her picture. She hands Buzz some money and a box of laundry detergent. Manny takes another picture. Buzz pockets the money and gives her a shove. Not a playful shove but a hard push that sends her crashing into the steps where she sits, head in hand, crying. Buzz grabs the laundry cart and starts walking toward the road. He's yelling at her over his shoulder as Manny takes another photo with his cell phone.

"Damn," he says, "this thing takes good pictures." He puts it back in his pocket and starts the car. We pull away, silent as a submarine. I haven't seen him looking this happy in weeks.

* * *

The next morning, we find Pence in his office, preparing for a staff meeting. His right cheek is swollen and he's worrying the inside of his mouth with his tongue. His secretary offers him breakfast from a tray of pastries she's about to take into the conference room. He looks longingly at the bagels but chooses a sugar-glazed air-filled donut on the grounds that he can't eat anything chewy.

"Soup, milkshakes, and Jell-O. That's all I've had to eat for the past three days. I'm starving."

He doesn't look like he's starving, but he does look uncomfortable. He brushes flakes of sugar off his jacket and starts to pick up his notebook when Manny looks in the door.

"Hey. What are you doing here?" the chief says. "You're not due back yet."

Manny smiles. He looks rested. "The doc cured me," he says. "I'm ready to roll."

"Cured you how?"

"With information. And a new suspect."

"In my office, now," Pence bellows at Manny. I start to walk away. "You, too, Dr. Meyerhoff. Staff meeting is canceled."

We go over all of it from our first visit to the Dollar Store to finding Buzz and Maldonado's truck.

"You took the doctor with you on surveillance to see a guy who just might be involved in a murder-kidnapping?"

"It was perfectly safe. I wasn't going to do anything, just take pictures."

"Supposing he had seen you? Come after you with a gun?"

"He didn't. He doesn't even know he's involved. Anyhow, judging from all the parking tickets he's got, he knows the locals are looking at him. He's a tweaker. So's his girlfriend. They're probably cooking meth and the locals know it."

"And now what?"

"We need an ID on him. All the intel we have is that his name is Buzz. No last name. I'm going give the sheriff's office a call. See if they have a mug shot we can show Chrissy's parents."

"And you feel ready to take this on? You still have more time coming to you."

"Staying home was killing me, Chief. This is exactly what I need to do to feel better."

"Not by yourself. Use the task force. If you need extra help, let me know. I'll reassign anyone you need from the PD. Anyone that is, except the doc."

"Why not me?"

"Because, Dr. Meyerhoff." Pence leans down until his face is opposite mine. "Meth addicts can be armed and dangerous. If I had to choose what to bring to a gunfight, I'd bring a big gun and a friend with a big gun. Not a psychologist." He laughs, then yelps in pain and grabs his cheek.

CHAPTER SIXTEEN

I HAVE A late afternoon appointment with Dr. Randall. I promised to check back with him, let him know how things are going. Bette Randall answers the door before I knock. She walks me into the living room.

"He's not feeling well. Hasn't been out of bed today. The doctor says he may be having a series of little strokes. Last night he was trying to say something to me and he couldn't find the words." She tears up and turns away.

"Should I leave?"

"No. He's been looking forward to your visit. He needs the stimulation. And he needs to be needed. Just remember, his acuity is compromised and he tires easily. I don't know how much you can rely on what he says." She takes my hand and leads me up to their bedroom. Charles is sitting upright in a hospital bed wearing a ball cap and a 49ers sweatshirt over his pajama top.

"Excuse me for not getting up," he says. "Nurse Ratched is keeping an eye on my every move."

"Stinks in here," Bette says and opens a window. "Smells like old men." She pushes a rolling table next to the bed. "Need anything else? Tea, coffee?"

"Privacy." Charles glares at her. She sticks her tongue out at him and makes for the door.

"Call me if you need something," she says to me over her shoulder. "Like a tranquilizer gun or a martini."

I give him a sketchy overview, nothing Pence or Manny would object to. He listens and then shifts around in the bed looking for a more comfortable position. He reaches under the covers and winces.

"Leg cramps. From the medication. Go on, please."

"What if someone, actually two people, failed to mention that they bought a blanket identical to the one Chrissy was wrapped in when she was found?"

"Didn't mention it or lied when asked? Because equivocation is another indication of lying. Same as skirting the issue or giving indirect responses."

"No one asked."

He looks at me over the top of his glasses. "If they weren't asked, they didn't lie."

"I asked. Not the police. One of them answered the question directly, even told me where she bought the blanket. The other woman didn't say yes and didn't say no. All she said was she bought her blankets at Nordstrom's."

"So she skirted the issue. What about her face? The corrugator muscles near the eyes? You should be looking for tiny facial movements that last less than a second. Barely noticeable indicators that the person is lying. Attempting to conceal some emotion from the inquisitor or from themselves." He pushes himself up higher in the bed. "Liars prefer concealment because they don't have to worry about remembering what lies they've told and to whom. Pay less attention to what your suspects say and more attention to how they say it. Truth-tellers will be genuinely emotional. They will provide unique sensory details and use more arm and hand movements to illustrate what they're saying. Liars tend to talk in a passive voice with a lot of moderating adverbs and tentative words."

"The first woman's response was straightforward. The second woman . . ."

"Your two prime suspects are women? Very rare for a pedophile to be female. Mostly it's brothers, fathers, stepfathers, or Mommy's boyfriend."

"It's not certain that this is a case of pedophilia." He raises a bushy gray eyebrow. "I can't say anything more. It's classified."

"If not pedophilia then . . ." He freezes. "Don't tell me that you suspect JoAnn Juliette of murdering her own child? That's not possible. She was here in my house. Sat in my living room. Drank my tea. I thought she was a loving mother. Careful. Concerned." He grabs for his notepad and pen. "I don't mean to be ghoulish, but I need to write this up."

He picks up a cowbell sitting on his night table and shakes it. "Bette's idea of an intercom." He rings until she opens the door. She's breathing hard and trying not to show it.

"Now what, your highness?"

"Help me into the library. I need my computer."

"No." She puts her hands on her hips. "You are on bed rest. Doctor's orders."

He throws his legs over the side of the bed and gestures at me to bring him his walker. Bette looks at me, "don't you dare" written all over her face. She moves his legs back under the covers.

"I don't need a computer to know from your face that you are tired and need a break." She touches me lightly on the arm and taps the face of her watch. Charles leans back against his pillow, eyes closed.

"Don't get old, Dot," he says. "It's very boring."

* * *

Frank is waiting for me at my house. My usually dark rooms are lit and glowing in the night. A swell of gratitude washes over me. Late as it is, he's waited to start dinner. He leans over, gives me a kiss and a long hug. If I had a lick of sense I should take a shower, change my clothes, and get him to elope to Las Vegas. I take the first step, a quick shower, wrap myself in a towel, and head for the closet when Frank opens the bedroom door and hands me the telephone.

"It's Manny. He's working late." Frank gives me the once-over. "Too bad you're not on Skype."

I pull the towel tighter.

Manny is bursting with news. Buzz has a bunch of aliases and a minor record for DUI, petty theft, and bar fights. The sheriff's been to his house a couple of times for DV, but his girlfriend refuses to press charges. The image of her, sprawled on the front steps of that ramshackle house, head in hands, rises in front of me.

"I didn't think the victim had to press charges in domestic violence. The sheriff can do that, can't he?"

"Can if he wants. Hard to get a conviction if the victim won't testify. In this case, the battery was mutual. They have mug shots of Buzz and his girlfriend to prove it. With his-and-hers black eyes."

"Sounds like a successful day's work."

"Not entirely. I was hoping Buzz was a 290 reg—registered sex offender. If he was, by law he should have reported in to the sheriff's department. Doesn't mean he isn't; it just means he hasn't been caught. Yet."

"What's his connection to Kathryn Blazek?"

"Don't know yet."

"So what's next?"

"I'm thinking about a knock and talk tomorrow morning. A friendly chat. Consensual. No warrants. Nobody under arrest. Buzz is free to ask me to leave anytime. I'll make something up like we just arrested a guy for child porn and your name was on his distribution list. I'd like to get your side of the story. That kind of thing."

"And you think Buzz will go for that? Voluntarily?"

"I do. I've done it lots of times. Pedophiles love to talk. Know why? Because they think if they tell you what you want to hear, you'll leave them alone and they can get back to downloading files. They're obsessed."

"Look, Manny, I don't mean to tell you how to do your job, but aren't you afraid that if you move on Buzz he'll get scared off? Leave town? At the moment, he doesn't know he's under suspicion. Doesn't it make more sense to keep it that way until you have more evidence to connect him to Kathryn and Chrissy? All you have now is the guy from the Dollar Store who says he sold a blanket to a woman we think is Kathryn Blazek and she drove away with a man we think is Buzz. The Dollar Store guy is not a credible witness. You said so yourself. You thought he was stringing us along to get more money. And now he's gone to Mexico and didn't leave a forwarding address."

"I got a deadline, remember? You were there. One month or I'm single again."

"I understand you're feeling under pressure from Lupe. Buzz has a history of violent behavior. I doubt she would want you to take chances with your safety to meet her deadline. You need to think this over carefully. Can we meet at Fran's tomorrow morning? I just got home. It's late, I'm tired, and I don't think well on an empty stomach. Give it a day. Twenty-four hours isn't going to make that much difference."

"It would have to Chrissy." He gives a low, airy whistle, like a punctured tire.

"Have you talked to anyone else about this? The team? Or the chief?"

"Not yet. I wanted to talk to Buzz first. See what I got."

This is crazy. No way should he go to Buzz's house without backup. Without telling anyone but me where he's going. It's impulsive and dangerous. Not the careful, by-the-book Manny I know.

"Manny, I have never minced words with you. So listen carefully. I don't care if you never speak to me again or if you tell everybody in the department I'm a snitch. But if you don't meet me tomorrow at Fran's, I'm going to the chief and tell him where you are and what you're doing."

* * *

I walk into the kitchen in my bathrobe, barefoot with wet and stringy hair.

"You didn't have to dress for dinner, you know." Frank whacks me on the butt with a dish towel. "What's up?"

"Manny's going to get himself killed if he's not careful. He's not sleeping, he's drinking, his wife is about to kick him out of the house, and from a tactical point of view he's making bad decisions. Something's off with him."

"He's working a kid case. You've always said it's the kids that get to cops."

I wonder if that's because every cop was once a kid.

* * *

My stomach doesn't stay empty for long. Omelets, salad, crunchy French bread, and a glass of pinot noir plus a foot rub and I was not capable of thinking about anything but getting a good night's sleep. Which is why I'm only interested in a cup of coffee at Fran's the next morning. The place is a madhouse. Orders to go, orders to stay, customers lined up out the door waiting for seats. I shove my way inside and ignore the dirty looks. Eddie and Fran are behind the counter. I don't see Manny.

"He's in the back," Eddie shouts at me, his face red and slick with sweat. "At the VIP table. Only the best for my buddy. Both of you."

I squirm past the counter patrons. As always, there are half a dozen KPD cops race-eating through breakfast before they're dispatched to a call. Manny's tucked into a booth, his back to the door. Uncharacteristic for a cop. He doesn't move when he sees me. That's another thing that's changed. He used to have old-fashioned manners.

"Hiding out? Didn't want anyone to see you drinking coffee with the department shrink?"

"There's enough cops at the counter to stop a dozen terrorists."

"Coffee, crazy lady?" Eddie fills my cup and hands me a plate of toast with a side of bacon that I didn't order. "So what's going on? Is my man losing his mind because he misses me so much?" He slides into the seat next to Manny. "You alright, buddy? You don't look too good. Working that kiddie porn shit? It's a drag."

"Eddie." Fran's voice sails over the chatter. "I need you up front."

Eddie rolls his eyes. "A fry cook's work is never done." He squirms out of the seat. "Hold that thought, I'll be right back."

Manny sticks his fork into a half-eaten pile of now cold pancakes, pulls it out again, and pushes the plate away. "I have a new strategy. I'm going to make an appointment with JoAnn Juliette. Go over the mug shots of local sex offenders with her once again and slip Buzz's mug shot into the photo lineup. See if she recognizes him. If she doesn't, I'll move on to the father and the stepmother. To be super thorough, I faxed the photo to Norway on the chance Buzz might be the nanny's American boyfriend. The cops interviewed her. Same story. No American boyfriend and she doesn't recognize Buzz. Still doesn't explain why she ran."

Eddie slides back into the booth. He wipes his hands on his apron. Cop talk, bad guys, unsolved homicides. This is what he misses, what he longs for. "So, my man, making any progress?"

Manny shakes his head.

"Can't talk about it, right? Especially not to a recovering drunk." He looks at me. "Emphasis on recovering." He turns back to Manny. "My money's on the mother. Nice-looking broad. One of them free-spirit, earth-biscuit types. Here's my theory. Think about the cops you know—got married young, had babies, and spent all their time working, because work's more exciting than changing diapers. They get divorced, move on, get married again, have another child, but this time the job's not so interesting anymore. Now the only thing in life that matters is the new wife and the new baby. It's like they're making up for what they missed the first time around. Maybe that's what happened here. Pop made a pile of money. Now he wants to play house, move in, settle down, and be a full-time daddy. But Mommy likes her freedom. Doesn't want the old—emphasis on old—man around. It will cramp her style. So she kills the kid. Or gets someone to do it for her. See what I mean? Life's a bitch. First you marry one, then you die."

Manny's face goes pale.

"Shit," Eddie says and whacks his forehead. "I've stepped into it again, haven't I? Wife giving you a hard time, buddy?" He slips his arm over Manny's shoulder. "Take it from one who knows. You may love your job, but it don't love you. As a matter of fact, the only time you need your vest is in the station, because that's where they stab you in the back. Take care of things at home first."

I can't tell if Eddie is talking about himself or Manny. Maybe both.

"On the other hand, I'm definitely not the person you want to get marital advice from." He slides out of the seat. "Take care of him, Doc. He's a good man."

I push my toast and bacon to Manny. He pushes it back.

"Eddie loves you, you know."

"At least someone does."

He waves his hands in the air and shakes his head. I don't have to dig deeply to know this is not the time to talk about his and Lupe's relationship.

"So. I like your new plan much better than the one you proposed last night. Much safer, and if someone identifies Buzz, then you have a real link to Chrissy." I take a sip of coffee and chew off the end of a piece of bacon. Manny doesn't say anything, doesn't look at me.

"I'd like to ask you a favor. Is that okay?" He doesn't respond. "As part of my graduate work in psychology, I studied the detection of deception. I've become interested in it again. Done a little reading, even visited my old professor, Dr. Charles Randall. He's an expert in pedophilia and the detection of high-stakes lies. And, coincidentally, one of the psychologists JJ consulted before she mounted the show with Chrissy's photo in it. She wanted to know whether her photographs would entice pedophiles. He's happy to talk to you if you ask. But I have to warn you, he's sick."

Manny makes a notation on his clipboard. Why is it that I'm the one who has to point out things he may have missed?

"What did he tell her?"

"That it's impossible to predict who will be aroused by what. He encouraged her to go on with the exhibit."

"And this is the guy you're taking advice from? Brilliant."

"There's enough blame to go around for everybody. I don't think it helps. Do you?"

Manny doesn't answer. He's rubbing his index finger over a burn mark on the Formica tabletop, around and around as if getting this ages-old scar off the table is the most important thing in the world. I wonder what else he's trying to erase.

"Would it be possible, Manny, for me to observe JJ, Kathryn, and Bucky when you show them Buzz's picture? Please don't misunderstand. I'm not implying that you can't do the job yourself."

"Or that you're spying on me for the chief?"

"Manny, I'm sorry I told the chief you looked stressed."

Once again he waves his hands in the air. "Go on."

"The detection of lying has strong evidence-based research behind it. It works. All I need is a one-way mirror with a sound system, just like the one in the conference room. I can sit there and take notes. Nobody will even know I'm around. What have you got to lose? It might even help the investigation."

"I can give them a polygraph."

"It's my understanding that the polygraph can be useful if there are facts known only to the police and the killer."

"That's what we got. The makeup. The heart atrial thing. Nobody knows about those but the killer."

"But polygraphs aren't admissible in court. Plus, they aren't always accurate. Some produce results as high as 95 percent accuracy and some are no better than chance. There can be sizable false positives. Ditto for false negatives where the guilty person looks innocent because they're good liars. That's why they're not admissible in court—too much depends on the examiner and the person being examined. Randall's theory is based on a coding system of facial actions. I think it's more reliable. If I get nothing, then you can reconsider polygraphs."

"I'll have to run it by the chief."

"Of course. I can come with you when you talk to him. Explain how it works."

He smiles for the first time. "I'd better handle this one myself, Doc. The chief will take it better if it comes from me."

* * *

The minute Manny leaves, Eddie sits down. I need to go to headquarters to meet with three records clerks who have some sort of personal dispute. Eddie takes twenty minutes I don't have to be convinced that what he said won't damage Manny or destroy their friendship. He's still highly reactive, but at least he's talking instead of medicating his anxiety with a six-pack of beer.

As soon as I get to headquarters, I go to the personnel and training department and ask to see Manny's file. My ex, Mark, did Manny's pre-employment interview. Whatever I can say about Mark and his former intern and now current wife, Melinda, they wrote good reports. The full psych report is online in the city's Human Services department. All I need is a paper summary sheet that the PD keeps for its own purposes. The on-duty personnel secretary is not too happy to be interrupted. Judging from her voluminous sighs as she removes the key from its hiding place and blocks my view of the open file drawer, the poor woman is carrying the weight of every employee, past, present, and prospective, on her shoulders. She hands me Manny's file with the admonition that I cannot take it out of the office nor can I remove any material. What she fails to do is offer me a chair.

Manny's file is thin, mostly commendations and letters of appreciation. There's a personal information sheet with instructions for funeral arrangements and beneficiaries should Manny be killed in the line of duty. Filling out this form and keeping it up to date is a practice I instituted when I started working for KPD. Nothing complicates grief more than finding out your dead husband left everything to his first wife.

The pre-employment summary sheet is basically a checklist of potential areas of concern to the psychologist and a statement about the applicant's stability. Psychologists don't comment on suitability or make hiring recommendations—that's up to the chief. Mark would have asked about childhood abuse and his testing would have exposed unresolved trauma. I scan the sheet. There are no checked boxes. I hand the file back to the secretary, who appears annoyed that after going to all that trouble to give me the file, I haven't spent more time examining its contents.

I'm relieved. I don't want Manny to have been a child victim. Manny is a hardworking officer, not the star of some grade B novel where the hero's actions can be explained away by a secret, single traumatic incident. Dedication is dedication. Why am I trying to twist it into a neurotic manifestation of childhood abuse? My father's voice echoes in my ear so loudly I wonder if anyone walking by me in the hall can hear him.

"Cops become cops because if they didn't they'd be crooks. You don't grow up in a normal household so you can beat people up for a living." My father was wrong, of course. Cops become cops, not because they want to beat people up, but because they want to make a difference in the world. He was right about one thing. Too many of the cops I've interviewed over the years have come from dysfunctional families. Putting on a uniform makes them feel safer. Protecting others from abuse infuses their own victimization with meaning and purpose.

CHAPTER SEVENTEEN

JJ IS FIRST to be interviewed. I take my seat on the observer's side of the one-way mirror. Manny is standing at attention, a paper album of mug shots on the conference table in front of him. Unlike the cop shows on TV, there's no computer, no high-tech digital imaging, nothing to suggest that he works in Silicon Valley. This is the real world, not CSI.

The door to the conference room opens and Pence walks in with JJ followed by Pence's secretary holding a tray of coffee, water, and cookies. Manny and JJ shake hands in a pantomime of civility. I switch on the speaker. Pence is falling all over himself with apologies. He's sorry about a number of things, inconveniencing JJ, cutting into her day by asking her to look at these mug shots, causing her to revisit such a painful time. He apologizes for everything but the abysmal failure to find her daughter's murderer. JJ doesn't react or respond to anything he says. She simply settles in her seat and sips water until he excuses himself and backs out of the room, fawning all the way.

A minute later, the door to the observation room opens and Pence comes in. He looks at my open notebook and facial action coding sheets.

"Manny tried to explain what you're doing. I didn't get it. That's why I told him you could observe, but only if I was in the room with you. Just give me the Cliff Notes while he's giving JJ instructions."

"I'm looking for micro-expressions, subtle movements that occur often in less than a second. Like now, what you just did with your eyebrows tells me that you are trying to conceal something."

"Like the feeling that you're feeding me some new-age psycho-babble BS?"

"Yes. Those feelings."

He sits down.

"Actually, there's nothing new age about this. Recording universal expressions of emotion started with Darwin who coded seven emotions—anger, fear, disgust, surprise, enjoyment, sadness, and contentment."

"So which one was I?"

"Somewhere between anger and disgust."

He laughs. More of a snort.

"The system is not without its problems, the most challenging being the difficulty discerning whether a person is deliberately lying or unconsciously concealing their real feelings from themselves."

Pence puts his fingers to his lips. "Here we go."

Manny places the album in front of JJ as though he were handling a rare and delicate book. JJ starts to turn the pages. She works slowly, deliberately, bending over each photo, her long braid obscuring her face. Manny flicks his eyes toward us and shakes his head.

Pence puts his face next to my ear. "See that expression? That means no progress."

Ten minutes pass in silence. I'm beginning to wonder if I have the patience to sit through this when JJ sits up, grasps the side of her chair, and twists, first toward us and then away. She looks up at Manny and smiles. "My back hurts. Sorry."

"Can I get you something? More water?"

"Water would be lovely. Thank you."

Manny leaves the room. JJ flips her braid over her shoulder and bends to the book, carefully turning back two pages. Manny returns with a bottle of water, opens it, and sets it on the table. Pence picks up his cell phone. Manny excuses himself to answer. A minute later he's in the room with us and Pence is on his feet.

"The minute you left the room to get water, she flipped back two pages. Ask her if she recognized someone."

"Too direct," I say. "Don't put her on the spot. Tell her you noticed she turned back a few pages. Ask her if there is something bothering her. Anything you need to know."

Manny looks at Pence for permission. Pence shrugs.

By the time Manny reenters the room, JJ has closed the book and is sitting quietly with her hands on the cover. Her eyes are closed and her mouth is a smooth crescent.

"Anything I need to know, Ms. Juliette?" He sits down next to her so she has to turn toward him with her face in full view of the one-way mirror.

"These photos are amazing. Fascinating. Such detail. The range of expressions from contempt to fear to I-don't-know-what. This is a treasure trove of portraiture. I'm wondering if you have more of these and if I might borrow them. I can imagine assembling a collage of faces. It would be very powerful."

Manny's eyebrows scramble across his forehead. "Don't know. I'd need permission." He stumbles over his words. "Did you recognize anyone?"

She shakes her head and sighs. "I'm sorry. I can see I've disappointed you. As a photographer, I'm used to studying people's faces. I'm sure if I'd seen any of these men before, even briefly, I would have remembered."

JJ stands and extends her hand to Manny. "Thank you for all your efforts. Please thank the police chief, too."

"I may need you to come back again to look at more photos."

She lapses into herself for a moment, eyes closed. "I do appreciate all you're doing, but please don't ask me to do that. I could look at a thousand mug shots if I was creating an art project. But it's very different and quite disturbing to be looking at these men thinking one of them might have killed my daughter. I don't mean to be uncooperative, but I need to move on with my life."

"I understand this is painful for you, Ms. Juliette. I wouldn't ask you to do this except that the man who murdered Chrissy is still out there. As long as he's out there, other people's daughters are in jeopardy."

"I would never want to see another child harmed or another parent go through what Bucky and I have gone through. But life is full of suffering and there's little you or I can do to prevent it."

Manny's eyebrows pull down. His lips fuse into an angry line. "I don't get it. Don't you want to see this creep punished for what he did to your daughter?"

JJ backs away, just a little.

"You may find this hard to understand, but I refuse to live a life of ill will. I prefer to spend my life with loving-kindness and compassion."

"So you're telling me you're not angry."

"What I am is sad, heartbroken, and agonized. Desperately longing to touch Chrissy, to hold her, kiss her. But I am not angry."

And now I see it. The corrugated lines around her eyes pulling down on her eyebrows at the same time her lips tighten to thin red margins. She's lying. I make notes. My only question is whether she is deliberately masking her anger or hiding it from herself.

* * *

"Did you hear that?" Manny's face is red. His lips bared. "She'll come back but only if I give her mug shots for an art project. When John Walsh's son was kidnapped and murdered, he spent the rest of his life helping to find missing children. That woman whose daughter was killed by a drunk driver founded Mothers Against Drunk Driving. This bitch just wants to sit on her meditation pillow and think kind thoughts about the man who murdered her daughter. What the hell is that all about?"

Pence puts his hand on Manny's shoulder. "You're a little too agitated. If you want out of the next two interviews, I'll do them myself."

Manny stiffens. "Don't pull me off the case, boss. Next interview is not until tomorrow. I'll be good to go."

"I'm going to make sure of that. Go home. Now. I'm ordering you out of the building."

I want to warn Pence that being at home won't stop Manny from working the case or that, given the tension between Manny and Lupe, home is not a haven.

Pence claps Manny on the back. "You did a good job in there."

"I lost it."

"No you didn't. Your timing may have been a little off. It's understandable. The mother's a hard case. Ask the doc—she's been writing down numbers and letters like crazy." He gives Manny a collegial squeeze on the shoulder. "You and I. We don't need hieroglyphics, do we? With all due respect, Dr. Meyerhoff, even a blind man could see that, underneath all that nicey-nicey stuff, Ms. JoAnn Juliette is hiding something big."

* * *

I walk Manny to his car. He's disgusted with himself, convinced that he so alienated JJ she'll stop cooperating. I tell him that's catastrophic thinking. He doesn't know what she'll do in the future. Neither do I. He opens the door to his car.

"What is it, Doc? I can tell, you've got something on your mind."

"I've been thinking about you. How this case seems to be eclipsing everything else in your life. I'm wondering if there's anything personal about it?"

"What do you mean personal?"

"Something that happened to you. Some wrong you'd like to set right. Something you've never told another soul."

"Like was I molested as a child? You sound like Lupe. She asked me the same question."

"What did you tell her?"

"That she's been watching too many novellas on the TV."

* * *

Where JJ's wardrobe is artsy and edgy, Kathryn Blazek's taste in clothing tends toward the school of fashion favored by politicians' wives, knit suits with big pins, her hair sprayed into a wavy nest. She digs a pair of reading glasses out of her purse and carefully unfolds them. Pence inquires if she has enough light, would she like another cup of coffee, a different chair perhaps? He's treating her like a guest, not a witness. Or a suspect. She's the wife of a powerful man with a dead daughter whose killer he hasn't caught. The situation calls for a little extra finesse.

"I'm a bit nervous," Kathryn says. "I'm not very good at remembering faces or names. It can be quite embarrassing." She smiles. Only the muscles around her mouth move. Genuine smiles involve the orbicularis oculi, a muscle that raises the cheeks and creates crow's feet around the eyes. I warn myself not to jump to conclusions. It would be hard for anyone to be genuinely happy when asked to identify a child killer in a police station under the watchful eyes of the chief of police and who-knows-who sitting behind an obviously one-way mirror.

"Well then," she says, still smiling. "Whenever you're ready."

Pence thanks her again for being so helpful. His smile looks as fake as hers.

Manny enters the room as Pence leaves. He looks way more rested than he did yesterday. He's wearing a sports jacket, a collared shirt, and a tie. His hair is shower-wet. Marks from his comb run in parallel tracks through his glossy black hair.

Pence opens the door to the observation room and sits down next to me, arms crossed over his chest, legs stretched in front of him. All that he's missing is a ball cap and a hot dog.

"Looks better today, doesn't he? Glad I decided to send him home."

I start to respond and stop when Manny lays the album in front of Kathryn. He asks if she has spoken to JJ since yesterday.

"Poor woman. Did she have to look at these photographs, too?"

She puts on her reading glasses, adjusts them, and pats the hair around her ears searching for any unruly bits poking out from under the temple pieces. Manny opens the album.

Kathryn's pace is slow and deliberate. She tracks her place with the index finger of her left hand. The overhead light splinters reflections from her diamond wedding band into multicolored fragments that splay across the ceiling. Five, then ten, minutes pass. I look for fine movements in her face. A slight wrinkle in her nose, a downward tug at the corners of her mouth. Nothing. It's like she's looking through a book of upholstery swatches, not the faces of men who do hideous things to innocent children. She takes off her glasses, folds them in half, and puts them back into a hard-metal cylindrical case. "I'm sorry, but I don't believe I know any of these men."

Don't believe or don't know? She's skirting the question the same way she did when I asked her about buying the blanket at the Dollar Store. She never said yes and she never said no.

She picks up her purse and stands. "I do wish I could be of more help. My eyesight isn't what it used to be. I think I need something stronger than over-the-counter reading glasses these days. I told your chief that I'm terrible at remembering faces anyway. It's quite embarrassing not to remember someone I've met the week before. We all forget names. But faces?" She shakes her head in mock self-disgust. She's going on longer than she needs to, producing extraneous information that means nothing. Her words float aimlessly like confetti in a ticker-tape parade. I wish I knew what was under her chirpy patter or hidden behind a face so motionless it might have been cosmetically frozen with Botox.

* * *

An hour later, Bucky bangs his way into the conference room, irritation written all over his face. Pence offers his hand and Bucky just looks at it. Same with the coffee, cookies, and water.

"I'm a busy man. Let's just get this over with."

"Too busy to help us find his daughter's murderer?" Manny is standing next to me, looking through the one-way mirror, waiting for his cue to enter the conference room.

"I am sorry to inconvenience you," Pence says. "Your cooperation is appreciated."

"I wouldn't have to be here if you were doing your job."

Pence winces. "I understand your frustration—"

"No you don't. Don't pretend to. It's not your daughter who's dead."

"My apologies. I didn't mean to infer—"

"Can we get on with this?" Bucky yanks a chair from the table and sits facing the one-way mirror.

"Certainly." Pence takes a chair, positioning himself at a right angle to avoid staring into Bucky's face. "The reason I've asked you to meet with our investigator is that we have developed some additional suspects. We need you to look at this set of photos and tell us if you recognize anyone. We've already showed these pictures to Ms. Juliette and to your wife. Have you spoken to either of them about their experience?"

"I don't talk to JoAnn and I haven't seen my wife for two days. I've been away on business. I just got home this morning." He looks at his watch.

"So you don't know if they did or did not recognize anyone."

Bucky shakes his head.

"Are you aware that your wife has difficulty with faces because her eyesight is poor?"

Bucky hesitates for a second. "She wears reading glasses." He shakes his head again, more forcefully. "Are we going to get on with this anytime soon?"

Manny starts to open the door of the observation room. I stop him. "Ask Bucky if Kathryn has ever had Botox treatments. I'll explain later." He shrugs and walks out the door into the conference room. Pence stands, shakes Manny's hand, and leaves as we rewind back to the beginning. Manny offers his hand to Bucky. Bucky refuses to shake it, looks at his watch, and demands to know when they are going to get started because he's running out of time and patience.

Pence opens the door to the observation room and sits down. "Nasty son of a bitch. Likes to throw his weight around."

"Thank you for coming in, sir," Manny says. "I realize you're a busy man. Before we start, I need to ask if you have discussed these photos with Ms. Juliette or your wife."

Bucky throws his head back and his hands in the air. "Don't you people talk to each other? The chief just asked me the same question two minutes ago and I told him no."

"Thank you, sir. It's an important question because witnesses can influence each other's perceptions."

Bucky's face goes red. "I am not a witness. I am a victim." He spits the words out between clenched teeth.

"My apologies, sir. My mistake." He starts to lay the album on the table. Bucky reaches for it just as Manny pulls it back.

Pence shakes his head. "Not sure that's the way to go. I know what he's trying to do. Taunt the old man, rattle him, get him off his guard." I can't tell if he's talking to me or to himself. "Could be trouble."

"One more question before we start, sir. Has your wife had Botox injections?"

There is a moment, a silent second hanging in the air before Bucky tries to grab the folder from Manny's hands. Pence races into the room, kicking over the chair he was sitting in. He pushes Bucky off Manny and forces him back into the seat, his hands pressing down on Bucky's shoulders. "This is the second time you've tried to assault an officer of the law. I could have you arrested and I will if you don't calm down. Your grief does not entitle you to break the law. Do you understand me?"

Bucky's black eyebrows lock together.

"Do you understand me? Say it." Pence is in full command presence mode. His training as a street cop rising up like muscle memory without thought or hesitation.

Bucky's voice is robotic. "I understand."

"What do you understand?"

"That if I don't calm down, you will have me arrested."

Pence lifts his hands off Bucky's shoulders. "Now, answer Officer Ochoa's question."

"I have no idea if my wife has had plastic surgery."

"Botox injections," Manny corrects him.

"Or Botox injections. My wife goes to a spa. I don't know what she does when she's there. I just pay the bill. Now, may I please see these photos?"

Manny places the book on the table. Bucky starts to flip the pages.

"Take your time, please, sir. Look at every picture."

Pence pulls out a chair and sits down. Just in case.

Bucky gives a big sigh and starts turning the pages slowly, making a big show of looking at every mug shot. Suddenly his body jerks. His mouth opens and just as quickly compresses into a thin line.

"See someone you recognize?" Manny asks.

"No."

"Are you sure? You reacted to something." Bucky turns the page forward.

Pence reaches over and flips it back. "Look again, please."

"I thought I did, but I don't."

"Could be, sir, that whoever you recognized looks different in person than how they look in the picture. Older, younger, dressed differently. People don't look their best in mug shots." Manny moves closer.

"Don't tell JoAnn that."

"I thought you said you haven't talked to Ms. Juliette or your wife about this."

"I didn't. I just know how she thinks." He turns another page.

Pence stops him. "One more time. Look at that page one more time."

Bucky's hands curl into fists and his chest inflates. Manny and Pence stiffen, getting ready for a fight. Bucky assesses the situation. He's outnumbered and outgunned. "My mistake," he says. "This guy looked like someone I used to know. But it's not him. I'm sure of it."

"Which man? Point him out to me." Pence bends over Bucky. As soon as he does, I see his shoulders slump.

The rest of the interview is pro forma. The minute he's finished Bucky leaves the room without a word. Manny and Pence's words of appreciation and regret for taking up his time bouncing off his back. I go into the conference room.

"Right page, wrong guy," Pence says. "Bucky picked the page with Buzz's picture on it, but he pointed to another guy."

"What are the chances that the one person he thought he recognized just happens to be on the same page with Buzz? C'mon, Chief. Let's call him back. Show him some pictures of Buzz with his hair cut, in a suit, something different."

Pence holds up his hand. "Stop, please. We're not getting anywhere. I know you've tried your best, Manny, we all have. No shame, no blame. But the truth of the matter is . . ." His face bleaches with the effort of whatever he wants to say next. "I think it's time to call in the FBI."

"Please don't do that, Chief. I'm sure it's Buzz he recognized and he was—"

"Listen to me, Manny. You're not getting close. What you're getting is exhausted and desperate. Trying to make the pieces fit when they don't. Go back to your regular assignment on the ICAC team. Let the FBI do their magic. They've got bells and whistles we don't have."

Manny starts to protest again, and Pence stops him with a raised hand.

"I run a police department, Manny, not a democracy. I just gave you an order. I don't need your approval and I'm not interested in your opinion." He turns to me. "Do you have something to add, Dr. Meyerhoff?"

"Yes. You can't just cut him off like this. It's cruel. He's put his heart and soul into this case. Let him work with the FBI."

Pence's face turns red. "I am not asking your opinion about my decisions, I'm asking you to comment on these interviews. You've got a notebook full of hieroglyphics. Do they mean anything or am I paying you to scribble meaningless crap?"

Adrenaline washes through my body, stinging my cheeks and sending a hot flush up my neck. I stand. My heart is pounding hard enough to hear. I'm not sure I can speak without my voice quavering.

"In my opinion, they're all lying. What I don't know is what they're lying about and why."

"Very helpful. Anything else?" His voice is dripping with contempt.

I suck in my gut. Military style. "You are the chief of police and this is not a democracy, I understand that. But neither your rank nor the authoritarian nature of a police organization gives you the right to treat me or Manny disrespectfully because we're telling you something you don't want to hear."

* * *

As soon as Pence leaves the room, Manny turns to the wall, half-sitting on the edge of the table, his back to me. I'm pretty sure he's tearing up. I want to reach out, reassure him that this is not his fault. Point out that it may be for the better that he is relieved of an assignment that's causing him and Lupe so much anguish. But I keep quiet. He's just lost his dignity. He doesn't want me to see him in tears and he surely doesn't need a lecture.

"This is not the end of your career. Only a setback."

"You don't know that. Pence gave me a special assignment. I screwed up."

"Bucky Stewart is a powerful man. The chief doesn't want him as an enemy and he certainly doesn't want a lawsuit. He has to think about these things and protect the organization."

Manny doesn't answer. Rationality never trumps emotions. Manny's discovering that he is a limited human being and the bluntness is devastating. He started out in this job, as they all do, thinking he was part of an elite group of invulnerable people, smart, strong, and determined. This is not narcissism, it's a necessary fiction. Without it, Manny or any other cop couldn't do what society needs him to do. Or see what society doesn't want to acknowledge. Manny's mistake is believing that he could work without sleep. That he didn't need a break. That the job came before his family. That if only he worked harder and faster, no more little girls would be stolen and killed.

The door to the conference room bangs open and Pence barges in. "I'm putting you on notice. One more week and then I'm calling the FBI. I don't want the FBI doing my job for me. I don't want Bucky Stewart crawling up my ass. And I don't want my primary investigator to turn into a mental case." He turns on his heel. "Happy, Doc?" He doesn't wait for my answer.

CHAPTER EIGHTEEN

"THIS IS WHAT I get for not following my own instincts." Pence's face turns to a scowl the minute he sees me coming into the break room for a cup of coffee. It's late in the day and I need the caffeine after a particularly trying conflict-resolution session with the records division. The few cops that are standing around scatter.

"After he left here yesterday, Bucky decided to take matters into his own hands. If the locals hadn't shown up Code 3 after Buzz's meth-head girlfriend called 911, I'd be holding him for homicide."

"Manny was right. Bucky did recognize Buzz's photo. Where's Bucky now?"

"After a trip to the emergency room, he's downstairs in my holding cell waiting for his attorney."

"And Buzz?"

"In the hospital." He dumps the remainder of his coffee down the sink.

"Don't be so hard on yourself or Manny. This is progress."

He laughs. "Some progress. What in hell am I going to tell the media? I have two suspects in custody. One won't talk and the other can't."

I break a dinner date with Frank and stay at headquarters waiting for Manny. It's going to be a long day. I hear his voice on the scanner telling dispatch he's on his way back to the station. The police garage is empty of people, only patrol cars and a mournful police dog barking impatiently for his master. The electronic gate goes up and he drives right by me, parks, gathers up his clipboard, and gets out of the car. He jumps the minute he sees me, his startled response in full throttle. I give him a thumbs-up. He gives me a thumbs-down.

"I guess you heard. If his tweaker girlfriend hadn't called the locals, Buzz might be dead. My bad."

"You couldn't have predicted what Bucky would do."

"I could have pushed harder."

"You pushed as hard as you could. You and the chief. I was watching, remember?"

"I don't think the chief sees it the same way."

He takes a deep breath and starts up the stairs to the chief's office, one step at a time, like a man on his way to the gallows.

* * *

Frank is engrossed in a photography tutorial by the time I get home and barely acknowledges me as I walk in the front door. I change into my bathrobe, pour a glass of wine, and sit down on the couch next to him. He shuts the lid to his laptop.

"It's okay. I've seen this one before about six times." He looks at me. "What's going on?"

"I can't talk about it."

What's the matter with me? Why am I acting like I work for the Secret Service? It's going to be all over tomorrow's news.

"Chrissy's father is in custody and another man is in the hospital because Chrissy's father beat him up. Manny doesn't know who this other man is—I mean he knows his name, but not how he's related to Chrissy's father, only that Chrissy's father recognized him from a photo lineup. You can't tell anybody that. Swear?"

"That Bucky murdered his own daughter?"

"No. That he recognized this man in a photo lineup. Especially not JJ. You can't say anything about this to JJ."

"JJ does not want to talk about Chrissy. Not to me or to the other students. Why can't you tell me what's going on?"

"I just did, didn't I?"

"I don't think so. There's something more."

"It's Manny. He's under a lot of pressure. He's lost his confidence and . . . you can't tell anybody about this . . ."

Frank gives me his "I've-told-you-a-million-times-that-you-can-trust-me" look.

"The chief is on the verge of kicking Manny off the case and calling in the FBI. Manny thinks he's about to lose his job. And I think he's about to lose his marriage."

"And you can do what about any of this?"

"That's the problem. I don't have a clue."

* * *

At my office, the next morning, I have a message from Bette Randall.

"Charles isn't doing well. He keeps asking about you, and it would cheer him immensely if you called and gave him an update about the case you and he talked about."

I feel a flush of guilt for not having followed up with him. I skip lunch and call after I finish my scheduled pre-employment screenings. It's all I can do to keep from warning the eager-beaver applicants, all shiny-faced and enthusiastic, that police work isn't what they see on TV, all cops and robbers and heroics. But I don't because they won't believe me. They're in that nothing-bad-will-happen-to-me phase. Warning them about job-induced psychological damage is as futile as doing premarital counseling to a couple in full lust mode.

Bette answers on the first ring.

"I thought you might be his doctor. I'm glad you're not. Too much doctoring going on in our lives. Makes it hard to enjoy whatever life we have left. Hold on."

I can hear noises, voices, sounds of furniture being rearranged.

"Just a minute. He's got the damn phone cord tangled around the leg of his walker."

Dr. Randall gets on the phone; I can barely hear him.

"Here, you old fool. He's got the ear part to his mouth and the mouth part to his ear."

"Dot? Are you there?"

We go through the usual back and forth banter. I ask how he is and he tells me not to get old. He shouts at Bette to leave him in peace and asks how the case is going. I give him a short summary: everybody's lying and I don't know why.

"People lie to avoid being punished," he says. "Or to help another person. Or to control someone else. Or simply because they enjoy duping people. Some get away with it because people readily accept a certain amount of lying. For example, if you told me I was looking strong and healthy, I might not challenge you because I prefer hearing that to hearing that I'm old and decrepit."

Bette yells at him to stop talking like he was about to keel over.

"And that I married a witch."

I can't imagine how either one of these two dear people, their endless mock quarrels camouflaging the pain of sickness and the nearness of death, will survive on their own.

"The police need to do something different. Forget photo line-ups. You need drama, fireworks, an element of surprise. The line-up process is too antiseptic. Raise everyone's level of discomfort, make them afraid that whatever they're concealing, for whatever reason, is about to be exposed. Get them together. Face-to-face."

* * *

Pence isn't impressed with the face-to-face idea even after telling him I consulted with Dr. Charles Randall. Foolish me for expecting him to be impressed that I've gone way beyond the call of duty to consult a renowned expert on deception and pedophilia. And did it on my own time.

"The guy with the doodles? The one who told JoAnn Juliette not to worry about pedophiles? 'Go ahead, hang up your naked pictures of children. No problemo.'"

"It's called a facial action coding system."

"No."

"No what?"

"No face-to-face."

"Why not?"

"The last time Buzz and Bucky had a face-off, Bucky almost killed him."

"They wouldn't be alone . . ."

Pence cuts me off. "Bucky's lawyer won't let him say a word."

"He doesn't have to. His presence alone may be enough to spook Buzz into talking."

"Buzz has a broken jaw. I don't think he's talking yet." He looks at his watch. "Anything else?"

"Even if he can't talk, you can learn a lot from someone's nonverbal behavior."

"Dr. Meyerhoff." Pence enunciates his words as if he is talking to a mentally disabled deaf person who doesn't speak English. "Help Manny with his stress. Help Manny with his home life. Do whatever you can. Just don't try to work this case for him. Or for me."

* * *

By the time I get home, the evening news is on. "Thought you'd want to see this. They've been promoting it for the last half hour." Frank gives me a kiss and goes back to the kitchen. Something with curry is simmering on the stove. "You just missed your chief who announced that Bucky Stewart has been released on his own recognizance after surrendering his passport."

Suddenly the TV screen swarms with banners announcing the coming of breaking news with as much fanfare as the coming of the Messiah. A graying man in a gray suit with hair, skin, and teeth to match appears. "And now," the announcer says, "an exclusive interview with Bucky Stewart's lawyer." Hardly exclusive—there are reporters from a dozen stations mobbing the front of the police department. Their cameras clicking like angry insects.

The gray man steps to the microphone. "My client is a grieving father who was defending himself against the man he believes kidnapped and murdered his daughter. Mr. Stewart should be commended, not arrested, for identifying and trying to detain this dangerous individual. This was a job for the police, not a grieving father."

"Can we have a name?" someone shouts.

"I'll leave those kind of details up to the police. I can only say that the person currently in custody is a distant relative who has not been seen for years."

I think back to how Bucky lurched when he saw Buzz's photo. And how he lied when Manny asked him if he recognized anyone.

"We believe this individual is a methamphetamine addict whose motivation for kidnapping Chrissy was to get money to support his habit."

"Why did he kill her?"

"It is up to the police to make this determination. Are there any other questions?"

The camera reverts back to the news anchor who interrupts the briefing to announce that Chief Pence will shortly be giving a briefing of his own. Frank leaves the kitchen with instructions for me to keep an eye on the curry and not let it boil.

"I'm going to call JJ before the cops do. She doesn't have a TV. She won't know what's going on."

I stir the curry with a vengeance. Frank is back in a matter of seconds.

"I was right. She didn't know Bucky was arrested and has no idea who this other guy is." He ladles some liquid out of the pot, tastes it, pronounces it done, and turns off the burner.

"Do you think she's telling the truth?"

"Why wouldn't she?"

"Everybody involved with Chrissy seems to be lying about something."

"Lying about what? About hiring a meth addict to murder her own daughter? Jesus, Dot. Is there anybody you trust? You're worse than a cop."

He fills two bowls with rice and ladles curry on top. Drops of red liquid splash the front of his shirt.

"You don't understand JJ, never have. You don't like her photos, you don't like her relationship to me, and you don't like that I want to help her. That's all I want to do—help her; not sleep with her, not run away with her. If I've given you the wrong impression, and I don't think I have, I'm sorry."

I start to turn off the TV.

"Go ahead. Leave it on. You know you want to watch it."

He begins to eat, head down, without waiting for me to start. "Delicious," I say. He doesn't respond.

Pence steps to the podium. It's barely two hours since I saw him last and he looks as though he's had a total makeover. His hair, his clothes, all neat and pristine. Manny, wearing a sport jacket and rumpled shirt, looks like he hasn't slept in days.

"I have a brief announcement. The person of interest in custody is Bucky Stewart's half brother."

"His name," someone shouts.

"He uses several aliases. I'll let you know as soon as we determine his real name."

Another shout. "Why did he kill Chrissy?"

Pence raises his hand. "We are at the very beginning of our investigation. I can't confirm who killed Chrissy."

"Is he talking? Do you have a confession?"

"No and no. What I do have is a written request for a lawyer."

Frank refills his bowl and sits down again. I turn off the TV. The only sound in the room is our spoons, scraping against the sides of our dishes.

* * *

A cold, slick February rain is fouling traffic as I drive to headquarters the next day. I can hear the traffic team calling for backup on the scanner in my car. Directing traffic in the rain is more hazardous than chasing crooks. Nearly half of all police deaths involve vehicle accidents. I drive through an intersection. Two cars are mashed together, their snouts blunted by the impact, the drivers comfortably warm inside their vehicles, talking on their phones. A young cop, rain pouring off the plastic cover of his hat, redirects a line of growling drivers. Horns blare. The citizens of Kenilworth are on the move, getting to where they're going far more important than the welfare of anyone other than themselves. The line creeps forward. I lower my window as I pass the officer.

"Thanks. Tough duty. I appreciate it."

He doesn't take his eyes off the road and the line of cars behind me.

"Move ahead," he says. "You're blocking traffic."

I unlock the door to my office at headquarters, dripping water on the floor. I put my briefcase on the desk, hang up my raincoat, and mop my face with a wad of tissues.

"Hey, Doc." The young redheaded PIO stands in the doorway, careful not to step in my office and give anyone the impression that she needs my services. "Manny was looking for you. He's got some screaming woman in the conference room. I think he needs your help before he 5150s her to the nuthouse."

I hear her yelling before I reach the closed door to the conference room. I let myself into the observation area. Pence and Manny are at the conference table, a uniformed officer stands at the door, another stands to the left of the one-way mirror. The woman at the table is the same woman Manny and I saw when we were watching Buzz's house.

"Buzz didn't do anything. It's not his fault."

"We're not accusing you of anything, Miss . . . I'm sorry, your name again, please," Pence says.

"Finister, Brenda Finister. I'm twenty-seven years old and I live at 190 Old County Road with my common-law husband, Buzz Stewart, which is why you can't make me testify against him. And I want my phone call. And coffee."

She spits out the words like a prisoner of war: name, rank, and serial number.

"You are not under arrest, Ms. Finister. You came to us voluntarily." Pence's voice is tired. I don't know how long they've been at this. "I'd be happy to get you coffee."

The officer in front of the mirror moves toward the door.

"And a blueberry muffin. I'm hungry."

Her eyes flicker around the room.

"Is that one of those one-way mirrors? Is somebody watching me?" She half rises out of her seat. "Is it you, Buzz? I love you, baby." She kisses the tips of her fingers and flicks them at the mirror. The black hoodie sweatshirt she's wearing falls open and I can see her wasted torso under a baggy pink tank top. Her hair is matted and her once tiny nose flattened into a smudge.

"No one's looking at you, Ms. Finister. Please continue." Manny hunches forward.

"Is she behind that thing?"

"Is who behind that thing?"

"I want my coffee and my muffin." Brenda crosses and uncrosses her legs. Her jeans ride up, revealing scrawny, scratched legs.

The door opens and the officer returns with a paper cup of coffee and a muffin wrapped in plastic. He sets it in front of Brenda and digs in his pocket for a handful of sugar packets, three small capsules of fake milk, and some paper napkins. Finister empties four packets of sugar into her coffee and tries to unwrap the muffin with shaky hands.

"May I?" Manny says. He unwraps the muffin and puts it in front of her on a paper napkin.

"Buzz called her Mother Teresa. She worried about me and Buzz. Tried to get us to go to rehab."

"Who did he call Mother Teresa?" I can hear a wedge of irritation in Pence's voice. Under the table, Brenda's tiny feet are pedaling an invisible bicycle.

"More coffee?" Manny says.

"Later. Maybe."

"We appreciate your cooperation. Your willingness to help us identify the person who murdered Chrissy. It's very helpful." Brenda looks at Manny as though he's speaking a foreign language. Praise is not something I imagine she has heard much of in her life. "This person you referred to as Mother Teresa . . ." He makes air quotes with his hands. "What's her real name?"

"I don't want to get anyone in trouble."

Pence rolls his eyes. "I thought you want to get your boyfriend out of trouble. You're not going to help him if you don't give us a name."

"He's not my boyfriend. He's my common-law husband."

Pence comes at her like a barking dog.

"Frankly, lady, I don't care if you're brother and sister. If you want to help him, you're going to have to give us names."

Brenda jerks and raises her hands in front of her face as though she's going to be hit. Manny leans in. "He's not going to hurt you. He's just asking you to give us some names."

Good cop, bad cop. I can't tell if he and Manny planned this or if Pence is running out of patience.

Brenda moves her chair closer to Manny. She cups one hand next to his ear and whispers loud enough for the rest of us to hear. "I'm not talking if he's in the room. Only you."

Manny glances at Pence and flicks his eyes at the door. Pence stands.

"I could use a break. I'll be back in a while."

Manny cocks his head at the other two officers, and they follow. Brenda waits until all three men are out the door.

"He's mean. He makes me nervous."

"He makes a lot of people nervous." Manny laughs. Brenda looks at him, checking his reaction to see if she should laugh, too. This is a woman who feels her way forward, never makes a move without first testing the waters. And even that doesn't guarantee that a fist or a foot won't fly out of nowhere.

"Let's change the subject. Tell me about Chrissy."

Brenda shrugs. "Can I have some more coffee first? I'm cold."

"Sure," he says. "Maybe even a sandwich?"

"I'm not hungry. Just coffee."

The minute Manny leaves the room, Brenda starts pawing through the pockets of her sweatshirt. She throws back her head and swallows whatever she's found. The effect is almost immediate. The muscles of her face loosen and she releases a long breath, as calm and content as the Mona Lisa.

Pence comes into the observation room. He looks tired and frustrated.

"Brenda just swallowed something when Manny left the room," I say. "Probably a downer."

"Manny left the room? What in hell is he thinking about?" He sits heavily. "I'm bushed. Maybe I should ask Ms. Finister if I can borrow some of her uppers. She's playing us. Playing Manny. She's a hype. After something. They all are. She better catch on quick. This is a tit for tat game. We give her something, she gives us something back."

"Like a blueberry muffin in exchange for information that could send her and her husband to jail? Not a particularly appealing deal."

"She's pulling his leg. Two hours. Not a minute longer. If he hasn't got something we can use in two hours, I'm going to pull more than his leg."

The door to the observation room opens. Manny sticks his head in and gives us the thumbs-up.

Pence gives him a thumbs-down. "This is going nowhere. She's wasting our time. When you left the room, she downed a handful of drugs. She's getting ready to nod off. She won't open up. She's loaded."

Manny's eyes move from me to Pence and back again. He presses his fingernails into the palms of his hands. It's stifling in this tiny room. And rank with the stink of anger.

"She needs more time," Manny says.

"We haven't got more time," Pence hisses between clenched teeth.

I hiss back. "Brenda is an abused woman. Probably been abused all her life. She won't talk until she trusts. And trust doesn't come easy to a woman like this. Don't try to force her." I turn to the mirror. Brenda is asleep, her arms folded on the table and her head resting on her arms like a schoolchild during nap time. "I don't know what she swallowed. Maybe a downer, maybe an aspirin. Whatever it is, she feels safe enough, at least for the moment, to take a nap. I suggest you both do the same. Take a break. Do something to clear your heads and calm your minds. Anything but drink coffee."

Brenda is still sleeping when Manny gets back to the conference room, her battered face in repose. He sets the coffee on the table. She stirs, sits up, and looks around. It takes her a minute to remember where she is. Manny smiles. He looks relaxed. The stage is set, just two old friends talking over coffee. Nothing threatening. Nothing to be worried about. He takes a sip. Brenda follows.

"Sorry I fell asleep."

"You're tired. It's okay. I got a little shut-eye myself. My mother used to call it a catnap." He's enticing her with small personal tidbits in the hopes that she'll respond with revelations of her own. He takes a second sip of coffee. Brenda watches him like a hawk. This kind of friendly exchange with a police officer is new territory. "Before you fell asleep, you were starting to tell me about Chrissy. I'd like to know more about her."

"Not much to say. We couldn't get near her. Bucky didn't want anything to do with us. Treated us like dirt. Never wanted us around."

"Are you saying you never met Chrissy?"

"I didn't say I never met her." She tears up and pinches at the mouth. "Are you going to question everything I say? I can't always say stuff right."

"Not a problem. We can come back to this later. No rush."

She pouts and shoves her hands deep in her pockets. "I have to go to the bathroom."

Manny watches her hands. "We're almost through here. You can go in a minute."

"I'm going to pee my pants."

"Who broke your nose? I know it's broken, I can see it. Nothing to be ashamed about. And it's not your fault. I know he hits you. I saw him when I was watching your house."

She stiffens.

"I shouldn't tell you this, but I will because I know you're being up front with me. The reason I was watching your house is because we're pretty sure Buzz is involved in Chrissy's murder." She backs up in her chair. "Let me be perfectly clear. I'm talking about Buzz. Not you. I don't think you had anything to do with it. Or if you did, I bet Buzz forced you to get involved. I can help you. If you're afraid of him, I'll take you to a safe place."

"I need to go to the bathroom." Brenda stands, stumbles, and sits down again. "I can't go to the bathroom?"

Manny shakes his head as though it pains him to refuse her request. "Sorry," he says. "When we're finished talking."

And now the tantrum she was working on comes to fruition. She knots her hands. Bangs on the arms of her chair. Her bottom jaw juts forward. She kicks at the table leg and then folds forward, her back quivering with sobs. I can see her hands fumbling at her pants pockets. She appears to be talking to herself.

"I can't hear you." Manny taps her gently on the shoulder.

She sits up. Her eyes are dry. "All we had to do was watch Chrissy for a few days because bad things were happening to her."

"What kind of bad things?"

"They were doing things to her and taking pictures while they did it. Sex things. I wasn't going to let that happen. She's only a baby."

"Who was doing bad things to her?"

Brenda flings her arms wide, knocking hot coffee into Manny's lap. He howls and starts frantically pawing at his groin. The minute his back is turned, Brenda swallows a handful of pills.

"Sorry," she mumbles. "Are you okay?" Her head is turned to the wall. She is so thin I can see the muscles in her neck distend as she swallows whatever is still in her hand.

Manny's face is the color of old plums. He grits his teeth.

"I'm fine. Would you turn around, please?"

Brenda turns. Her face a frozen grimace. The pupils of her eyes glinting like glass marbles.

Manny gestures for her to sit and lowers himself gently into his chair.

"Let's continue."

"At first it went perfect. But when I tried to feed her, she wouldn't eat and she started to cry."

"Who took her from her bed? Was it you? Was it Buzz?"

"Buzz didn't want to at first, but when she offered money for rehab, he changed his mind. Said we could start over."

"Who offered money?"

"She just kept crying, and I couldn't make her stop. We tried everything. We let her crawl around the house, go anywhere she wanted, but she wouldn't stop crying. So we put her in a room and locked the door. For safety. In the morning, when I got up, I went into her room first thing because I knew she'd be hungry. She didn't move. Her little hands and feet were cold and her face was a funny color." Brenda waves her hands in the air as though trying to bat away the terrible raw memory. "Buzz said we shouldn't tell anyone because it wasn't our fault. And we needed to go to rehab. I said she wouldn't pay because Chrissy was dead, and Buzz said she would if we helped her get rid of Chrissy and not tell anyone she was involved."

"Please, Brenda. *Who* wouldn't pay?"

"She loved Chrissy more than anything."

Manny's body inflates as if he's going to explode. He looks toward us, through the mirror, like a tympanist waiting for the conductor to signal that now, this moment and not any other, is the time to bring down his mallets. Pence scoots to the front of his seat, his hands against the mirror. I hold my breath.

Manny takes Brenda by the hands. "I'm going to ask once more. Tell me who you're talking about. If you don't or can't, I'm going to leave the room. You'll never see me again. You'll see plenty of cops. You'll see Chief Pence, but you won't see me."

"Why not?"

"Because the chief is going to fire me if I can't get you to tell me who you're talking about. I have a baby daughter. About the same age as Chrissy. I need this job."

CHAPTER NINETEEN

No one really knows why an abused woman fiercely protects her abuser. Why she confuses enduring pain with commitment. Self-sacrifice with love. How desperately hungry, yet so coiled with a sense of unworthiness, she must be to fall for the delusion that a cruel relationship is better than none.

"I don't want to get anyone in trouble."

"You're a kind person. I get that."

"I don't want to get you fired."

"I'll make sure everyone knows how you helped me."

"You won't tell that I told on her?"

Manny slices his finger across his lips. "Zippo lippo."

Brenda sways. Her eyes wander aimlessly around the room. She grasps the edge of the table to steady herself and inhales deeply.

"She's the only one in the family that ever treated us nice. Like we were her kids. She never had her own, you know."

"Who is the only one that treated you nicely?"

"Kathryn." Manny's body buckles, just slightly. "You won't tell her I told. I had to help. What Kathryn said was happening to Chrissy was horrible."

Manny draws a deep breath and forces himself up in his chair.

"Of course, you did."

"Me and Buzz. We had to."

"Kathryn put you in a very bad situation."

"We had to do something. Kathryn can't climb a fire escape."

Brenda pushes her chair back from the table.

"How much did Kathryn pay you and Buzz to take Chrissy?"

Brenda swings into high dudgeon. "I didn't do it for money. I did it for Chrissy. And to go to rehab."

"Why did you give Chrissy meth?"

Her eyes go wide. She starts to panic at the familiar smell of betrayal in her nostrils.

"I never . . . I wouldn't give a baby meth."

"There was meth in her system when she died. If you didn't give it to her, who did?"

She starts to hyperventilate, sucking air in great noisy gulps.

"Is that how you tried to stop her crying? By giving her meth?"

Brenda pushes out of her chair, sending it squeaking and squealing across the room. "Motherfucker. You want to send me to jail so you can keep your fucking job. I came here to help you and you're going to send me to jail." She twists in a rage, screaming and banging her head against the wall. Her forehead splits open, spraying blood everywhere. She claws at her face. Manny reaches to stop her and backs away. An addict's blood can be deadly. Pence charges out of the observation room, yelling for help. By the time the medics arrive in their protective gear, Brenda has battered herself into unconsciousness.

* * *

Pence has his raincoat on and is ready to leave the building by the time Manny gets back from the psych ward at the county hospital. He looks exhausted. The both of them have been working for almost fifteen hours straight. "The ER doc put Brenda on a seventy-two-hour hold."

Pence puts his briefcase down. Rain is hammering against his office window, car lights moving like fingerpainting over the glass. "Did the doc check you out?"

"She gave me a shot and some pills. I'll know in six weeks if I picked anything up."

"I should never have left you alone with her."

"You didn't have a choice. She wasn't going to talk with you in the room."

"Do you believe Brenda?" I say to Manny. "Is Kathryn behind Chrissy's death?"

The chief steps in front of me. "Brenda is a stone-cold addict. I don't believe anything she says. Neither will a jury."

"Why would she lie about her and Buzz kidnapping Chrissy if it wasn't true?"

"You're the psychologist," Pence says. "I don't know why addicts do what they do. I just know you can't trust them. Brenda's looking to pin the blame on someone. Kathryn's an easy mark."

Manny moves forward. "Supposing it is true, Doc. Why would Kathryn get mixed up with these two ass-hat tweakers? What does she have to gain by getting them to kidnap Chrissy? And why kill her?"

"I have a theory," I say, "but you'll need to give me a minute."

"Take your time," says Pence sweeping his arm in a circle, making a big show of looking at his watch. "Sixty seconds and counting."

There's something I want to say, but how can I say it without laying myself bare? Do I want Pence and Manny to know how I know what it's like to lose your husband to a younger woman? Do I want them to know that I understand how two people can pretend to be content not having children, can convince themselves that they are enough for each other? How do I describe the pain I felt when the man I married, who swore he didn't want children, didn't have time for children, started a family with someone else?

"Your sixty seconds are up." Pence puts his hand on my shoulder. "You okay? You got quiet all of a sudden." He and Manny flash eyes at each other, unwitting companions traveling in the emotionally volatile world of women.

I take a deep breath. "Bucky's a man who's used to getting what he wants. What he wants is JJ and Chrissy. JJ's self-sufficiency is an elixir. The more she pulls away, the more he wants her. Kathryn has tried hard to convince everyone that Bucky's love for Chrissy, his affair with JJ, and the fact that she and Bucky have no children of their own doesn't matter and doesn't threaten their marriage. She's been good at lying to us, especially me, but I guarantee that if you put her in a room with her husband, face-to-face, she's going to find it much harder to lie to herself."

* * *

For whatever reason, Pence has included me in the meeting with Kathryn and Bucky. Maybe he's merely taking advantage of the fact that I'm the only female in the department old enough to empathize with Kathryn Blazek's state of infertility.

We're sitting in Bucky Stewart's living room. Coming here was Pence's idea of a suitable and comfortable environment for a face-to-face meeting. The entry hall and the living room are filled with oversized furniture, gleaming metals, and enormous abstract paintings by famous artists. Hand-blown glass fixtures the size of small helicopters descend from twelve-foot-high ceilings. Kathryn is seated on an Italian-made red leather sectional sofa. A modern silver tea service sits in front of her on a chrome and glass coffee table big enough to stage a ping-pong tournament. She's wearing a cashmere sweater set, tailored slacks, and a bracelet of thick gold links. Bucky, dressed for business in a pinstriped suit and silk tie, is seated on the shorter section, his face and hers at right angles. Pence, Manny, and I are in separate chairs covered in glove-soft off-white leather.

Pence begins. "I appreciate your meeting with us without your attorney."

"Not my idea." Bucky crosses his legs.

"Of course," Kathryn says. "Anything to help."

"As you know, Mr. Stewart, we are holding your half brother, Buzz, in custody. We've been unable to interview him because of the damage to his jaw." Bucky's face remains static. "On the other hand, we have learned some things from his common-law wife, Brenda Finister."

Bucky flicks a thread off the cuff of his jacket. "Never met her."

Kathryn's spine stiffens slightly.

"Ms. Finister said some things about you, Ms. Blazek, that caused us concern. We'd like to share them with you. Give you the opportunity to comment."

"Was she sober?" Kathryn's voice is dispassionate, scientific. "It's hard to believe anything she says when she's under the influence." Bucky's eyes cut in her direction and then back to Pence. Kathryn settles against the sofa in studied casualness, barely interested in Pence's response.

"That's why we're here, Ms. Blazek. She said some things we found hard to believe."

Kathryn's fingers play across her bracelet as though it is a string of worry beads.

Bucky leans forward. "I don't understand. I haven't seen my half brother for years until the other day. I didn't even know he was married."

"I'm curious how you found him, given that you haven't seen him in years."

Bucky looks at Pence as though Pence has just woken up. "I have a staff. They have computers. Their computers have search engines. Should I continue?"

There's a tiny twitch under Pence's right eye.

"Why is it that you and your half brother are estranged?" I ask. If Pence wants me here, I'm going to participate.

Bucky releases a loud, impatient sigh, letting us all know that he is not used to suffering fools. "My half brother, by my father, is an unrepentant addict whose only interest in life is his next fix. He lies. He steals. He broke my parents' hearts."

Pence interrupts. "Ms. Finister suggested that you, Ms. Blazek, masterminded Chrissy's abduction."

Kathryn has a small, involuntary spasm in her neck, hardly more than a tick. I wonder if an innocent person, accused of such a terrible crime, would be so calm and composed.

"You didn't believe her, did you? She's an addict. Unstable. Quite a torment. So is Buzz." She sighs. "Me, masterminding anything? That's amusing. But hurting my beloved Chrissy? Unthinkable."

Pence pauses for dramatic effect. "Ms. Blazek, did you tell Ms. Finister that Chrissy was being abused by her mother and that she and Buzz needed to abduct her to save her?"

"Wait a fucking minute!" Bucky jerks his arm away from Kathryn. "What are you implying? Do I need my attorney here?" He starts to get up, changes his mind, and swivels to face his wife. "Is this true? Have you been talking to Buzz? He's dead to me and you know it. I don't want anything to do with him and I don't want you to have anything to do with him."

She smiles. Something between a hostess-with-the-mostess smile and a hand-caught-in-the-cookie-jar grin.

"Have you been talking to him? Answer me. Now."

"Please don't be upset. I know he's been a tribulation to you, but he's family. You can't cut family off. I've never felt right about that. I've kept tabs on him for years. I help out when I can. Sometimes he and Brenda don't have enough to eat. I can't live with that." She looks at me. "That's what I was doing at the Dollar Store, Dr. Meyerhoff. Buying them cigarettes and food. I'm sorry I lied to you."

"He's a junkie. He's been to every rehab in California. Nothing works." Bucky's face is flush.

"I had hoped that one day he would go into recovery and we could welcome him back into the family."

"You're a fool. A goddamn fool." Bucky bats her hand away and sits heavily, head in hands.

Kathryn turns to Pence. "Amphetamine produces paranoia. I'm sure you know that. How can you possibly believe anything that Brenda says? She's delusional and paranoid. And easily intimidated. She would tell you anything to help Buzz."

She turns back to Bucky. "I'm so sorry. I was just trying to help. I can't stand seeing people suffer." She crumples forward until her head covers her knees. She appears to be crying. I can't see her face, but I can see that she needs a touch-up to cover the gray roots in her burnished auburn hair.

"Fuck." Bucky slaps himself on the leg.

Kathryn sits up. Her cheeks are dry. "I know what you think. All of you. Stepmothers are evil. Everyone has read Cinderella and Snow White. We're practically iconic." She crosses her hands over her heart, defending herself against our as yet unspoken accusations. "If I'm guilty of anything, it's being naive. Brenda and Buzz like to tease me. Say they are going to kidnap Chrissy. They would play at guessing how much money Bucky would pay to get her back. One million. Two million. A billion. And then they would talk about how they were going to spend the money. Open a restaurant. Go to Kathmandu. Stay high for a year. They were joking. I never thought they were serious."

She looks to Bucky for confirmation, some visual evidence that he believes her. He remains still as a stone, staring at the wall.

"But now that I think of it, sometimes they joked about kidnapping in front of their friends. They're all addicts. Maybe one of them got the idea and took Chrissy. Oh, God. Bucky, what have I done?" She reaches for him and he swings hard. His wedding ring catches her cheek. Blood zigzags down her face. She sinks back, covering her head with her arms. He dives at her and they struggle, flailing at each other until Manny pulls Bucky away and pushes him into a chair. He sits, arms wrapped around his middle, shaking his head and spraying tears.

"Why didn't you contact us?" Manny turns to Kathryn. "Tell us about Buzz and Brenda."

She's whimpering. Patting her cheek. "They're addicts. They lie about everything. They belong in a hospital. I thought they were just making some sick joke to upset me. I never thought they would go through with it. Take me to see them. They'll tell you I thought they were only joking."

"Why didn't you tell us about them after Chrissy went missing?"

The front of Kathryn's cashmere sweater is muddy with blood and mascara. A huge bruise is starting to show on her face. She wheels back around toward Bucky. "This is not my fault, Bucky. I asked you to put a security guard on Chrissy. Repeatedly. Don't you remember? But you refused because JJ thought it was unnecessary. And oppressive."

Bucky struggles to his feet as though he were hefting a thousand-pound weight.

"Why did you listen to her and not to me?"

Bucky starts for the door.

"Don't you dare walk out on me. I'm your wife."

Bucky turns around. He has aged twenty years in less than twenty minutes.

"Chrissy's dead. Nothing else matters."

"I matter. Me. I matter," Kathryn howls at Bucky's back. A long, doleful caterwaul that bounces off the ceiling and the walls.

CHAPTER TWENTY

Buzz is groaning as we walk into his hospital room. His face is a mass of bruises.

"Milking it for everything it's worth," Manny says under his breath. "Trying to get the nurse to bring him more dope." He smiles. "Hey, Buzz. How you doing? Thought I'd come by to congratulate you on getting unwired."

"Where's Brenda?"

"Not to worry, man. She's getting good care at the county psych ward."

"County? What'd the bitch do now?"

"Nice to know you're so concerned about her welfare. She took a bunch of pills. Had to have her stomach pumped before she got 5150'd. The doc took some X-rays. Told me he found a couple of old broken ribs and a broken nose. Know anything about that?"

"Clumsy skank. Gets loaded. Falls a lot." He looks at me. "Who's this?"

"My name's Dr. Dot Meyerhoff. I'm the department psychologist. I'm just here to observe."

"Him or me?" He laughs. His teeth are a jumble of blackened stubs.

"And I'm Jay Pence. Chief of Police."

"Whoa. The police chief and a psychologist? I must be one badass crazy motherfucker."

“I got somebody else with me who wants to say hello.” Manny opens the door for Kathryn. She’s still dressed in her blood-spattered sweater set. Her face, bare of foundation and blushers, is lined and blotchy with age spots.

“What the fuck? Look who’s here. Mother of the year.” Buzz starts to clap, slowly, one clap after another in mock applause.

“Hello, Buzz,” Kathryn says, her voice coated with maternal honey. “How are you doing? I feel terrible about what Bucky’s done to you. So does he. I hope you can understand. He’s been out of his mind with grief.”

Buzz laughs. More like a cackle.

“I wanted to check in on you earlier, but the investigation into Chrissy’s death has me so upset. The police have been talking to Brenda. She’s made some horrific accusations against you and me. I was hoping we could straighten this out.”

Buzz’s mouth is half hidden in shadows cast by his sharply angled cheekbones.

“Really? How you gonna do that?”

“I’ve told the police that you and Brenda couldn’t have done this terrible thing. That it was probably one of your friends who knew that you had a rich relative who had a little daughter. Please tell them who that might be so they can investigate.”

“I don’t have any friends. Brenda and me. We don’t socialize much.”

Kathryn looks panicked. She’s handed Buzz an out, and he’s thrown it back in her face.

“Of course you have friends. Don’t be ridiculous.”

Buzz counts on his fingers. “I got suppliers, customers, and tweaker buddies who want to steal my shit and fuck everything in sight.”

"Is it possible that maybe one of those people wanted to, you know, have sex with Chrissy?" She looks as if she can barely stand to say the words.

"Yeah. Probably. They'd have sex with the refrigerator if the door was open. Problem is they're so busy fucking and tweaking, they couldn't sit still long enough to kidnap anyone who wasn't sitting on their lap."

Manny steps closer to Buzz's bed. "So who did it? You? Brenda? The two of you?"

"Brenda's not well. She's delusional, you know how she can be, don't you, Buzz? What she says is not reliable." Kathryn's breathing through her nose, her nostrils moving in and out like tiny bellows.

Buzz shrugs. "Sometimes she is, sometimes she isn't."

"I'm listening," Manny says. "Talk to me and things will go better for you. The DA likes a cooperative witness."

"You shitting me? I ain't no witness. I'm a suspect."

"Buzzy." Kathryn steps to the side of his bed and gingerly lays her hand on the pillow next to his scabby face. "It's the dope that makes you do things. Don't say anything. Anything you do or say under the influence doesn't count. I suggest you be quiet until I get you a lawyer."

"That ship has sailed, baby. We're all screwed."

"I'm going to help you. Just give me a little time. In the meantime, the less said, the better for everyone." She puts her finger to her lips like a mother hushing her child.

"Fuck that." Buzz sweeps the sheets back. His body barely more than a scarred skeleton. He reaches for Kathryn. She skitters away, grabs my arm, and wedges herself behind me as though I could protect her. Manny pushes Buzz back onto the bed. He rolls on his side. "I'm done with you, bitch. I'm done with my whole fucking life.

They can take me to jail, I don't give a shit. I have a crap life. And it's going to get worse. Why prolong the misery?"

Kathryn brings her face close to my ear. "He's irrational. You can see that, right? Probably high on some drugs as we speak."

"I'm not going to wait for you to set me and Brenda up. Let you tell everyone you had nothing to do with it."

"I didn't have anything to do with it, you have to believe me."

"Bullshit." Buzz cups his hands around his mouth like he's holding a megaphone. "Hey. Who wants to hear what I got to say?"

"At your service," Manny says stepping to the side of the bed. "I'm all ears. But first, just to be on the safe side . . ." He pulls a card out of his pocket and reads Buzz his rights.

"Don't listen to him." Kathryn pitches into a shriek. "He's crazy. He'd say anything. Remember what Bucky said about him? He lies, he steals."

Pence moves to her side. "Perhaps it's time for you to take a break. Let Manny do his work. We can straighten all this out later." He places his hand on Kathryn's back and propels her toward the door. I can hear her arguing with him, her voice getting louder and louder as he pushes her down the hall.

"My brother been saying shit behind my back? *Que sorpresa*. He's hated me all my life. I'm scum to him, and he don't even know the half of it." Buzz struggles to sit up again, pulling his hospital gown down to his waist as he twists in the sheets. "First the bitch gives us a pile of dough and tells us to snatch Bucky's kid out of her bed and keep her for twenty-four hours. What the fuck did she think we were going to do with all that money? Put it in the bank? Sign up for rehab?"

"What did you do?" Manny asks.

"What'd you think? We got glassed on some quality ice. Fucking amazing run."

"Why did Kathryn want you to take Chrissy?"

"Dunno. She got Brenda all in a fit saying Chrissy was being abused by her mother. Brenda'd believe anything." He turns on his side, wincing. "Chrissy's mother is a good-looking bitch. You ever seen her?" He stretches. Winces again. "If my old man was boning a chick like that, I'd be green, too."

"They didn't have a current relationship," I say.

Buzz looks at me as if he'd forgotten I was in the room. "You a psychologist? You don't know fucking A about people." He sits up higher. "I ain't as stupid as I look, Doc. I'm a doper, not a dope."

"You're doing great," Manny says.

"I don't worry about Brenda cheating. The only man she wants is me. And nobody wants her old bag of broken bones. Not after what I done to her." He flicks his head away but not before I see some emotion splash across his face. He waits a minute and turns back to Manny.

"Brenda goes where I take her. She don't have a mind of her own. She's in trouble because she follows me. She needs treatment. She's got mental problems. Depression. Nervosity. Drugs and alcohol. The whole shebang. I talk to you, you got to help her."

Manny looks down at him. "I can try. But it's not always in my control. The DA decides what charges to press."

"All she did was follow me. I did it for the money. She did it because she's a sucker for anything that's abused—kids, cats, dogs, it don't matter."

"I'll do what I can, I just can't promise."

Buzz shrugs. "After we took the baby, we got loaded like I said. The baby was crying like she was sick or hungry or something. She mighta ate some of our stash. We put her in a room to keep her quiet. By the time we found her, she was dead."

"What did you do next?"

"Called Kathryn. She went bonkers. Said we were going to go to jail for murder. I told her to calm down. It was an accident. Not the same as murder. Anyone can have an accident. Shit happens."

"Who decided how to dispose of the body?"

"Kathryn came over. Looked at the baby."

"Was she upset, crying, did she try to hold her?" I ask. I can't imagine how it feels to see a beloved child dead. I don't even want to try.

"She's one coldhearted bitch. I cried harder over a dead dog I once had."

I lean in so close that I can smell his rotting teeth through the mouthwash he's been drinking. "Were you sober? Are you sure you are remembering things accurately?"

"I got to tell you, lady, there's nothing like finding a dead baby in my house to sober me the fuck up."

Manny gives me a look. He wants me to back off. "So then what happened?" he asks.

"Kathryn pulls out a bag of makeup and starts putting it on the baby . . ." He can't say Chrissy's name. "Makes her up like a hooker so everybody will think some porno dude took her. Says there's a whole task force looking for kiddie fiddlers, why not give 'em what they're looking for?"

"Where's Brenda during this?"

"Hysterical. Hiding in the bedroom. She couldn't watch."

"Who put Chrissy in the dumpster?"

"That bitch asked me to put the body in a dumpster behind where the mother lives."

"And did you?"

"Absolutely not. Brenda and me. We were finished with this caper. We cooked up some more crank and went to bed."

* * *

Pence and Kathryn are still at it in the hall by the time we finish with Buzz. The minute she sees me and Manny, she charges toward us.

"What did he tell you? He's a born liar, you know. You can't believe anything he says."

"Then why are you interested?"

"I need to know what lies he's telling you about me."

"So you can what, tell lies about him?" Manny's starting to lose his equilibrium, like a runner growing more impatient the closer he comes to the finish line.

"Did he tell you I gave him money?"

Manny nods his head.

"What did he say I gave him money for?"

"To kidnap Chrissy."

"Oh, God." She crushes her face into a handkerchief, then wipes her eyes before I can see if she has any tears to be wiped. She sucks in air, bracing herself. "I need to tell you something. Please forgive me, but I haven't been entirely honest with you. And I certainly couldn't say what I'm about to say in front of Bucky. I did give them money. For rehabilitation. And when I began to be suspicious that they were planning this horrible thing . . ." She takes another deep breath. "I gave them money *not* to kidnap Chrissy." She checks our faces for reactions. "I'm being totally honest with you. I am so ashamed of myself. I told them I'd give them whatever money they needed so they didn't have to resort to such an unthinkable act."

"So you knew all along what they were planning." Manny starts to pull out his Miranda card.

"I thought I'd bought them off. I never thought they'd go through with it. I may be a fool, but I'm not guilty of hurting my beloved Chrissy."

"Buzz says you were instrumental in moving her body."

Kathryn stiffens. Her eyes narrow and her lips compress, pulling at the spidery lines around her mouth.

"And you believe them? There is no evidence, none, to tie me to any part of this despicable act. I loved my stepdaughter, I would never hurt her. I am a respected citizen with no criminal background, not even a parking ticket. There's something very wrong if you're taking the word of two mentally disturbed drug addicts over mine." Once again, she dabs at her eyes with her handkerchief. "Are we finished here? I need to call my lawyer. And my husband, if Buzz and Brenda haven't destroyed my marriage with their insinuations. Where's the elevator?" She looks around. "Where's the bathroom?"

Before we respond, she marches down the hall following the signs toward the public restrooms. Her shoes slap against the floor in righteous indignation. As soon as she rounds the corner, Manny says, "She's right, we don't have a shred of physical evidence."

"You have the blanket she bought," I say.

"JJ has the same blanket, so could half of East Kenilworth."

"Buzz knew about the makeup. The one detail that never got into the press."

"That doesn't connect Kathryn to the scene, only Buzz."

* * *

I find Kathryn in the public bathroom washing her face over the sink. She gives a theatrical sigh when she sees me. "Are you following me? What did you think I was doing in here, planning my next murder?"

"Sorry, I have to pee."

She snorts and closes her eyes. "Whatever. No need to be graphic."

By the time I leave the stall, she's carefully applying concealer over her skin. I wash my hands.

"I'm going to try to get Bucky to meet me." She takes a long breath. "I don't know if he'll ever forgive me. Or how I'm going to forgive myself for being so naive. I run boards, I have a business background, you'd think I would know when people were lying to my face." She looks at herself, examining her so-easily-lied-to face in great detail.

I watch as she smooths foundation over spidery clusters of broken capillaries and the shadowy circles under her eyes.

"Good makeup hides a multitude of sins. I could use something like that myself," I say.

She looks at me, not sure if I've complimented or insulted her. This is how narcissists act. Filled with inflated importance, they accept praise as their just due at the same moment they are fearfully sussing out hidden criticisms.

"This is hardly the time to be discussing cosmetics. I've been probed and prodded all day by people who think I'm guilty of the most heinous crime imaginable."

"I'm sorry. That was very insensitive of me. It's just that . . ." And now I'm riding the crest of my own narcissistic injury. I should get back in therapy, but I can't face telling a thirty-year-old shrink whose parents paid her way through college about how my ex dumped me for a younger woman.

"Are you worried about getting old, Kathryn?" She turns around so that I'm no longer talking to her reflection. "I know what it's like trying to hang on to someone you love who seems to love you less every day." She looks pleased. Nothing more satisfying than discovering that the acclaimed shrink and author of several books who has been persecuting you has emotional hot spots no different than yours.

"If you know how I feel, why are you tormenting me?"

I grab the memory by its tail. Shove it back where it belongs.

"I loved Chrissy with all my heart. How can you think I killed her?"

"Because you love Bucky more."

There's a twitch on her upper eyelid, and the muscles around her jaw go slack. I can hear just the tiniest puff of air leave her lungs. It's the look all therapists are after. Visceral evidence that they've struck pay dirt.

She turns back to the mirror.

"I get this at a spa. They make it exclusively for their clients. You can't buy it in a department store." She hands me the bottle of concealer. "I'm sorry I can't let you try it. It's mixed especially for my skin tones and reacts to my unique chemistry."

"Thank you," I say with sincerity. "You've been very helpful."

CHAPTER TWENTY-ONE

I GO BACK to the coroner's office where JJ and Bucky identified Chrissy's body. I sit in the same room and talk to the same medical examiner's investigator with the same cotton-candy hair wearing the same dark business suit. She kindly, but vaguely, remembers me.

"You are a friend of the family's and you also work for the police department? Do I have that straight? How can I help you?"

"When you showed the parents Chrissy's photo, her face was washed clean. I know that when her body was found, she was made up like a grown woman. What I want to know is whether or not the coroner kept any samples of the makeup before Chrissy's face was washed." She refuses to answer my question. I call Manny on his cell, promise to explain myself as soon as I get back to the department and ask him to authorize the investigator to talk to me. She takes the phone, nods a few times, and hands it back to me.

"The coroner did preserve some samples in case the police wanted to test them chemically. It's possible to separate the oils and waxes in lipstick from the remaining residue and analyze the molecular structure using gas chromatography. This gives you the unique formula of that particular brand of lipstick. Same for makeup. Liquid makeup especially." She opens her notebook and flips through several pages. "When you apply makeup on a deceased individual, it is like applying it to a waxed surface. It takes a lot to cover the surface properly. We have several samples on hand. It is possible to compare and contrast makeup formulas, although it would be very labor intensive considering the number of cosmetic companies and the number of products they offer. It would cut down considerably on the investigation if this were a rare cosmetic not widely available for sale."

Exactly what I was hoping she'd say. I thank her profusely and head out with the good news. She stops me at the door.

"I rarely get involved emotionally with the bodies we examine. I'm sure as a psychologist you can understand the need for me to keep my distance in order to do my job properly. But I do remember this case. I remember looking at Chrissy and thinking that whoever applied that horrid makeup did so carefully. With love."

* * *

"What do you want me to do?" Pence says to me. "Ask a judge to issue a warrant to search Kathryn's house for mascara?"

"Call the spa."

"And say what? They're not going to turn in a client. And I don't have any jurisdiction in Southern California. I could ask my wife to go down there. Undercover. Maybe they could do something for her." He looks at Manny, hoping for a laugh at his beleaguered man joke. Manny manages only the barest grimace.

Pence's phone rings. He picks it up.

"When was the last time you went home, Manny?" I ask.

"I can't remember."

"And when's Lupe's deadline?"

"Four days ago."

"Go home," I say. "I'll write you a doctor's note prescribing a five-day extension."

"You can't go home," Pence says hanging up the phone. "We've found Bucky. He's at JJ's commune. So is Kathryn."

* * *

I head for Frank's. I've seen him about as frequently as Manny has seen Lupe. Sneaking into bed next to a sleeping body who barely manages to acknowledge my presence with a snort before rolling over back to sleep is not my idea of quality time. But tonight I'm early enough to find him at the dining table cleaning his camera lenses.

"Do I know you?" he says.

"In the biblical sense. On rare occasions."

He makes a grab for me. I duck and run into the kitchen, babbling over my shoulder about having to make an important phone call that can't wait.

* * *

Whoever answers the telephone at the Belle Aqua de la Vida spa is exceptionally happy I called. When I tell her I'm a friend of Kathryn Blazek's this makes her even happier. Close to giddy. I ask if I can take her into my confidence. Her name is Miki, with an I. She assures me that when it comes to keeping secrets, she is a perfectionist. I tell her that Kathryn's birthday is coming up and a few of her friends want to surprise her with a basket of her favorite Belle Aqua de la Vida cosmetics. I wonder if Miki could text me a list of Kathryn's custom-formulated items so that we could choose what to order.

"Absolutely, right away," she says, dismissing whatever plans she had for the evening in lieu of creating a gift list with some additional suggestions from their newest line of argan oil, urea, and Dead Sea minerals. Argan oil, she croons, comes from the nut of a tree grown only in Morocco and used as a dipping sauce for bread.

I know where urea comes from and don't want to embarrass her by asking about the benefits of massaging pee into my face. Ditto for the youth-promoting properties of an ancient sea so salty nothing can live in it but bacteria and microbial fungi. "It really works," Miki, the guardian of secrets, says. "Miss Kathryn has been using our product line for years, That's why you'd never guess she's in her sixties."

Frank is leaning in the doorway to the kitchen looking at me when I hang up. "Why are you ordering cosmetics for Kathryn Blazek?"

"We have to go to JJ's. She's going to need you. I'll explain in the car."

* * *

Frank slams both hands on the steering wheel. "Kathryn? And the guy who bought Maldonado's truck? So JJ's off the hook and so is Anjelika?"

"Looks that way."

"I knew it." He's grinning from ear to ear. "Contractors are good judges of people. We have to be. I remodel someone's house, we're practically living together for months. I have to be able to tell which clients are going to be easy to work with and which are the complainers who'll nickel-and-dime me to death." He slams his hands on the steering wheel a second time. "I know JJ is a little eccentric, but she's not capable of hurting Chrissy. And Anjelika is a naive kid. Innocent as the day she was born. The cops were barking up the wrong tree with her."

Ten minutes from JJ's commune, he looks at me.

"This might be a good time to tell you something."

My heart slips a little in my chest.

"I got a letter from Anjelika a couple of weeks ago. A thank-you note. I didn't tell you about it because . . . just because. She's happy to be home and wanted to know if the police have caught the person who took Chrissy. Now I know what to say."

"What was she thanking you for?"

"I'm the one who encouraged her to go back to Norway while she still had her passport and wasn't under arrest."

"You? She was a murder suspect."

Almost. I remember Manny telling me after she fled that he was never really interested in her. She was a decoy. A way for him to make the real suspects think he was after someone else.

"As far as I know, I didn't do anything illegal. I didn't give her money or drive her to the airport. I just couldn't stand the way the cops were treating her. They were overzealous. Scared the poor kid to death. I may be your all-around good guy, but I do have a little larceny in my heart when it comes to the mistreatment of innocent women. Are you going to turn me in?"

"I'll have to think about it, although I do find larceny a bit sexy."

* * *

The doors to the gallery at JJ's commune are open. Light is spilling out into the night. There's a worried clutch of seven or eight people standing in the parking lot talking to Manny and Pence.

"One person," Pence shouts. "I can't listen to all of you at once."

A tall, skinny man with a ponytail and Van Dyke goatee takes the lead. "We all live here. I was in my studio and I heard loud voices. Angry voices. I went to the gallery to investigate. I saw three people. JJ, JoAnn Juliette—she lives here—and two people I didn't recognize. A man and a woman."

"Any weapons?"

"I didn't see any guns, if that's what you mean, but there's a lot of glass and metal and heavy objects on display. They could be weapons—"

Pence and Manny head for the open door. Pence is shouting over his shoulder, telling everyone to stay outside. Manny is calling for backup.

"Does he mean us, too?" Frank asks.

"Better not." I grab his hand and we run toward the building.

JJ, Kathryn, and Bucky are standing in the gallery, their forms barely distinguishable from the life-sized sculptures surrounding them. The fresh bruise on Kathryn's cheek blooms through her custom-blended Belle Aqua de la Vida foundation.

"Come home with me, Bucky," she says. "I can explain."

"Why did you kill Chrissy?" JJ's voice is quavering, watery. Bucky puts his arm around her shoulder. She shrugs it off.

"It was an accident. I had nothing to do with it."

"I don't understand," JJ says. "You knew they were going to take her. Why didn't you tell someone?"

"I didn't think they'd do it."

"How could you take the chance?"

"Me? Taking chances? You're the careless one. Letting her live here with all these hippie types. Everyone coming and going."

Bucky's hands curl into fists. "Crazy fucking woman. I fixed it. I had people in here all the time. Watching her."

We are standing in the shadows, just inside the door. Pence starts forward. I put my hand on his arm to stop him. This is the face-to-face we need.

"I can't lose you, Bucky."

"I don't want Bucky," JJ says. "Bucky doesn't want me. We barely speak."

"Don't be stupid. Bucky wants Chrissy. His affairs come and go. But you're different. You're Chrissy's mother. You'll never go away."

"That's why you killed my daughter? Because you're jealous of me?"

"I didn't kill Chrissy. I loved her."

"You killed her," JJ shouts, over and over. Her face a torment. She lunges at Kathryn.

Kathryn's cry wails through the gallery. She rips away from JJ. "It wasn't supposed to happen. I only meant for her to be missing. Long enough to frighten Bucky. Make him hate you. Brenda and Buzz, they're the ones who killed her with their drugs."

"I would have given you Chrissy if it would have saved her life. Moved away. Whatever I needed to do to stop you I would have done." She spins around, arms flailing. A display of ceramic pots crashes to the floor, splintering into shards. She picks up a shard. Waves it in the air. Uncertain where to slash. Who to cut. All she has been trying not to see—the waste, the loss, the banal evil—hits her full on. She plunges toward Kathryn.

Frank's voice spins by my ear. "JJ, no."

She stops mid-step, frozen, one foot raised in the air, her eyes luminous with panic. Then runs to Chrissy's tapestry, clawing at it with the sharp end of the shard, tearing at the pieces she so lovingly stitched together. Clumps of cotton batting float in the air like tiny clouds.

"She killed you. She killed you. You're dead." Droplets of tears and saliva spray the bare wood floor around her. She yanks hard on a dangling fringe, the ripping sound like a muted scream. Chrissy's eyes, the same eyes that once gazed serenely over the room, collapse at an angle, deforming her innocent face.

JJ falls to the floor, hollowed out by the rage she has finally released, leaving her with only enough strength left to weep.

Frank moves to her side, drops to his knees, and puts his arms around her.

"Let it go," he says. "Let it all go."

"Get away from me!" Bucky shoves Kathryn against a wall, hard enough to send a large painting clattering to the floor. She stumbles and rights herself.

"Leave her," Kathryn says to Bucky. "Come home with me. I love you."

"No you don't." I move toward Kathryn. Pot shards crunching under my feet. "You don't love Bucky. You took Chrissy to punish him. That's not love."

"I didn't kill her. Why won't anyone listen?" Kathryn's voice pitches through the gallery.

"Doesn't matter," I say. "You didn't kill her with your own hands, but you're the reason she's dead."

* * *

It takes nearly an hour to calm JJ down and help her to her feet. One by one her commune mates sit with her, stroking her back, whispering in her ear. Someone opens a bottle of wine and passes it around. A whiff of marijuana floats in the air.

"Thank you, everyone," she says. Her voice is reedy. She steadies herself against a table. "I'm so sorry to involve all of you in this. And for the damage to your work. I don't know how to make it up to you."

"No worries," the man with the goatee says. "I'm going to take the broken pieces of my pots and build something new with them." There are murmurs of reassurance from the group and offers to help repair Chrissy's tapestry.

JJ's face fills with unbridled grief. "I need time to think." She turns to the tapestry. "I may change my mind, but for right now, I don't want to repair the tapestry. I want to learn to live with it. As it is. As I am. Damaged and torn."

* * *

Frank is unusually quiet in the car as we drive home in the dark.

"You were great," I say. "The way you stopped JJ. She might have killed Kathryn. And then you held her until she stopped crying when everyone else was afraid to touch her."

The light in front of us turns red. We sit in silence waiting for it to change. I have something I need to say but I'm afraid I lack the courage to say it.

The light changes. We move forward.

I find the courage I need at the next stop light.

"Before we marry, I have some work to do in therapy."

Frank grimaces.

"Is this about feelings you still have for your ex?"

"No."

"Then why do you need therapy?"

Two parallel tears slowly inch down my cheeks.

"Kathryn fooled herself into thinking she didn't care about Bucky's affairs or that he had a child with another woman. JJ fooled herself into thinking she could avoid her anger and her loss. I've fooled myself by not acknowledging my own grief."

"What grief?"

"Grief over not having children. Mark didn't want kids. At least not with me and I went along with it. I was so focused on not losing him that I lost touch with myself, with what mattered to me. My insecurities, my suspicions, they're all part of my grief. I don't want to lose myself again. You deserve better. And so do I."

"We're too old to have children, Dot. Unless we adopt. And we're too old for that."

"Feelings don't grow old the way people do. Especially feelings that aren't worked through. It takes guts to look at painful emotions.

But if you don't, those feelings take you places you don't want to go. I think that's what happened to Kathryn and JJ and to me. I don't want to do that again. You're the best thing that's happened to me, Frank. I want to be the best thing that's happened to you."

CHAPTER TWENTY-TWO

I GO TO headquarters the next morning directly from Frank's house, dressed in yesterday's clothes. No shower. No hair gel. Pence is in his office in sartorial splendor working on his comments for the morning's press briefing.

"Tell me what you think." He picks up his script and gives a short preparatory cough. "Ladies and gentlemen of the press, citizens of Kenilworth." He shakes his head. "Wrong. Should be citizens of Kenilworth first." He scribbles something and starts again. "Citizens of Kenilworth, ladies and gentlemen of the press, I am happy to announce that, after more than two months of nonstop investigation, we have three suspects in custody for the tragic death of Chrissy Stewart: Kathryn Blazek, Chrissy's stepmother; Buzz Stewart, Chrissy's father's half brother; and his common-law wife, Brenda Finister. It is not anticipated that there are additional people involved. The district attorney plans to charge all three defendants with felony murder under the special circumstance of kidnapping. The punishment for murder committed in the perpetration of a kidnapping is severe. The district attorney determines the charges to be filed. But I can tell you with certainty that all three defendants are facing the death penalty or life without parole plus five years. If there is anything positive to emerge from this tragedy, it is this: Chrissy's kidnapping and subsequent tragic death was not a stranger abduction. What we feared at first, that the person or persons responsible for her death were trafficking in child pornography, turns out not to be the case. Why? Because the task force on Internet Crimes Against Children is working. Are there any questions?"

I want to ask how he knows this, since it's impossible to prove a negative. And doesn't he feel responsible for creating a convenient narrative for Kathryn to use, one that sent the investigation on a wild goose chase and prolonged JJ's agony?

"I do." Manny is in the doorway. I have no idea how long he has been standing there listening to Pence. He walks into the office and leans against a chair. His eyes are sunk deep in their sockets and his clothes are more rumpled than mine.

"If the ICAC team is so successful, how come there are still more than thirty thousand child porn links on the Internet?"

Pence turns around and gives Manny the once-over. "Speaking of how-come questions, how come you look like you slept in your car?"

"Because I did. Lupe kicked me out. I missed her deadline."

"What deadline?" Pence puts his paper down. "I never gave you a deadline. Anyhow, it's all over except the shouting. Or the applause."

"It's not over and Lupe knows it. Not until the trials are done and those guys are in prison. Until then it'll be nonstop testimonies, depositions, you name it. She wants a husband with a nine-to-five job."

"Then she shouldn't have married a cop." Pence looks at his watch. "We have a briefing to do. Get yourself cleaned up. You've got ten minutes."

Manny doesn't move.

"Look, if it helps, I'll call your wife and tell her how much we appreciate her support. I'll give her a framed certificate of appreciation. Send her some flowers. A gift certificate to get her nails done. Tell me what she wants, I'll get it."

"I think she wants more than getting her nails done," I say. Flowers and a mani-pedi may satisfy Pence's wife. What Lupe wants is engagement, participation, a full partner in life, not someone whose identity is dependent on his job.

Pence walks up to Manny and claps his hand on Manny's shoulder. "Isn't this what you've been waiting for? To stand up with me in front of the press and tell everyone Chrissy's murder is solved? The community's gonna love you."

"The doc got the physical evidence. We already got confirmation from the lab that the makeup on Chrissy matches the stuff Kathryn Blazek buys. The doc's the one who found the Dollar Store and Maldonado. She's the one who should be on TV."

I flash with anger toward Lupe. Couldn't she have waited? Let Manny feel the relief, the pride that comes with arresting the guilty? On the other hand, addiction to work is like any other addiction. All promises and good intentions with multiple relapses. Actions speak louder than words. She's been fooled before.

"Nobody solves a murder by themselves, Manny. I was glad to help. This is a day to feel proud of yourself, not badly."

"I feel bad because my marriage is on the rocks."

Pence raises his hands in the air. "Marital counseling is above my pay grade. I'm going to the briefing. By myself. Straighten him out, Doc. He only gets one pass."

* * *

As soon as Pence leaves the room, Manny slumps into a chair.

"Talk to me, Manny. What's going on?"

"She doesn't want me. Says I'm not the person she married. I told her, I can't change back. Be the person I used to be. Not after what I've seen."

"Of course you can't. You're older. Wiser."

"Also more cynical, more suspicious and paranoid according to Lupe. She's been telling me that ever since I started with the nanny-cams so I can check on Carmela." Before I can say anything, he puts his hand up. "Don't you start on me, too. I need to make sure Carmela is safe. Lupe can't protect her from people so bad she doesn't even believe they exist."

"I'm not going to start on you. I don't even know what a nanny-cam is. But I am going to challenge your underlying assumption that because Lupe's a civilian and you're a cop, she's hopelessly naive."

"That's right."

"Let me give you another interpretation. You're judging 90 percent of the people in your private life by the 10 percent you encounter at work. That's a sampling error, get it?" He shrugs. "Do you do this nanny-cam thing while you're at work?"

"I'm good at multitasking."

"Really? So how come you can't be a cop, a husband, and a father at the same time?"

He pushes back in his chair, rolling away from me toward the door. He's had about enough of my hectoring. What he's looking for is kindness and understanding. Kindness and understanding have their place, but there are times when what's most therapeutic is a kick in the ass. Or a two-by-four between the eyes.

"Do you want Lupe back?"

"Of course I do."

"Well then, go and get her."

"Won't work. She's finished with me."

"That's because you didn't stand by her. Change that and maybe she'll change her mind."

* * *

Manny walks into my office on A-level an hour later and shuts the door. His eyes are red from crying.

"I did what you said. I called her."

"Didn't go too well?"

"I got conditions. Get therapy and quit the task force."

He flops in a chair and pokes at his chest.

"Policing is what I do. The task force is what I do. I can't change."

"Of course you can. You change every day. We all do until the day we die. Exercise changes your brain. Meditation changes your brain. PTSD changes your brain. You can change if you want to, but you'll need help."

"I'm not taking any medication."

"Get into therapy like Lupe said." He winces. "Not with me. I'll find you somebody else. Maybe someone who used to be a cop and is now a psychologist." There's a slight tilt to his eyebrows. My guess is he didn't even know about the new breed of cops with doctorates in psychology. "Let me tell you something. This case has stirred up a lot of unexpected feelings for me, too. It happens when you identify with the victim. Carmela and Chrissy were almost the same age. It brought things too close for you."

He leans forward in his chair. "We got a conniving liar, a bully, two dope addicts, and an earth-biscuit mother. Who did you identify with?"

I start to answer and stop. I'm pressing Manny to have some boundaries between his home life and his work. I need to practice what I preach.

"I talked to the guys on the task force after I talked to Lupe. They don't want me to quit. They're getting hammered. They need me."

"So does Lupe. And Carmela. For that matter, you need you. You said so yourself. You're not who you used to be. Do you even know who you are anymore?"

"The chief needs me."

"It's nice to be needed. Feels good. But know this first. Pence is your boss. He's not God. And he's not family. He'd throw you under the bus in a hot minute if it served his purposes."

"Lupe kicked me out. How's that for family loyalty?"

"She's trying to get your attention."

"She's picked a helluva way to do it."

There's a knock on the door. Pence is standing in the hallway, all smiles.

"It went perfect." He walks into my tiny office. "There were a ton of questions, most of which I had to deflect, because my main man wasn't there. I gotta tell you, Manny, everyone was asking for you. You are a hero."

Manny squirms in his chair. Nothing embarrasses a cop more than to be called a hero.

"So, did you get everything straightened out here, Doc?" he says as though we are talking in code and Manny isn't sitting right in front of us.

"You have to ask Manny."

"How about it, Manny? Take a few days off, get a little rest, talk to the wife, and then get back in the saddle?"

Manny struggles out of his chair and stands, feet apart, hands behind his back, in parade rest position. "Thank you, sir, but I am requesting an immediate transfer back to patrol, preferably swing shift with weekends off."

"I told you. No can do."

I stand, too. "If he's a hero, doesn't he deserve some consideration?"

Pence gives me the stink eye.

"Bad move, Manny. Take my advice. Cases like this don't come along every day. Take advantage of the moment. Could be good for a promotion. Funding for the task force. FBI National Academy. Who knows?"

"Sorry, sir. I want to go back to patrol."

"Because of the wife? Man up for Christ's sake. Make your own decisions."

I can hear Manny take a sharp breath.

"I refuse your request for a transfer. End of discussion. Blame it on me. Tell the wife I ordered you to stay on the task force until further notice because I don't have anyone to replace you."

They stand face-to-face, eyes locked.

"Do you understand me, Officer Ochoa?"

"Yes, sir. I understand that you have the right to refuse my request."

"Alright then, that's settled."

"And I have a right to find a job with another department."

Pence's back goes ramrod straight. "That would be a very poor decision. Think about it. You'd have to start all over. Low man on the totem pole. Dog watch. No vacation for a year."

"Shouldn't I take advantage of the moment like you suggested?"

Pence recoils, unused to having his own words thrown back in his face.

"Don't kid yourself, son. Finding another job won't be easy."

Manny takes a step back, widening the space between them.

"With all due respect, sir, I am not your son, I am an employee of the city of Kenilworth." He moves again until his back presses against the wall. "Furthermore, and after serious consideration, it is my opinion that finding a new job will be a damn sight easier than finding another wife."

* * *

Manny leaves first. Pence stands there, clutching his script.

"What kind of fix is that? You just wrecked his career."

"I did nothing of the kind. Anyhow, that's his decision. Not mine."

"And you didn't coach him?"

"He's suffering on this assignment. His family is suffering. Where is all that care and concern you told me you have for your employees?"

He opens his mouth to say something and closes it. "Pussy-whipped. That's what I call it. He can't stand up to the wife and he can't stand up to you."

"And you just want to parade him around in front of the media like your pet dog."

"He deserves the attention."

"You're the one who likes attention, not Manny. In my opinion this investigation has been as much about your love of the spotlight as it has been about solving Chrissy's murder."

"Out." He points to the door. "Now."

"I beg your pardon. This is my office."

"Not for long," he says and stomps down the hall.

I think for a minute about following him upstairs. Doing damage control. We're all exhausted and on edge. Not the best time to have a serious conversation or make important decisions. What I really want to do is go home, take a shower, and change my clothes. Frank is coming over with dinner and a bottle of champagne to celebrate. Last night, when we finally got to the truth about Chrissy's death, celebrating seemed like a good idea. Tonight everything looks different. Manny's marriage is in shambles and his career is on the edge. Bucky's a broken man with no child, a wife who's bound to spend the remainder of her life in prison, and a domestic violence charge hanging over his head. Buzz and Brenda are facing years in jail. A tough way to cure their dependence on drugs and on Kathryn, who, I suspect, has been grooming them for months to do her bidding by supporting their habits. JJ's heart is shattered. Chrissy is still dead. And I may be out of a job.

* * *

Frank pours. I watch as the champagne bubbles fizz to the rim of my flute and then retreat. It's my second glass. "Better eat something," he says pushing a dish of salmon mousse and crackers in my direction. I take a half-hearted nibble.

"Pence is not going to fire you. You're like an old married couple, always grousing at each other. He'd be lost without you."

"I doubt it."

"Who else would put up with him? The guy's a chameleon. Acts one way one day and totally different on another. He threatens to fire you every other month. Doesn't pay you benefits because you're a consultant. I treat my subs better than he treats you."

"I'm worried about Manny."

"You should be because he's just like you. Can't let go of the job when he's at home."

"What if Lupe won't take him back, no matter what?"

Frank shrugs. "Not my circus, not my monkeys." He spreads a cracker with salmon mousse and wolfs it down. "I dropped by to see JJ this afternoon."

"How's she doing?"

"I'm not a psychologist but I'd say she's consumed with guilt. Why didn't she see how tormented Kathryn was? Why didn't she and Chrissy move away? Could she have saved Chrissy if she hadn't been so caught up in her work? On and on. She's second-guessing herself to death."

"And the tapestry?"

"Still hanging. Still in shreds. I offered to help her take it down, but she wants it where it is, the way it is. On the positive side, she is willing to cooperate fully with the cops and the DA. Eager even. She thanked us again for our help. Wants to show her appreciation by offering us the gallery at the commune for our wedding. Might be a nice venue. Certainly the right price." He finishes his glass of champagne and pours another, waiting for me to respond.

"What do you think?"

"I can't talk about this now, Frank. I may not have a job."

"What's that got to do with it?"

"Everything. I'm not going to let you support me when I'm perfectly capable of supporting myself."

"So what you're saying is I can't respond to JJ's offer until you and Pence decide if you're going to get divorced."

"I'm under a lot of stress and I'm sleep deprived. This is not a good time to have this conversation."

"Seems to me there's never a good time to have this conversation."

"A few days, that's all I need."

"What about your psychoanalysis? You told me last night we can't get married until you figure yourself out."

"Now you're mocking me."

"Call it what you want. You're the psychologist. I think I'll go home."

* * *

As soon as Frank leaves, I take another swig of champagne and burst into tears. I'm tired. I'm confused. I may be out of a job, one of my favorite clients is in serious trouble, Frank hates me, and I may be drunk. I think about calling my mother. But if I tell her about our fight, she'll launch into a tirade about taking supplements to improve my attitude because whatever problems we're having can't be Frank's fault. Ditto for my girlfriends who are perpetually worried that I'm going to chase Frank away if I don't get over my cold feet. I stare at the wall wondering what therapist to call when the phone rings.

"Were you ever going to call me? It's all over the newspapers." Dr. Randall sounds hoarse. "That face-to-face thing work for you?"

"It did."

"Then how come my name wasn't in the paper?" He laughs himself into a coughing fit and drops the phone. Bette picks it up. I can hear her shouting at him to drink some water.

"Sorry, Dot. Laughter apparently isn't the best medicine, at least not for Charles."

"How is he doing?"

"About the same—no worse, no better. He's been following the case, wants me to get all the newspapers. It's been a great distraction. Hold on a minute." She muffles the phone. "Charles wants me to tell you two things. First he wants you to bring that young man of yours over for dinner so he can check him out. He doesn't want you making another mistake."

"Frank's hardly young. He's in his fifties."

"When you're our age, dear, fifty seems young."

"We've just had a fight."

"You and your young man?"

I muster a mumble.

"Are you crying?"

I nod my head yes and somehow she hears me.

"Fighting is nothing to be afraid of. All couples fight. If they don't fight, that means they don't trust each other. God knows Charles and I fight. It's unavoidable. Think about it. Marriage is a cosmic joke. How could two people who have different ways of living on earth be expected to get along without fighting? I don't like to eat what Charles eats and I don't want to sleep when he sleeps. He thinks I talk in riddles. I think he talks like a textbook. The trick about fighting is not to avoid it, but to know how to make up afterwards. You can do that, can't you? After you sober up a bit?"

There's noise in the background.

"Hold on a minute, Charles wants something. He can't stand to be ignored." She muffles the phone again.

"Still there?" she says after a minute. "Charles wants you to investigate another murder. He hasn't had this much fun consulting with anyone in a long time. Which only goes to show you how dull our lives are these days."

"Remind Charles that I counsel cops. I don't investigate murders. It was only by accident, because Frank knows Chrissy's mother, that I got mixed up in this." She deadens the phone again, apparently repeating what I just said to Charles.

"Well then, Charles says you'll just have to find someone to murder yourself. But don't let it be your young man."

I can hear Charles coughing.

"One more unsolicited piece of advice before I rescue Charles from himself. Don't let things fester. Fish or get off the pot."

* * *

Saturday passes, then Sunday afternoon with no word from Frank, Manny, or Pence. I do the laundry. Clean the house. Water the plants. Pull a few weeds in the yard. My withered winter garden looks as bad as I feel. My mother calls to see what I'm doing over the weekend and I lie. I tell her Frank and I are going to the movies and out to dinner. She instructs me to tell him hello and hopes we'll both come to visit soon. She's certain Frank would enjoy the activities at her senior living complex. Maybe even come for the Valentine's Day Dance. She wants to know if he likes Golden Oldies. He must, I say. He likes me.

I call a few girlfriends. No one's home although they all hope I'll leave a message so they can call me back as soon as possible.

By Sunday night I've convinced myself that Frank is over at JJ's proposing to her, Pence has just about finished the wording on an ad for a new psychologist, and Manny is teetering on the edge of the Golden Gate Bridge. I sit on the couch watching the setting sun take the light and leave behind a gloomy wet sky. Bette's words do hot laps in my brain.

Manny has to repair the damage he's done to Lupe. Pence has to repair the damage he's done to Manny. And I have to repair the damage I've done to Frank. In a perfect world, Lupe would make up with Manny, Pence would apologize to me, and I would apologize to Frank for treating him as though he has nothing else to do with his life but wait around for me. I dial his number. Now I know for sure he's at JJ's because all I get is voice mail.

* * *

Monday morning, I get up extra early and dress for success in a pantsuit and silk shirt. I stop by the local bakery for almond croissants and cappuccinos, Pence's favorite morning snack. It's blatant pandering, but I don't care. I don't want to look for another job. I like the job I have and I'm willing to kiss up to Pence to keep it. He looks up from his desk as I juggle my purse, my briefcase, and try not to spill the coffee.

"I wondered if you'd be coming in today."

I open the box of croissants and offer him one.

"It's my usual day. I'm just a little early."

I hand him a cappuccino. He accepts it without a word as though I do this every day.

"I thought maybe you thought I had fired you on Friday."

"I wondered, but before we talk about that, we need to talk about Manny." I'm willing to bribe Pence with pastry, but I'm not willing to give up advocating for my clients if that's what it takes to keep my job.

"What do you mean, talk about Manny?"

"Are you going to let him transfer to patrol?"

"Is my answer contingent on your decision to continue working here?"

"Maybe."

He takes a bite of his croissant followed by a slow sip of coffee.

"It costs me over a hundred thousand dollars to hire and train a new recruit. Why would I do that when I already have a perfectly capable officer on staff." He takes another bite of croissant. "I spoke to him over the weekend and approved his transfer." He sits up in his chair. "So what about you? Do you want to continue to work for me?"

I want to tell him I work for KPD, not for him. But this is not the right moment to point that out.

"Absolutely."

He sets his coffee down and leans forward, both hands flat on the top of his desk.

"Let me be perfectly clear. I don't give second chances. I'm going to put a letter in your file. I won't tolerate another act of insubordination."

I want to ask—what file? What insubordination? But once again, this is not the time.

"So you're not firing me?"

"I need a psychologist on staff. As my wife pointed out, 'Better the devil you know than the devil you don't.'" He looks at his watch and stuffs the last morsel of pastry in his mouth. "Are we both clear now?"

I nod. He thanks me for breakfast and starts walking to the staff meeting. The front of his suit is dusty with flakes of powdered sugar and almonds. I start to tell him but change my mind.

* * *

I head to Fran's for lunch after the staff meeting. Eddie's slinging hash behind the counter. He sees me and orders a customer to stand up and give me his seat.

"Nice customer service. I'm surprised Fran has any customers left."

"That guy finished his burger ten minutes ago. Plus, he's a lousy tipper. Coffee?"

My stomach is still roiling from the cappuccino I had this morning. And from tension.

"A cup of the soup de jour and a glass of water."

"What's with Manny? He's been sleeping at my place all weekend. Wife throw him out?"

"A married man stays at your house all weekend and you don't ask what's wrong?"

He shrugs. "Not my problem."

"He might need a friend. Someone to talk to."

"Am I paying you to provide entertainment to the customers?" Fran comes out of the kitchen, wiping her hands on her apron, her cheeks red and glossy with sweat. She whacks Eddie on the rear with a long wooden spoon and bends over the counter to kiss my cheek. "Long time no see. How's that man of yours?"

"I'm doing fine. Thanks for asking."

She slaps my hand and turns to Eddie. "What are you waiting around for? Bus some tables. Stir the soup. Do something besides talk."

"Hear that?" Eddie says to the customers at the counter. "That's workplace harassment. I'm gonna sue." He stomps off.

I love the way they joust with each other. If Pence ever offers Eddie his job back, and I doubt that will happen, Eddie could do way worse for himself than staying here.

"So?" Fran leans over, elbows on the counter. "Set the date yet?"

* * *

On Tuesday, I call Lupe. I don't want to change her mind, I just want to see how she's doing.

"He's back on patrol starting next shift," she says. "And he's willing to go to therapy. I guess I have you to thank for that."

"He did this on his own. He was willing to quit if the chief wouldn't let him rotate out." I can hear her gasp. "Didn't he tell you?"

"Is he going to hate me for forcing him to quit? Someone on his team called him a candy-ass."

"I doubt it. I think that the fact that you had a bottom line and held to it will give Manny the courage to resist peer pressure. It certainly gave him the courage to face off with the chief. Give yourselves some time. Somebody once said that police work is a greedy mistress. It's going to take both of you to figure out how to balance work and family."

There's a soft knock on the door to my office. I've kept my next client waiting. I tell Lupe I have to go.

"One more question," she says. "When it comes to balancing home life and work, how do you do it?"

* * *

As soon as my next client leaves, I call Frank and ask him to meet me for dinner.

"What's up?"

"What do you mean *what's up*? I want to talk to you. I haven't seen you since Friday."

"What do you want to talk about?"

"Wedding plans."

No response. My heart does some jiggly thing. My head goes into catastrophic mode. I'm too late. He hates me. I've let him down too many times.

"Are you there, Frank?"

"I'm listening." His voice is flat.

"JJ's offer of her place was very sweet. I've thought about it a lot and decided it's not a good idea. Too many bad memories."

"And?"

"If we can get my mother on a plane, what do you think about getting married in Pick City, Iowa?"